Brownies
& Betrayal

Heather Justesen

Also by this author

The Ball's in Her Court
Rebound
Full Circle
Family by Design
Blank Slate
The Switch
Shear Luck
Homecoming
Second Chances
Identity
Safe Haven

Other Sweet Bites Mysteries

Pistols & Pies
Muffins & Murder
Eggnog & Extortion

Brownies & Betrayal

JELLY BEAN PRESS
FILLMORE, UT

Heather Justesen

ISBN: 978-0615698083

Published by Jelly Bean Press, 90 S Main, Fillmore, UT 84631
Brownie by Noodledoodle, Vecteezy.com
Wedding dress by 1001graphics, Brusheezy.com

Cover design by Bill J. Justesen
Cover design © 2017 by Heather Justesen
Typeset by Heather Justesen

Dedication

For Danyelle—thanks for the years of friendship and support.
There's nothing quite as sweet as finishing a project, and having
good friends to celebrate with.

Chapter 1

I pulled into a parking spot and took a deep breath. What was I doing here?

Okay, so I knew what I was doing. I was bringing moist, delicious, award-winning brownies to the wedding rehearsal of a woman I'd known for years and always disliked, in the pathetic grand ballroom of a three-star hotel. It was a long fall from the Best-in-State hotel restaurant in Chicago where I'd created cakes and pastries for the past nine years. I tried not to let that bother me.

And the whole thing made me as nervous as a preteen at her first bakeoff with much older kids—an event I remembered clearly almost twenty years later.

My cell phone vibrated in my pocket. "Honey," I greeted my best friend after a glance at the Caller ID. "This is a big mistake. I can't believe I let you talk me into it."

"Don't be ridiculous. This is nothing—you've baked cakes that cost more than my car. This is a batch of brownies. Have you left for the hotel yet?"

"I'm here. And don't talk down about our award-winning brownie recipe."

Honey laughed. "See, you'll be fine."

"If I fail at this, I may never forgive you, so you know." I climbed from my Mitsubishi Outlander and walked around to the back to retrieve the box of brownies.

"You've never failed at anything, and we need a good custom bakery in town. Not to say anything against ours at the store, but our staff is hardly cut out to do fancy wedding cakes." She spoke of Mark's Foodtown, her in-laws' grocery store, which her husband now managed. The suggestion that I start my own bakery here in town wasn't a new refrain; Honey had been singing it for several years.

The quiet town of Silver Springs, Arizona, wasn't exactly a hotbed of socialites willing to pay thousands for custom cakes, but with everything else in my life crumbling to ashes, she'd convinced me to give it a go. I hoped having the much larger city of Prescott close by would bring in extra business to keep me running since my savings account would only stretch so far. "I ought to go," I said as I clicked the button to lock the vehicle's doors and headed for the hotel. "Have to face Bridezilla."

"She's not your first."

"And I'm sure she won't be the last," I agreed as I pushed through the double glass doors and headed toward the grand ballroom. It wasn't particularly grand, but it would fit the needs of most locals. The new reception center wasn't supposed to be up and running for a couple more months.

"Hey, at least you only had to put up with her for a week—it could have been worse."

When I looked back at the hurried cleaning and planning to renovate my grandma's old restaurant into a pastry shop, I had a hard time believing that I was still working in Chicago seven days earlier. I felt a tug of longing for what I had thrown away, but pushed it back as I entered the left half of the ballroom, which had been sectioned off for tonight's meal while the wedding party held their rehearsal on the other side. Muffled voices leaked through to me as I set the pastry box on the table and checked to make sure my short, dark-brown hair was still tight in its little ponytail at the nape of my neck. Then I pulled on a pair of food-grade gloves and began to set the rocky road brownies on the provided tray.

"Valerie, this is my wedding. Can't you let it go for one night?" A woman's voice drew my attention as two women walked into the room. It was the bride, Analesa.

"It's not like I'm trying to seduce Tad. Shawn is an adult, remember?" the woman who must have been Valerie answered. She gestured expansively, and her jeweled bracelet caught my eye. The voices went low again, and I heard a few phrases like *control yourself* and *get a grip*. The conversation was punctuated with angry eyes and finger jabs to the air.

So not everything was smooth sailing with this wedding. Since I'd done cakes for hundreds of weddings, I knew that was hardly unusual. And Analesa had never been particularly easy to please. Though we never hung out on my long summer visits to Silver Springs to see my grandma, I remembered well what a control freak she was.

I glanced at the two women, the blonde bride and her brunette maid of honor—I hadn't met many of the members of the wedding party, but I recognized Valerie's name from when Analesa paid for the cake.

Both women were tall, tanned and had long hair flowing down their backs, but that was where the similarities ended. Analesa was the picture of conservative upper class—the poster wife for her attorney fiancé—though she'd been raised at lower-middle class at best. Valerie was dressed like a loaded call girl, from the strappy red Jimmy Choo's, which I admit made my knees weak with envy, to the formfitting dress that showcased her ample cleavage.

I tried to pretend I wasn't listening while I strained to catch more of the conversation. Valerie turned toward me and approached, all but stomping in her heels, if anything so graceful could be considered stomping. "Quit being so uptight, Ana. I'm just trying to have a little fun."

Analesa looked like she intended to continue the conversation, but her groom-to-be, Tad, entered the room and caught her by the elbow. I thought he looked far less handsome in person than in his engagement picture, which I'd seen around town. And more geeky, with his slicked-back, tawny hair and silver-rimmed glasses. Maybe it was the stress of dealing with warring women, I mused. I added the last brownie to the trays the kitchen staff had provided me, then shifted them all around for the perfect presentation. I added another item to the growing mental list of equipment I would need for my new shop and imagined my savings account shrinking.

Valerie dragged my attention back to her. "Brownies? Aren't you Tempest Crawford? I heard you were supposed to be some amazing pastry chef, a woman who creates *fabulous* desserts capable of awing the most *discerning* of customers. And yet we have *brownies*." She stared down her nose at the delectable delights. "Are all your awards invented to make you sound impressive?" She snatched one from the tray. Her bracelet sparkled, almost blinding me at this proximity, the colored stones catching the light, the dangles jingling as she moved. A matching necklace with a large, gaudy pendant and cluster earrings glittered, completing the set.

I couldn't help feeling defensive, but determined to stay professional, I clenched my jaw and forced a smile. "You should wait until dinner. You're ruining the presentation. And this is what Analesa asked me to make. These brownies are award-winning."

"I'm sure they are—in tiny burgs like this one. Even in Prescott they're probably considered fancy fare. I doubt you'll have any trouble fitting in here." She took a large bite, looking smug.

I held in a growl at her disregard for etiquette as the other guests entered the room. I needed to make a good impression, as this was my first opportunity to showcase my pastry skills since my impulsive relocation. I knew any work I found here would be a far cry from my previous employment, but I was determined to make my business succeed.

Valerie tipped her head to the side, looking at the ceiling as though considering the dessert's merits as she chewed and swallowed. "They're fine, I suppose. But I know this chef in Mesa—Roscoe Marks. He'd bake circles around you. Sorry, sweetie." With a gleam of meanness in her eyes, took another large bite before she turned and walked off.

I couldn't help myself. Roscoe? She was comparing my award-winning brownie recipe to Roscoe? He was such a poser! If she'd wanted to offend me, she could not have done better—besides comparing my work to Karen's, that is, but as my former boss wasn't a pastry chef, such a comparison was unlikely to happen. "That idiot wouldn't know a turkey roaster from a double boiler." I said this low so no one else would hear, but I must have been louder than I thought.

Valerie twisted back, amusement in her eyes. "Hit a mark, didn't I? I know why you're here—you were let go by your former employer. Surprised I heard about that, aren't you? Small towns have big mouths. In your late thirties and you're already a washed-up has-been." She turned and trotted off.

I saw red. I was only thirty-one, for heaven's sake, and I didn't get fired, I quit. I had them begging me to come back. Knowing that didn't stop a shaft of hurt from accompanying the anger, though.

A tall, blond man who did serious justice to the navy designer suit he wore—Armani, if my guess was right—followed Valerie into the hall, a look of determination on his face.

Tad approached and addressed me. "Ana's been telling me all about your fabulous desserts. The brownies look great, and I'm looking forward to seeing what you do with the cake on such short notice." He extended a hand. "Hi, I suppose I ought to introduce myself. I'm Tad Richardson. I'm the anxious groom." He stepped in front of me so I couldn't tear off after Valerie and mar her pretty little face before the wedding. I don't know what he was worried about. It's not like I would do anything permanent.

I sucked in a breath and admitted to myself that I wouldn't have hurt her. We would have crossed verbal swords again, and since she had my measure, she was more likely to come out ahead. Reining in my emotions, I focused my attention on tomorrow's groom and forced a polite smile as I took his hand, which was cool and dry. He had a nice, firm grip—something I appreciated.

"It's good to meet you. I know Analesa is very excited about becoming Mrs. Richardson. And I promise tomorrow's cake won't disappoint. You've had the benefit of my almost undivided attention, which didn't hurt." I admit, my vanity was mollified by his words. Smooth talkers—I always seemed to fall for them, which was why I've had two failed engagements. But now was not the time for dwelling on my relationship failures.

His grin transformed his face from a serious, but pleasant-looking, geek, to someone considerably more handsome. Even his green eyes seemed to sparkle. Ah, the man in the photos *did* exist.

A tall, platinum blonde who ought to have had some gray in her hair, but instead looked fresh and young as a forty-year-old, came over, putting a hand on Tad's elbow. "Sweetheart, can you find out what's keeping the food? And track down Jeff and Valerie—he took off after her and we're ready to sit down, don't you think?"

"Of course, Mother."

Mother, like they were some high-fashion set. All polite façade and no warmth, but then I changed my mind. There was warmth in both mother's and son's eyes when they looked at each other. Yet she wasn't Mom, she was Mother. I let the thought go—there were too many odd characters in this group.

Tad turned to leave as a little girl ran over to him. She had dark hair and a sweet pixie face with huge green eyes and a smile that would light up a high-rise. "Tad, where you goin'?"

"To find your mom. You want to come along?" He held out his hand to her with a fond smile. She accepted both as her due and they wandered out together. That adorable little girl was Valerie's? Really?

I offered my hand to Tad's mother. "Hello, my name is Tempest Crawford, but you can call me Tess. I'm about to get out of your way for the evening."

"I'm Caroline Richardson. Tad's mother, of course. Well, your brownies look delicious. I've heard such great things about your desserts. I look forward to sampling one." Her smile was genuine, but I doubted the woman had eaten a brownie in the past ten years. She looked slightly better fed than an Ethiopian during a drought.

I appreciated the kind words, however, so I thanked her and made a final adjustment to cover the hole Valerie's theft had made. I collected my things and headed for the exit. As I reached it, I nearly bumped into the man who'd been chasing Valerie. He was coming through the doorway from the other direction. I moved to the side and ran into a table nearby, which held a huge Chinese vase of pale pink roses.

I reached out and grabbed the vase in time to stop the whole thing from toppling, though the empty pastry box I'd been carrying ended up on the floor. My heart rate kicked up for a moment when I realized how close I'd come to knocking the vase over, but my temporary lack of personal coordination wasn't going to cost me this time.

"Sorry," the blond said, picking up what I'd dropped. "I should watch where I'm going."

"No problem. It was my mistake," I answered. I took another glance at his suit, now that I was up close. Yes, definitely Armani. "I'm Tess, the pastry chef."

"I'm Jeff, the best man." He grinned and passed over my things. "Are your brownies a work of art too?"

"Of course. They may not look it, but wait until you've tasted them."

"I look forward to it." He backed out of the way and let me pass.

Rocky Road Brownies

2 cups sugar
4 eggs
1 cup plus 3 Tbsp butter
1 tsp vanilla
2 cups melted unsweetened chocolate chips
½ cup plus 1 Tbsp cocoa
Mix, then add: 2 ½ cup flour
¼ tsp baking soda
1 tsp salt
1 cup pecan bits
1 cup semi-sweet chips
4 cups miniature marshmallows

Mix the sugar, eggs, butter, vanilla and cocoa until smooth. Melt the chocolate chips in the microwave, stirring every twenty seconds until smooth Cool and mix in the rest of it.

Add the baking soda and salt, then the flour, mixing between cup fulls. Add the nuts and chocolate chips into the batter, mixing well, and pour into greased and floured 9x13 pan. I usually use a spray oil like Pam or Vegalene, then flour the pan to keep it from sticking. Bake at 350 degrees for 30-35 minutes, adding mini-marshmallows to the top of the pan for the final five minutes or until the marshallows on the edge just start to turn golden. *The marshmallows will cut better if you let the brownies cool most of the way first.*

9

Chapter 2

The cake was a masterpiece. I carried the final layers into the room where the meal would be held in two hours. Though many pastry chefs liked to assemble the cake at the bakery and have someone else deliver it completed to the site, I'd always preferred to do deliveries and assemble final details on site myself—especially since you never knew what could happen in transit.

I can't count the number of disasters I'd had to fix over the years. If a piece could crush, fall off, slump, or wilt, it had happened, and being on hand to fix and assemble was the best option in my mind. As I set the last pastry box on the table, I realized I was spoiled doing cakes at the hotel in Chicago, since I baked, assembled and displayed most of them at the same location. I would have to consider the issue before I finalized my policies for the pastry shop.

Wait staff scurried around me as I checked each bakery box and was relieved when I saw there had been no disasters en route to the hotel. I put in my ear buds and turned on my tunes. After flipping to my collection of songs from the nineties, I mouthed some of the words with Paula Abdul, though I was too conscious of everyone around me to sing any of it out loud—I saved that for the quiet of my kitchen at home.

Straightening the tablecloth on the table I'd used the night before, I set the cake base in the middle, checked my box of supplies to be certain everything was there, and began with the lower layers.

The mother of the groom entered and said something to me. I turned off my iPod, pretending like she wasn't interrupting, and that I wouldn't have minded if she had. It was a carefully honed talent of mine. "Sorry, what was that?"

She repeated the question. "Have you seen Valerie? She should have been up in the bride's suite hours ago for her hair and makeup. Could the woman *be* any more irresponsible?"

I blinked and watched her glance around the room as if she expected to find the missing maid of honor there with me. "No, I haven't seen her. If I do, I'll send her along."

Diamonds glittered at Caroline's ears, sequins adorned her long, cream-colored sheath and her hair was perfectly coifed. I thought she'd make a lovely bride herself. She pursed her lips. "I'd appreciate it. I told Analesa not to choose that woman for maid of honor. Millie would have been a much better choice. Valerie's daughter's running wild here with no one to watch her, and it's distracting having her in the dressing room. Why isn't Valerie keeping her under control?"

"The little girl I saw last night, with the big eyes and dark hair? Why would Valerie leave her running wild?" It seemed odd that the woman hadn't arranged for someone to watch the girl.

Caroline seemed to realize she had overstepped the bounds of propriety into the murky fields of gossip. "Valerie took her to a neighbor's house last night. The neighbor brought her back here this morning for the wedding, though why Tad insisted that she be here, I certainly don't know." She checked the slim gold watch on her wrist. "I guess Millie will have to fill in as maid of honor."

The woman swept out of the room again.

After I switched my tunes back on, I focused again on my task. Playing with butter cream and gumpaste, tinting and tweaking and manipulating it had always soothed and excited me, since the very first cake I had decorated when I was eight.

That was long before I had a clue what I was doing or how to use the very few tools my mom had in the kitchen. I'd never been great at drawing, though I could do a decent sketch in most cases—enough to please the clients—but with sugar, I could be an artist.

I stacked the bottom two layers, added plates and columns and arranged the gumpaste flowers I'd made earlier in the week. Next came the leaves I'd made and dusted with sparkling powders to make them realistic. Making a little sugar look like the real thing was my specialty, I thought smugly as I placed another rose and continued around the table. It was a labor of love.

"How are things in here?" The male voice made me jump, as it came from right over my shoulder—the only way I would have heard it while wearing my earbuds.

I yanked one out and looked back at Tad, willing my heart rate to return to normal. "Just fine, thanks. Don't worry—it'll be perfect, and I'll get out of the way long before the ceremony ends."

"Thank you, I appreciate everything you've done. Your brownies last night were amazing."

"Most of you thought so," I muttered, but not low enough.

"What do you mean?"

"Valerie seemed to have definite opinions on their quality." I tried to pretend I wasn't still offended. Roscoe, of all people!

"Funny, I swear she had two at dinner. Well, I better get moving. Guests will start arriving any moment." He nodded and smiled, then took off.

So Valerie had eaten not one, but three of my brownies over the course of the evening? I held the thought close, reassured. Like so many before her, she enjoyed causing a fuss. I'd had experience with her type.

When I got around to the back of the cake, I heard organ music start. Early arrivals, I thought. I checked my watch and

12

realized I was taking longer than usual. This would be my first opportunity to wow the locals, and I wanted to do it right. One more step and I saw a smear of chocolate frosting from the previous night's brownies on the floor at the edge of the tablecloth. Hadn't the hotel cleaned up everything after everyone ate?

I grabbed a paper towel and leaned over to wipe up the frosting, and saw the smear continue under the table. I lifted the pale pink tablecloth—did Analesa's obsession with pink have no end?—and saw the brownie lying on the floor, a bite taken out of it. What a waste, I thought as I reached for it, then noticed the red toe of a woman's shoe. I pulled the tablecloth up even farther and saw a bent leg, the tiny red dress and sprawled body of Valerie among shards of a china vase. In my earbuds, Jon Bon Jovi started screaming about going down in a blaze of glory, and I knew I'd never hear the song again without seeing her pale face.

Blood pooled on the floor beneath her head, and streaks led to the edge of the tablecloth. More blood soaked her dress and ran down from her chest, where a shard of china vase still stuck out from her heart. Her eyes were closed, her face gray, the earring twinkling in the reflected light. My breath caught and I dropped the tablecloth, taking several steps back. Was she dead? I wasn't sure, but my first thought was that she had to be. I held my breath for a moment, then started breathing again, faster than ever.

I dipped my hand in my pocket for my cell phone, dialed 911 and approached the body again. Body—was she dead? I asked myself again. Though there were still over twenty minutes before the ceremony was scheduled to begin, I heard the murmur of voices coming from the next room. My hand shook as the operator answered, "9-1-1, what's the address of the emergency?"

13

I gave her the name of the hotel and what I remembered of the address. I spoke haltingly, still not sure I believed what I'd seen. "There's a body, I'm not sure if she's dead, but this woman, at the hotel, she's been hurt. Blood. Lots of blood." Why was I freaking out? Most of the time, I was so level-headed. I'd encountered many an emergency during weddings over the years, and they hadn't thrown me. But I'd never seen so much blood before.

As she relayed the information to emergency personnel, I lifted the tablecloth and looked into Valerie's gray face again. Her eyes were closed, for which I was grateful, as I didn't think I could stand looking into her dark, almond-shaped eyes if they had been vacant. I smelled the tang of blood in the air, and wondered, vaguely, why I hadn't noticed it before.

One pink rosebud lay across her pale chest, as if put there as adornment while the rest of the bouquet lay scattered around her. Her legs were scrunched up in front of her, so she was in the fetal position—the only way she would have fit under the table.

A teenage girl approached me in her wait-staff uniform. "Is something wrong?" she asked.

I pointed to the body. The girl's eyes widened, and turning hysterical, she screamed. That made me feel almost competent—after all, I hadn't screamed, right? I almost wet myself with surprise, but I managed not to scream.

I heard a faint beeping in the hallway, the whisper of a voice over the radio—the same voice I heard in my ear, though slightly off-sync, and a tall, muscular man with serious, pale-blue eyes and strawberry blond hair entered the room, scanned it, zeroed in on me and strode over in long, ground-eating steps. "Where's the patient?" I wondered if he intended to kneel in the blood while wearing his gray pinstripe suit—which was definitely off the rack, not a product of Armani or any other designer of note. Strange, the details you notice when you're in shock.

I pointed to the table, and he flipped up the cloth edge, brushing my cake with it. I decided I didn't much care if he damaged the decorations as I collapsed into a nearby chair. He felt for Valerie's pulse, lifted an arm and pulled out his cell phone. A moment later, I heard him say, "This is Jack King with the Agave County paramedics. You can 1022 the ambulance—the patient is status echo. Trauma to the head and chest, rigor mortis has already begun."

I didn't get most of what he said—it was all gibberish. I did get the words "rigor mortis," however. That was hard to miss. I felt all the blood rush out of my head and I swayed.

Jack looked up at me, stood and hurried over, closing his phone and sliding it back into his pocket. "Hey, are you okay?" He touched my shoulder and forced me to bend at the waist so I folded in half. "Head between your legs. Feeling a bit woozy?"

"It's my first dead body," I told him. "Last night I saw her wearing that dress. She looked a little healthier then."

"Yeah, I bet she did." He touched my wrist for a moment—feeling for a pulse, I wondered? "Stay there, don't move." He stood and headed back to the door, where, when I turned my head to follow him, I saw people starting to crowd in. "Everyone out. The police will be here any minute. Go on, get out."

A distinguished man in a gray tux and wearing a pink rose boutonnière stood firm and argued with him, but Jack urged him out, promising someone would be by to explain in a minute. He requested that Mr. Richardson—which would make him father of the groom—wait for the police at the front door and show them in. I saw Tad standing beyond the door, looking in, shock on his unnaturally pale face. I thought it would be good if he put his head between his knees as well.

A minute later Jack crouched beside me. "Feeling better yet?"

"Yeah. Why did everyone come?" I asked.

15

"The screaming. Was it you?"

"No. Some young wait staff. Blond." My words were still halting, but I thought I might sit up without passing out now. When I straightened in the chair, I saw the body again, Valerie. One long, slim arm extended behind her. "How long has she been dead?"

"I don't know—the officers will have an idea. Feeling better?"

I nodded, relieved it didn't make my head spin.

He looked me over. "What are you doing here? Do you work in the kitchen?"

"No, I'm the pastry chef. Analesa asked me to make the cake."

He put two fingers on my wrist's pulse point again. "You sound like you're from the east."

"Chicago. I've only been back for a few days. Should've known leaving the city would put me in the middle of something. Bronson warned me." I was babbling at this point, not sure why, except that I needed to fill the silence with words.

"Bronson?"

"Bronson Daniel DeMille the third. My fiancé, or rather, my *ex*-fiancé." Lousy cheat. But I didn't need to spread my dirty laundry, and it appeared I did still have a tiny bit of self-control left.

"He warned you not to come to Silver Springs?" Jack stood again.

"Rednecks, he said. Hole in the ground. Waste of my potential." These were all things he'd said in a conversation we'd had on the phone the previous evening as he tried to convince me I should return to Chicago and work for him again, instead of staying in this backwater hole—as he called it. I was rather attached to this backwater hole. He also seemed to think he could sweet-talk his way back into our relationship. Stupid jerk. As if I

16

would ever forget the sight of him kissing Karen, of her smirk when she'd seen my hurt and surprise.

A sneer came over Jack's face. "I've heard that before. I didn't agree then, either." He moved away as the sound of sirens penetrated the room. "You seem fine to me. I suppose I should go where I'm useful."

I wasn't sure what I'd said to cause the attitude turnaround. Maybe he was just like that. Was he with the police? He seemed to know what was going on. I wished I did, but I didn't seem to have regained full control of my senses.

The sirens stopped, and a couple of minutes later, the doors opened and three blue-uniformed officers entered along with a man in a suit. Two went straight to the body, the other stayed to talk to Jack and the man in the suit, a tow-head in his early forties, came to my side. "Jack said he didn't get your name. I'm Detective Tingey. Can you tell me what you know?"

"I'm Tess, Tempest Crawford, and I made the cake." I told him everything I remembered from the moment I arrived, though I'm afraid it came out a bit jumbled and full of nonsense. I ran through the events, then he had me write them down. By that time, I felt more in control, and I hoped my written account made sense.

As he took the papers from me, he asked, "Is there anything you noticed that was out of place? You said she wore that dress last night. Is she missing jewelry, a purse, anything else you remember?"

I touched my ears, then my chest as I tried to remember. How had I missed it at first? "Her jewelry. She had a real flashy bracelet, necklace and earrings. I know she's still wearing the earrings but I don't think she has the necklace on anymore. I'm not sure about the bracelet." I took back the pages I'd written on and turned the last one over, doing a rough sketch of the set for him. "It was an expensive set, probably worth several thousand dollars. Do you think it might be a robbery gone wrong?"

17

"It's too early to tell. Thanks for the sketch—it helps." He took the pages back and moved away.

Everything seemed to happen in a blur—the people, the officers, the noise and confusion—but above the din, I heard Analesa's clear, distinctive voice wailing. At first I thought it was over the death of her friend, then I realized that was only one component. "Val, Val is dead, how can I get married without Val? My wedding is ruined. This was supposed to be the most perfect day of my life. But Val. Val! And her poor little girl. Parentless." It sounded as though she wasn't sure whether she should be more upset over her friend's unfortunate demise, or the postponing of the ceremony. Tad patted her hand, a grim look on his face. It was his wedding too—I supposed he was more than allowed to be upset.

A moment later Valerie's little girl ran into the room, tears flowing down her cheeks. Tad took three long strides and snatched the girl up before one of the officers could stop her. She sobbed and hit and kicked Tad, calling out to her mommy. He cradled her to his chest, murmuring softly into her hair and walked back toward the exit. The girl grew limp despite her sobs, and her little hands wrapped behind his neck before they moved out of sight.

My heart wrenched for her pain as I remembered vividly the way I'd felt when I learned my parents had been killed in a train accident. Was it better or worse that I'd been old enough to really understand what dead meant? I rubbed the chill from my arms and forced the thoughts away.

Everyone milled around, shocked and muttering. Soon Honey approached, her long black hair hanging in cornrows and her dark eyes filled with concern. "Are you okay? Someone said you found Valerie." She leaned over and gave me a big hug.

I squeezed her back, grateful for her calming influence. I'd needed a friend. "I did. It's horrible. I can't even explain how awful." Honey and I had been best friends since we were little, despite the distance between our homes.

She let me talk about what had happened until one of the officers asked her to rejoin the others. Honey squeezed my hand, promising to stop by and see me later, but left without complaint, promising me to keep her ears open. I knew how she loved gossip; it was part of what made her the savvy, people-oriented person she was.

Eventually Caroline stopped by. "We're going to have the buffet set up in the next room though the ceremony isn't taking place today. The police say we'll be able to hold the wedding tomorrow, even if we have to set up on the grounds. Can you take the cake back with you, and bring it again tomorrow? It'll keep in the fridge, won't it?"

"It'll keep." I didn't mention it was covered in fondant, so the refrigerator wasn't an option, not unless she wanted it to sweat and get water spots on it. She wouldn't care about the details, anyway, and I could handle it. The pantry downstairs in the shop was cool, since I hadn't turned on the heat there yet, and it was still March. The problem was that my cake sat on top of the table above the body, and the police hadn't appeared too interested in letting anyone near it. Deciding it couldn't be helped, I went in search of Detective Tingey. I hoped he could work something out for me.

Ten minutes later, under my direction, an officer disassembled the tiers, as much as I dared let him, and brought it over to me. I lifted the plate off the second tier and drove several sharpened dowels through the two tiers. That would keep everything together until I brought the cake back the next day. I'd deal with any issues later. I loaded everything back into my SUV and headed home.

Chapter 3

Technically, I shouldn't stash the cake in the pantry at the restaurant. My shop still hadn't had a health inspection, and I hadn't heard back on my business license application yet. The decorating, which I did in the grocery store bakery—there are advantages to Honey's connections—and piles of paperwork to make everything legal, had kept me busy all week. I hadn't taken the time to clean the shop downstairs. Unable to settle after the events of the day, I changed out of my white chef's uniform and headed down to put things to rights.

I started by making a list of everything that needed to be done. I'd already ordered a commercial oven and a nice range, and placed an ad in a regional restaurant website to sell the grill.

I'd worked for half an hour when Honey showed up, changed from her bright, flowered dress into faded jeans with non-factory created rips in them, and an old, faded T-shirt with the grocery store logo on it. She had her cornrows pulled back from her face in an elastic, making her cocoa-latte features more pronounced. She had a gorgeous face with the perfect mix of her Jamaican and French ancestry. "I figured you'd be digging in to work and could use some help, and sustenance. Since your ovens aren't here yet, I brought something along." She opened the pink box to expose four chocolate éclairs.

My favorite. "You know me so well." My recipe would be better, but I wasn't about to complain—"any éclair in an emergency" is my motto. "Are you staying around to help, or are you leaving me with three?" I asked as I washed my hands at the sink.

She chuckled. "George's mom took the kids for the day, so I'm free, at least until seven."

Three hours would easily suffice for us to finish these babies off. I boosted myself onto the counter—something I wouldn't allow myself to do once the bakery was cleaned—and selected my first pastry. "So how 'bout that murder?" I took a big bite, closed my eyes, and savored the flavor. With all the excitement, I'd forgotten to eat, so this tasted extra good.

"Is it too cliché to say I'm shocked?"

"Only if it's too cliché that I nearly passed out when I found the body."

"I'm safe, then." Honey picked out a pastry for herself. "Analesa did say she wanted it to be an event everyone would talk about for years. I think she got her wish, though I don't think it's quite what she had in mind."

"Beggars can't be choosers," I said, as if the outcome was one of the possibilities anyone might have expected. "Can you believe the way she acted, though? I couldn't decide if she was upset about Valerie's death because she was a friend, or if it was about losing her maid of honor because the line would be messed up, or the ruining of her wedding day. Like it wasn't a far worse day for Valerie."

Honey laughed outright, covering her mouth since she'd just taken a bite of éclair. "I can't believe you said that. Oh, wait, it's you—of course I can. But you're on target. She was upset about all three, and I'm not certain the death was the strongest pull. Tad seemed genuinely upset, though—such a sensible man would have his priorities straight. And his mom is a rock; pale, looking like she was ready to crumple, she instead marshaled the troops and got everyone in line."

"Sweet woman, too," I agreed. "I think she's uncomfortable

in public and that's why she's so formal with everyone. I've been mulling over the way she acts with Tad. I think her kids are her world, and the social face she put on was just that. I could be wrong, but I'd bet I'm not." I dealt with people and relationships every day in my job. They fascinated me. "Valerie's little girl though, it nearly killed me, seeing how upset she was." Her tear-streaked face was going to haunt me for a long time.

The bell over the door pealed and Detective Tingey walked in. "I hoped I'd find you here," he said to me. "I had a few more questions for you. One of the wedding party said they saw you arguing with the victim last night. Can you tell me about it?"

I blinked at him for a moment. The conversation had completely blown out of my head after I discovered Valerie's body. It took me a minute to remember what he was talking about. "Right, she argued with Analesa about something, then came over and took a brownie off the tray I was arranging. When I asked her not to mess up the presentation and suggested she should wait for the rest of the party to join them for dinner, she made a snarky comment and ate it anyway. She insulted my food, saying it wasn't as good as Roscoe's. He's such a moron."

"She insulted you?" He scribbled something in his pocket-sized notebook.

"Yes. Well, she insulted my food, which was almost the same thing. If you'd ever tried those brownies, you'd agree. *Roscoe*," I put as much of my detestation as possible into my voice, "doesn't have half my flair for pastries."

The officer gave me a commiserating look. "Okay, I want you to tell me what the two of you said, as close to word for word as you can remember. You don't mind if I record it, do you?" he asked, pulling a small recorder from his pocket.

I didn't like it, but I agreed, and did my best. When he ran me through it again, I wondered what he expected me to remember. Then he asked what I did after I left the hotel last night. I told him I'd gone to the grocery store, finished work on the cake and headed home before ten.

"Alone?"

"Yes, alone. I'm single, I live by myself. Alone." And after the breakup with Bronson, that didn't look like it would be changing anytime in the near future.

"Hmmm." He wrote something in his notebook. "I bet you were fuming after the things she said. Artists like you have killed for less."

Secretly, I agreed with him, but I saw where he was going, so I pretended not to understand. "It was a petty slight," which had reached its mark, "and completely wrong." Okay, so maybe the last comment was over the line if I wanted him to believe I was innocent. I couldn't help myself.

"Sure. Petty slights are the cause for lots of accidents these days."

"Are you calling her death an accident? Because I don't think she crawled under there, knocked herself on the head with a vase, then stabbed herself with the broken shard."

His brows lifted. "How do you know how she was killed?"

"I saw the shards. I noticed the vase last night when I was there, almost knocked it on the floor. Might have been better for Valerie if I had." Except there had been another one on the other side of the door, so maybe it wouldn't have mattered.

"Mmmhmmm." He made another note. "So you've touched the vase?"

I felt my eyes widen as my heart rate picked up. "Yeah. I did. Oh, man." I felt light-headed and was glad I was seated.

"Really? Hmmmm." He scratched the pencil across the paper again, his face unreadable.

"Is there anything else you need?" Honey asked, breaking her self-imposed silence for the first time in twenty minutes. I'd never known her to be so quiet for so long except when she was asleep, and even then she tended to hold conversations with imaginary people. We'd had plenty of sleepovers while we were growing up.

He studied the notebook for a moment. "No, I suppose that's all for now." He looked at me. "Don't leave town. I'm sure I'll need to speak with you again." He turned and pushed back through the front door.

I stood gaping after him. "He thinks I killed her. My fingerprints are on the murder weapon. I'm totally going to get nailed for this." The thought of going to jail for something I hadn't done made me shiver. Not to mention that I'd look horrible in an orange jumpsuit.

"How can he think that? You'd never kill someone." Honey pushed away from the counter and crossed the undersized kitchen.

"Because she insulted my brownies—our brownies. How messed up is that?" I started pacing the customer area. "I've never hurt anyone for insulting my food—even when they deserved it way more than Valerie. Not that insults are a reason to kill someone . . . " I stopped because Honey didn't care what I said and I was only making a bigger fool of myself.

"We can't let this happen. He so cannot pin this on you. You have to open this place, and stay here, and meet some nice man and have a dozen babies so we can grow old together."

I put my hands up at that comment, completely pulled out of my moment of panic. "Hold on—there's no way I'm having a dozen anything more time-consuming than goldfish." I wouldn't mind meeting a nice man, but it could wait a while—like until the word 'man' didn't make me want to throttle one in particular.

She nodded as if conceding my point. "What did you think of the paramedic who helped you? He's divorced."

"Jack? Nice at first, ornery once I started to feel better. Idiot." I whirled back to her. "Why are we talking about guys?

I've got to prove this wasn't me. I didn't kill the obnoxious Roscoe-lover."

Honey met me on the other side of the counter, folded her arms across her chest and smirked. "Then we'll figure it out. Where do we start?"

Chapter 4

After Honey's kids were in bed that night, we hashed out the options we had considered earlier. First things first, I thought. Until we knew more about Valerie, we couldn't decide where she'd been or what she'd done. "How about if we start back at the crime scene?" I asked as we sat in my living room.

"What are we going to find that the police didn't?"

"I don't know, but let's walk it out." I grabbed my keys and she followed me down the stairs. "Your car or mine?"

Her mouth curved into a smile. "Well, unless you want to sit in cracker crumbs, candy wrappers and forgotten Cheerios, we better take yours."

There were advantages to singleness, and a clean car was one of them. It was a good time for the reminder when I was feeling my lack of a significant other so acutely.

In no time we pulled into the parking lot at the hotel. We hopped out and I locked the doors. We walked to the front entrance, studying all the walls and the long, covered parking area designed for unloading bags. "There has to be some kind of camera system here." I remembered the monitors in the security room at the hotel in Chicago. Even though this one wasn't nearly as nice, they'd have something recording, right? Just in case.

"And the front desk clerk would have noticed her coming in. Valerie tended to stick out."

"I bet he or she won't be here yet, though." I checked my watch. It was ten p.m., which was an hour from shift change if their schedule was like most hotels.

"There, in the corner," Honey said, gesturing to the right.

I spotted the camera up high, taking in most of the parking area, and knowing what to look for now, I scanned the rest of the space, but didn't see any more. We walked through the front door and I saw another one above the doors themselves, facing into the foyer, pointed toward the check-in desk. I nudged Honey and gestured to it. We both began looking again.

Another camera was directed out the entrance to the conference center hall, but when we entered the conference room, there were none in sight. Of course that would have been far too easy. If there had been a camera in the room, Detective Tingey would have known whom to charge with murder and he wouldn't have bothered coming to ask me more questions. The area where the murder took place was still blocked off with police tape, so we went through the other side to where the ceremony was supposed to be held, looking for another entrance to the ballroom.

We checked the hall where the catering people came in. There was a way for patrons to enter that hall from down by the stairs instead of through the normal doors. I looked closer and shook my head. "There aren't any cameras on this entrance."

"Great. So that's how both Valerie and the killer got in without being caught by cameras." Honey rubbed a finger over her lips, studying the halls.

"We don't know that Valerie didn't come in the same way we did," I corrected Honey. "She might have used the front door, headed for the conference room, then met her killer in there. Only the second person had to slip in undetected."

"We need more information," Honey said.

That was for sure. I considered our options. At this time of night, there weren't many. "All right, let's go pick the desk clerk's brain."

When we arrived, we found the clerk had stepped away. I called out, but no one answered. I really wanted to get a look at

Valerie's room, but doubted anyone would let me in. "Do you think they've emptied Valerie's room yet?"

Honey's brows lifted in question.

"It would be valuable to get in there and see if there's anything useful, wouldn't it?"

"I don't know. This isn't like sneaking into Collin's room when we were kids," she mentioned her older brother.

I grinned, warmed by the memories from our childhood. "It's not like we're planning to steal anything or compromise evidence. We just want to look." I waited to see if she would argue; she didn't, though she didn't seem convinced, either. "So, do you think the stuff's still there?"

"Could be, I think the room was paid for through tonight. How do you think we're going to get up there?"

I glanced at the key card machine. Working in a hotel for so long, even though I hadn't been stationed behind the front desk, I'd learned how the machine operated. This one was identical to the one at the hotel in Chicago. Without lifting my face to the camera, I glanced up at it, judged the angle and directed Honey to stand in the way. I slid behind the counter and picked up an empty key card. "Millie said Valerie was in room 327." I punched in a couple of numbers, and slid the key card through the machine. It lit up and I pocketed the card.

I got out from behind the counter and we headed for the elevators.

"I can't believe you did that," Honey hissed at me, without moving her lips as soon as the elevator doors closed behind us.

What, did she think the security people could lip-read? Or that they'd be sitting around watching the videos as if there was nothing more important to do? I'd be surprised if they had a security guy at all, and they definitely wouldn't look at the tapes without a good reason.

"Wait and see if I did it right when we test it in the door. They may have already checked her out of the room. A lot of hotels are cracking down to keep employees from using the rooms without paying."

Honey stared at me, fascinated. "People do that?"

"Bronson had to fire a clerk a year or so back because he found out the guy took dates up to a room. He'd add the room to the cleaning list and no one was the wiser. They weren't sure how long he'd been doing it."

"He probably insisted he'd never done it before," Honey said.

"Naturally." The door to 327 had a 'do not disturb' card in the key card slot. I pulled it out and slid the key card into the lock. Green light.

Bingo.

I hoped this was Valerie's room, and not someone else's. I opened the door. Inside, the suitcase had been opened and the contents were strewn across the king-sized bed, revealing a plethora of makeup, underwear and casual clothes. I poked through the items and noticed a number of designer tags.

"Hey, be careful about fingerprints," Honey reminded me as she used the hem of her shirt to open the top dresser drawer.

"Right." I followed her example, picking up a scarf and using it flip things over and poke through the clothes.

A few kid's clothes were in the room as well—her daughter's, I realized, and remembered the little girl's tears. I moved to the closet and found four dresses, including the bridesmaid dress that matched the others, though this one had additional flourishes at the waist—probably to indicate her elevated status. Then I wondered if Analesa had known about the additions to the dress, or if Valerie had added them without permission. Six pairs of dress shoes with four-inch ice-pick heels lined the floor.

"And we have liftoff," Honey said as I admired Valerie's taste in footwear.

"What?" I turned to find Honey flipping through a planner and some papers.

"Here's a statement for her cell phone. There's also one from the bank." She picked up the paper and scanned it, flipping it over to check the charges and deposits. "Looks like regular charges: home, car, gas, food, nothing special." Still, she pulled the notebook from her purse and scribbled down the account numbers for both.

"I wish we could see her cell phone or computer or something, see if she had a note written down about her schedule." Honey muttered this as she flipped through a few more pages, but didn't find anything useful.

"We'll have to see what else we can dig up, I guess." I checked my watch again. "It's almost eleven. Want to see if the same clerk is on duty tonight?"

"Let's go."

I closed the closet door and checked to make sure everything else was the same as when we arrived. I didn't want anyone to know we'd been there, and since we weren't taking anything with us—other than Honey's notes—I hoped there wouldn't be a problem. I dropped the scarf back with the clothes where I'd found it.

We arrived at the front desk in time to see the changing of the guard. A young Latino man and little redhead were swapping the computer and cash register. We walked over and both clerks turned and smiled. "Can we help you?" the young man asked.

"Yes. I'm Tess Crawford, the cake lady from the wedding. I wondered, were either of you working last night?" I folded my arms across the chest-height counter and directed my attention to the young man.

"I was," he answered. "It's spooky, thinking about something like that happening only a few rooms away, without me knowing about it." He shifted his shoulders almost in a shrug, but looked a little unnerved.

I couldn't blame him. I often saw the murder scene when I closed my eyes. I was totally not looking forward to my dreams. "Yeah, I bet. Do you remember Valerie coming in last night, or passing through the reception area? I know you probably have a lot of people through here, but she'd be hard to miss in her little red dress."

He blushed a little. "Oh, yeah, I remembered the dress. She came in around midnight. I know because I was in the middle of the daily reports."

His expression said he remembered the parts of her which *weren't* in the dress, rather than the other way around. I wondered why she had left the hotel and with whom. "Do you remember how she acted? Did she appear drunk or upset or anything?"

"No." He shrugged. "She came in chatting on her cell phone, like it was normal to hold conversations with people at midnight. She didn't look my way, but she was on those tall, skinny heels and didn't seem wobbly to me, so she couldn't have had too much to drink."

I thought it was sweet and rather naïve that he thought someone couldn't walk on stiletto heels while drunk. Some people were super coordinated. I was not so lucky. "Did you see anyone else around? Anyone who appeared to be looking for someone?"

"No. Like I told the police, I didn't see anyone else for a long time after that, and hardly anyone in the half-hour before it. Once the hotel restaurant closes, we don't get a lot of people in and out."

31

It didn't surprise me. Silver Springs was practically the polar opposite of Chicago and New York. "Yeah, the city all but rolls in the sidewalks by ten. Thanks."

I wiped the keycard on my jacket to get any fingerprints off of it, and on the way out the door, I dropped it next to a planter where a cleaning person would most likely find it in the morning.

"What do you think?" Honey asked once we were out of hearing of the clerks.

I wrapped my jacket closer around me and wished I'd worn something warmer. Arizona may be far warmer than Chicago, but in March, the temperatures still dipped to or below freezing at night. "I think whoever she met must have come down the back way. Valerie's room was in the same wing as the conference room, but I think Analesa mentioned they bought a block of rooms for the wedding party, so that's not much to go on."

"So we're no better off than we started?" Honey asked.

"Not unless we can get one of them to admit they saw someone leaving their room between midnight and one." I was discouraged, though I knew it was stupid to let it get to me. We'd barely begun to investigate.

"If we only knew why someone would want her dead," Honey said.

"Let's hope we only find *one* reason for her death." I grimaced as I thought of how rude she was. "The woman knew how to make enemies, that's for sure."

"Then we'll have to keep digging."

I frowned and tried to think of our next move. Since we were tired, though, we returned to my home for a snack. I still had a few brownies left from the batch I'd made for the wedding breakfast.

I unlocked the door to the apartment over the restaurant and headed up. The lamplight fell in pale splashes against the faded yellow paint on the right wall of the stairwell, showing rub marks and chips in a few spots. Family portraits and postcards from trips my family had taken littered the walls. The Acropolis, Eiffel Tower, Big Ben, Egyptian pyramids and St. Basil's Cathedral in Russia made appearances, many with me and my parents in the corner of the shot.

The little apartment still held a slight musty smell despite my having been there for a week. Everything was familiar, and contrary to the pain I'd felt on my more recent visits, comforting. The room held old, worn sofas covered with afghans Grandma had knitted, the fake plants standing sentinel in the corners and on tables. More faded paint in mint green, more pictures and knickknacks. Coming back here had been a balm to my broken heart.

The restaurant had kept me busy with cleanup and renovations, but I'd managed some basic cleaning in the apartment since my return to town. There was a lot still to be done.

While Honey plated up the brownies, I headed to my tiny room for a comfy sweatshirt. The thought of moving into Grandma's much bigger room hadn't occurred to me until she'd been gone over a year, but I was so rarely here, I hadn't bothered. Since it would have required going through her personal effects, the bigger space wasn't worth the time, or the pain it would have dredged up. Now some time had passed, I might be able to face it.

Two sparkling salad plates, now with a couple of brownies on each, and two tall glasses of milk sat on the coffee table when I returned to the living room.

With a sigh, I kicked off my newest pair of Monolo Blahniks and wiggled my toes. They weren't very practical for walking around the hotel, but they made my feet pretty, and had cheered me up when I thought of being arrested for murder. Okay, so nothing could make that thought less horrible, but I'd been focused more on my aching feet than my questionable future, so that was something.

Honey picked up one shoe and held it reverently. "How unfair is it that I can never borrow your shoes? I can't believe your feet are smaller than mine."

I knew the tactic was intended to delay the conversation, and decided to humor her. "It's all that coveting you did as a kid. This is Karma blowing back at you."

She pulled a face at me. "I don't need to be reminded of what a brat I used to be."

"Used to be?" I lifted my brows at her, but I was teasing.

Honey laughed, her voice like the sound of tiny seashells as they clinked together. She was so feminine, from her short frame and tiny hands to her womanly curves. She even looked the part of a mother of three, though I still struggled sometimes to believe her oldest son was already eight. "I'm much better behaved now. Most of the time."

"Good enough for me," I took a bite and moaned in appreciation over our famous rocky road brownies. Filled with walnut chunks and chocolate chips, topped with melted marshmallows and slathered with my famous fudge frosting, nothing on the planet tasted better than these babies. "Can we say heaven?" This dessert wasn't sophisticated enough for my Chicago clients' palates—or that's what the head chefs claimed when I suggested adding them to the menu. But I couldn't imagine anyone not melting into a puddle of fulfillment with a single bite—I was totally stocking them in my bakery and knew the repeat business would be phenomenal.

Honey stayed around for another hour. I waved goodbye to her, and turned to study the apartment. I'd rarely been back to Silver Springs since I settled my Grandma's bills and everything after the funeral. Honey had told me more than once that I was avoiding the pain, and I'd feel better if I faced it all instead of staying away.

34

I hadn't believed her, but now I was home again—and wasn't it funny that I'd already begun to think of Silver Springs as home?—I found the ache of losing my last parental figure wasn't what I'd expected. The intense pain I'd felt last time had softened a great deal, though the bittersweet pain of being around Grandma's things now made tears spring to my eyes and I longed to have a chat with her. I decided I'd make a trip to the cemetery to visit her tomorrow.

Despite the late hour, my cell phone rang and I listened to *Marry Me* by Train play through until it went to voice mail. I was still avoiding Bronson's calls. If I didn't answer, just let him leave message after message, all of them pleading, none of them sincere, would he eventually stop? I wasn't sure, but the last thing I needed right after my trying day was to deal with him. He had been the one to pick the ringtone for his number, the cheating, lying jerk. I'd actually thought it was sweet at the time. Gag me.

Bronson was another hurt I'd have to deal with, and maybe it was why I'd had to come home again. Isn't that what people did when they had wounds that needed licking? Go home? I was sure there must be some primal draw to this town, even if it hadn't officially been home at any point in my life.

Despite the comforting surroundings, the knife of surprise at walking into Bronson's office to find him kissing someone else still sheared through me when I let myself think about it. Though he'd been trying to get me to agree to marry him for months, I'd only accepted a few weeks ago. Apparently he got what he wanted—whatever that was—and was ready to move on. That hurt, even as I hated myself for thinking maybe he had an excuse. Maybe, just maybe, we could make this work after all.

No. Ignoring the calls was best.

It was late when I headed to bed, still smelling the sweet sachets Grandma always stuck in with her linens. It permeated the clean sheets I'd pulled out of the cupboard earlier. It was almost as good as having her arms wrapped around me.

Chapter 5

I kept a close eye on everyone as I stood at the table with my cake the next evening. The police had cleared the room for use again only two hours before the wedding ceremony was scheduled to start, which meant the hotel staff and I had scrambled to set up everything.

The ceremony was over and Honey mingled through the crowd, making a point of tracking down all the people who'd been in the hotel the night of the wedding rehearsal—which, according to reports, had been the entire wedding party.

Because I was the hired help, it was my job to stand behind the cake table or in the corner out of the way, rather than chatting with guests—a rule I mostly intended to follow. It gave me a chance to watch everyone and see how they interacted. It was a smaller group than originally planned, but that was okay by me. One hundred people instead of a hundred and sixty meant I could see all the possible suspects.

The tone of the event was far more subdued than it would have been a couple days earlier. Even from my corner, I could see the tears, comforting touches and delicate sniffles against lacey handkerchiefs. Was this a wedding celebration or a wake? It was hard to tell, and the answer was, of course, that it might have been a bit of each.

After everyone had eaten their dinners, the bride and groom went through the ritual cake cutting and serving. They were totally circumspect about it—no frosting on the face for this couple. Then they moved away for the next set of pictures and I took off the top layer for the bride and groom to freeze for their first anniversary and sliced the next tier to be served to guests.

There's a science to slicing wedding cakes so all the pieces are the same size and no one feels picked on if they get a smaller piece than their neighbor. I seldom had the opportunity to do the cutting when I worked at the DeMille Hotel—I'd trained several of the wait staff there to do the job properly. Despite people's regrets that the masterpiece had to be destroyed, no matter how gorgeous, how elaborate the confection, it was, at heart, still just cake—fabulous and delicious, but cake all the same. I never felt bad about seeing one massacred for the guests to enjoy. It was meant to be eaten. If I wanted my art to last forever, I'd have taken up painting instead.

Jeff, best man, and the guy I nearly plowed into Friday evening, was the first of the wedding party to amble my direction.

"Chocolate almond, or vanilla with raspberry filling?" I asked when he stopped at the table.

"Vanilla, thanks. Is this going to taste as good as it looks?" His smile was flirtatious.

"Better. I guarantee it." I flirted right back, leaning in and allowing my lips to curve. So I wasn't looking for love—did that mean I couldn't enjoy myself? My pride was wounded, my heart broken, but a good flirtation always helped me feel better after a breakup.

His eyebrows lifted. "That certain, are you?" He forked up a bite, smiled, chewed for a moment and muttered from the corner of his mouth, "Holy cow, you weren't exaggerating."

I grinned, always happy to see people enjoy themselves. "Never doubt that my food is as good as my reputation."

"Reputations are delicate things," he said.

"They can be, yes." I'd heard from Honey that Jeff and

Valerie were attorneys for competing firms. "But you would know all about reputations. Lawyers have to protect their names as carefully as pastry chefs, don't they? Too many losses and you become persona non grata."

His eyes flashed back to mine. "Who told you?"

I blinked, surprised by his defensive question. "About what?"

He paused, took another bite of his cake and chewed for a moment. The move was very deliberate as his legal mind seemed to consider his words. "I thought you were referring to the lawsuit I fought against Valerie. Our clients had a business deal go bad. Valerie magically came up with some crucial evidence which cost us the trial."

He stuffed another bite in his mouth, not paying attention to the food anymore. "*Fabricated* was more like it, though. And she couldn't have won without the evidence. I don't mind people playing hardball, using the loopholes of the law to get what their client wants, but I draw the line at making things up."

"I understand that," I said, making sure my voice oozed sympathy. "When I was in culinary school, there was a competition with the other students. We had to create a dessert, and one guy used a recipe he'd filched from a famous chef. He won the prize, and I know he didn't deserve it." Yes, I'm referring to Roscoe—so you see why I was so offended by Valerie's suggestion that he was the better pastry chef. What were the odds that we'd end up living only an hour apart?

"Then you understand where I'm coming from. I'm sorry to see her dead, but Valerie didn't play by the rules." Jeff's plate was already empty. He stared at it as if surprised to see the cake was gone, then looked at me. "It was delicious. Thank you."

Had he even noticed it after that first bite, or was he being polite? "You're welcome. I hope you remember me if you ever need a special-occasion dessert."

"I will." He set the dirty plate on the table.

He was ready to walk away, but I wasn't finished with him, so I hurried with another question. "Valerie must have been doing well at her law firm, considering all the fancy clothes and jewelry she had. Do you think that case helped her climb the ladder?"

"I'm sure it would have helped in the long run, but I doubt it did anything yet. Valerie's always had more money than sense, or at least, she spends as if she does. I know she doesn't make that kind of money at her job. I figured it was a trust fund or something." He shrugged.

One of the bridesmaids approached and requested a slice of chocolate cake. I tried to place her, but couldn't do it.

"I hope you enjoy it," I said as I handed her a plate. Her bottle-blond hair was teased into a chic halo around her head.

"Thanks. I'll try." Her words were dry and she shot Jeff a nasty look before heading back into the crowd.

He winced.

My curiosity perked, but I tried not to be too obvious. "Who was that? I don't think I caught her name earlier."

"Janice. She's Tad's sister," he answered. He started to move away.

"Things must have been pretty busy here the night Valerie died," I asked, desperate to get some more answers from him before he melted back into the crowd. "Was there a wild bachelor party after the wedding rehearsal that night? Bachelorette party?"

"No, that was a few days earlier. Both Tad and Analesa decided they wanted to be fresh and alert for their wedding instead of hung over. I understand the women were going to get together and do their nails or something, though." He shook his head as if to say women were incomprehensible to him. "Thanks again." He raised a hand in greeting to one of the other guests and headed off with a vague goodbye to me.

I made notes on the little paper I had stuck in my pocket.

I remembered Valerie's red fingernails when I found the body—the same color she'd been wearing during the wedding rehearsal. Had she chosen not to join the others, or did she just prefer red? Did she go hang with the other women for a while, then go out, or did she skip the girl time?

A dark-haired woman came over, holding the hand of the little girl I'd seen at the wedding rehearsal dinner Friday night. Valerie's little girl. "What can I get for you ladies? Chocolate or vanilla with raspberry filling?"

"Vanilla," the woman said. She looked pale and tired. "How about you, Dahlia?" she asked the girl.

"Chocolate." Dahlia was very decisive, though she also looked very sad and a little cross.

"Great choice." I handed the slices over. "I saw you here a couple nights ago," I said to Dahlia.

The woman answered as Dahlia stuffed a huge bite of the cake in her mouth. "Yes. She's Valerie's little girl."

I studied the woman more closely. "You must be a sister. You look a lot alike."

"I'm Lidia, Valerie's older sister. I arrived last night after they let me know." Her voice broke and she paused to get it back under control. "My apologies. Did you know my sister well?" Her pain was palpable.

"No. We spoke only the one time Friday evening." I chose not to tell her the subject of our conversation. No need to bring it up now, after all. "I'm surprised you're here tonight. It's such a tragedy for you."

Lidia touched a hanky to her cheek. "Yes, but Tad insisted that he wanted Dahlia here, to get her mind off things, so I brought her for a while." Her breathing hitched and she gave me a watery smile. "I think the plan backfired."

"I'm so sorry." My heart went out to this woman. Even if

Valerie hadn't exactly been the nicest person ever, it must still be hard for her sister. "Are you going to be in town for a while?"

Lidia nodded. "For the next few days while they sort everything out. Dahlia and I are all she had, so I'll be settling the estate." She turned her head as someone called her name from the crowd, and I looked up to see Tad gesturing to her. "Looks like I'm being summoned," she said to me. "It was good to meet you."

"Same here." I watched with sympathy as she led the little girl back into the crowd. Settling a family member's estate was never easy. I'd done it first after my parents' deaths, then with my grandma, so I was intimately aware of the stresses involved. Dahlia stretched her arms up to Tad, and he passed the cake to Lidia, then scooped up the little girl. She snuggled into him, tucking her face into his chest, looking lost.

My resolve to investigating the murder strengthened. That child needed answers, and knowing her pain, I was going to be make sure she got them.

A few minutes passed as I continued to hand out cake to guests before Honey ambled over and scooped up a slice of chocolate.

"Learn anything interesting?" I asked.

"It's hard to interrogate people without letting them know what you're doing, but I did manage to get a little information." She closed her eyes as she savored the first bite. "Oh wow, I forgot what this was like. You so need to live in the area where I can taste-test for you all the time."

I laughed. What was a best friend for if not to fawn and praise once in a while? "You've got me. Now, what did you learn?"

"Analesa's mom confirmed that all the bridal party, as well as family members, were staying here in the hotel. Their house has been leased, you know." She said this in all seriousness, as if I was in the loop on local gossip and of course I would know.

"Why did they do that?"

"Mr. Plumber's company transferred him out of the area a couple years back so they moved, but he plans to retire in another year or two. They didn't want to sell."

"But of course they couldn't leave the house vacant," I answered the question myself. "That explains why everyone stayed here." Honey consumed the cake with gusto while I reined in my own longing for a slice. Working with sugar and fat all day showed on my hips. I knew I needed to stay away from the goodies, or at least try to refrain from eating more than one piece.

Especially after enjoying two éclairs the previous afternoon and a brownie last night. Fat city, even if they were delicious. I really needed to start working out again.

Instead of obsessing about the food, I turned the conversation. "Okay, so everyone was here. Jeff told me the girls might have had plans to do their nails after the wedding rehearsal, but the wild parties were held days earlier."

"Okay, you noticed the fingernails, didn't you?"

I had, since I'd been watching after talking to Jeff. Analesa and her attendants all wore what appeared to be the same shade of pale pink fingernail polish. It matched the color of the bridesmaid dresses, and the sash around the bride's white dress. The pink rose bouquet and trailing pink ribbons were the same shade as well. "But Valerie's nails were still red when she died, so she didn't join them that night."

"That would be my guess. Here comes Millie now. She was the third roommate with Valerie and Analesa in college. You see what you can find out from her, I'll go interrogate the mother of the groom." She grinned and glided across the room while managing to greet and schmooze with everyone in sight. The woman was a marvel.

Millie was a pale blonde with a mole near her mouth

reminiscent of Christy Brinkley's—which had me wondering if it was real, or an affectation intended to draw attention. Her mouth was wide and sulky, and, despite the pink everywhere else, was slathered in Come Get Me red lipstick. "I want a little piece of the chocolate," she said.

I handed her a plate. "All the pieces are pretty much the same, sorry." I considered suggesting she not finish the whole thing, but knew from experience that once she tried it, she'd finish it off. Most people did.

I looked at her hands. "It's fun that your fingernails coordinate with all your dresses."

"Yes, we had a girls' pampering night after the wedding rehearsal." Her voice hitched and one of her hands fluttered to her chest. "Sorry, I'm just still so upset. I can't believe this happened to Valerie. I've known her for so long. Did you know we were roommates with Ana in college? Like three peas in a pod." She held back a small sob. "I'm sorry—it must have been so horrible for you. Weren't you the one to find her yesterday?"

A chill and twinge of revulsion came over me when I thought of the blood everywhere and the color of Valerie's skin and I had to swallow hard and beat it back. "Yes. It was so difficult. It could have been worse though. I didn't know her well."

Millie nodded, picked up a fork and tasted a bite. She made a humming noise in the back of her throat. "Wow. I never knew cake could taste so good." Her mournful air disappeared as she took another taste.

"Thank you. That's such a kind thing to say." Her sudden attitude change confused me. My cake was amazing, but I'd never seen it improve someone's mood so fast.

"Not kind—honest." She gave me a calculating look. "You're opening a shop here in town?"

"Yes, hopefully in the next few weeks. It depends on how

long it takes to get all the paperwork and supplies." I tipped my head and looked at Millie's perfectly manicured hands again. "Did Valerie go to the girls' night party? I could swear she hadn't gotten her nails painted between dinner and . . . you know."

"Oh, no. She said she wouldn't be there, that she'd take care of it in the morning while we all dressed. She had a date, I guess." She tried to act like it didn't bother her, but her voice held an edge of spite. "She always had a date, or three."

Under normal circumstances, I would have let that tidbit of information float on by, not the least interested in pursuing it, but this time I chased it. "Is that what she and Analesa were arguing about after the wedding rehearsal?"

"Yes, well, more or less. Not the date that night, but the way she was always had to have a guy around. Valerie flirted with Ana's younger brother, who's a bit tender-hearted, not up to dealing with such a barracuda."

I smiled as I remembered Analesa's brother. "Is he here? I haven't seen Shawn in years. I must have missed him when he came in." I glanced around for the grown-up version of the skinny kid I'd known as a teen. I'd expected to see him that day, but hadn't caught a glimpse of anyone who looked likely.

"I saw him earlier," Millie turned and studied the crowd. "The guy there, standing with the woman in teal."

I spotted Shawn, maybe thirty feet away, though it took me a moment to be sure it was him. It's amazing what twelve years and fifty pounds can do to a guy. He was hot now! Was it in the genes? Did the Plumber family members start out homely and become beautiful before they were twenty-five? Did they have a freaking fairy godmother or something? It was so unfair. Not that I was interested, because I totally wasn't, but *dang*.

"I didn't see him Friday." I know I would have remembered him.

Millie smirked. "Into younger men, are you?"

I must have shown more of my appreciation for his current look than I'd meant to. I caught myself. "Not particularly. I remember him as a scrawny, freckled little boy." And he was only a couple of years younger than me, anyway.

"He's not scrawny anymore, is he?" She glanced at him again with a look of female appreciation.

I realized I'd gotten off topic and needed to bring it back to Friday night. I watched the last bite of chocolate cake disappear as Millie ate it, and hurriedly said the first thing that came to mind. "Do you think Valerie could have met with Shawn after she left you guys?"

"What? Oh no, it sounded like she had plans with some local guy. I have no idea who. It couldn't have been Shawn, though, since Ana called him around nine, nine-thirty, and said he was shooting pool downtown with some old buddies." She paused and tipped her head. "I suppose he might have been lying. It never occurred to me. I hope that's not true, though, since he could be blamed for her death. He's a sweet kid."

I didn't remember him being a sweet kid. A bit of a terror, yes, hilarious and full of fun, absolutely, but not sweet. I supposed anyone could change. "So how late did your girls' night go? You must have been tired after the travel and practice."

"I don't know, sometime before midnight." She turned to look at me, as if realizing I'd been pumping her for information. "What are you, one of those nosy neighbors who has to have all the gruesome details? Because I have nothing to say to you people. I don't know anything about her death—I just came here to be with Ana and help her through her special day." She stomped off—not as gracefully as Valerie had managed, I noted.

45

Chapter 6

It was some time before I gave up on Shawn coming over, so I grabbed a slice of each cake flavor and two forks, and approached him and his companion. This time the breach of etiquette would be overlooked, I figured, for old friends such as we, um, weren't.

The pretty redhead turned first, her eyes locked on the dessert, and she greedily took the chocolate piece as I started to speak, "Would either of you like some?" The words were unnecessary, but I was happy to let her have the chosen flavor. I turned to Shawn, and offered him the vanilla. "If you'd rather, I could get you another slice of the chocolate." Up close, I studied him again. Yes, if I'd gotten a good look earlier, I would have recognized him. At least I would have realized he had to be related to Analesa.

A smile bloomed over his face. "Hello, Tess, right? I'm Shawn, Ana's brother. I haven't seen you in ages."

I feigned surprise, then recognition. "Well, my goodness. Shawn Plumber, I had no idea it was you. It has been a long time, hasn't it?" I let my eyes do a quick head-to-toe scan on him. "Grown up, haven't you?" He was anything but scrawny. His shoulders were wide, his face chiseled. Did he work out, or did he have a job that put all that muscle on him?

"Some time ago. You got too busy to notice when I was

around." His smile dimmed. "I was sorry to hear about your grandma. Cancer's such a hard way to go."

"It was hard," I agreed with a twist of pain in my chest. Even now a lump came to my throat, but I did my best to ignore it. "They say time heals all wounds, but it only softens them. Some never quite seem to go away." I should know. I still missed my parents every day, and we'd buried them more than a dozen years earlier.

"Yeah. I get that." He held my gaze for a long moment, causing a little shiver of excitement to slide down my spine.

The redhead looked from him to me, sighed and said she had someone to talk to, then slipped off.

The distraction was what I needed to break the strange attraction I felt to him. "I'm sorry if I interrupted your conversation. She's very pretty," I said, though more to feel out his relationship to her than anything else.

He laughed. "She's my cousin, so you're fine."

I felt a bit relieved, though I told myself I shouldn't care one way or the other. He wasn't exactly the only attractive man in the room. "What are you doing these days?"

"Border patrol. I'm stationed out of Nogales."

I blinked in surprise. I'd expected something more . . . white collar than that. "What a nice, calm, boring career with no danger whatsoever," I stated with more than a little sarcasm. In these turbulent times, it had to be as dangerous as being an inner-city cop.

He shrugged. "It has its moments, like most jobs." He studied me for a moment. "I bet you face your share of dangers from irate brides, angry mothers and maids of honor who skewer with words rather than weapons."

I felt my face flush. Did everyone know? It wasn't like many people had been in the room at the time. "Heard about that, did you? Was she naturally repellent, or was she having an extra good day?" As soon as the words came out, I realized how disrespectful they were and tried to backpedal. I'd been taught better than to speak badly about the dead. "I mean, I'm sure she had a lot on her mind, getting ready for her date and everything."

He finally tasted the cake. "This filling is incredible. This is almost as good as your brownies." He swallowed. "Sorry for the change of subject, but where did you learn to cook like this?"

I leaned forward and lowered my voice in a conspiratorial manner. "Cooking school," I whispered, then used a regular voice. "And a one-year internship with a master in France. This is a slight variation of one of his recipes. I'm glad you like it."

His eyes caught mine. "I have the feeling I'd like most anything you cooked." His voice had dropped slightly, turning smoky and deep. A dimple I'd forgotten about flashed in his left cheek. "Do you cook real food, too? I'll be in town for a few days, and I'd love to pop by, or take you out for dinner."

I doubted very much Millie's assertion that Shawn was tender-hearted and needed to be protected—he was way too smooth. I was the furthest thing from wanting to get involved in another relationship barely a week after I broke up with Bronson. But Shawn lived five hours away, so it wasn't like it was going to get serious. It would just be a diversion, which I could totally use. And I did need someone to help me shift around equipment—he definitely had the muscles for it. "I think I'd like that. Going out, I mean. What's good for you?"

"Tomorrow night?" He pulled a card out of his pocket with his rank and office information—he kept it in his tux jacket? During his sister's wedding? Yeah, totally naïve and likely to be taken great advantage of, I thought. Not. He handed me the plate, "Hold that for a moment, will you?" He pulled a pen from his pocket and wrote something on the card. "This is my cell phone number. Call me tomorrow and we'll set something up."

I swapped him the cake for the card. "I'll do that." A glance back over my shoulder and I saw the prepared slices were getting low. "I better get back to the table."

"I'll see you around." Even in the dimness, his hazel eyes seemed to twinkle at me.

"See you." I turned back to the table, my heart beating a bit faster than before and came face-to-face with Jack, the emergency-responder guy from the day before.

"Having fun?" He shifted a glance back to Shawn and then to me again. "I thought you were here to work. I didn't realize it was a social opportunity for you."

"Just saying hello to an old acquaintance. Would you prefer chocolate or vanilla?" I became all business, the good mood I'd been feeling vanishing in the face of his cold attitude.

His pale blue eyes narrowed. "Ah, touching base again. Is that what you were doing? It looked like more to me."

I didn't respond, as he was right, even if it was rude of him to say so. I plated up a slice of each flavor, setting them before him. He took the chocolate, a choice I could commend him for, even if I disliked him. "It's none of your business."

"Which is fine, because I don't care." Still, he stood there for a moment while he ate his first bite. Unlike most people, however, he had no kind words about the quality of my product. I suppose he was just that much of a Neanderthal. "You've worked through your shock from yesterday?" he asked after a moment.

Was he trying to be kind? The man was giving me whiplash. "I doubt I'm going to get over seeing a dead body anytime soon, though you seemed to cope well."

He gave me an irritated look. "I'm a paramedic. It's not exactly old hat, as we don't get many murders around here, but I've seen my share of dead bodies."

That explained the pager he wore even now, and the muscles that rippled under his cotton shirt. That must be from the heavy people and equipment he had to carry at work. He'd already taken off the jacket I'd seen him wearing earlier. From the way his tie was loosened and a bit askew, he appeared ready to get rid of it as well.

"That explains a lot," I said, though there was still a bit of vitriol in my voice. I paused, trying to bring my emotions back to level. It had been stressful, and he didn't deserve to be treated badly, even if he did act like a jerk. Besides, I was hardly going to drum up new business if I was rude to the locals. "Sorry. Have you heard anything about Valerie? When she died?"

"I ran into Detective Tingey. He thinks it was around midnight, one o'clock, though he's still waiting for the official word. She sure didn't die under the table, though. They found blood traces all over the floor in there, swirled around, like someone had cleaned up after they hid the body."

That seemed so cold and calculated. "I wonder what happened to her jewelry."

His lifted a brow. "Her jewelry?"

"Yes. She had this really beautiful," Gaudy, "necklace, earring and bracelet set on earlier in the evening."

His brow furrowed. "Maybe she'd already taken them off?"

"Hmm." I doubted it; she was still wearing her stilettos. That told me she hadn't been back to her room. After so many hours, even a fashion-conscious woman would be groaning over the pain in her feet with those babies—and I don't care how many women claimed they found the shoes comfortable. They were all lying. Don't get me wrong, I wear heels often, but comfortable as slippers, they weren't.

"You think it was about theft?"

I realized he was buddies with the guy who wanted to pin this all on me—the detective told him time of death, didn't he—and I didn't want to give him any ammo. I had nothing to do with it. "Who knows? I just noticed they were missing. I mentioned it to Detective Tingey. He seems very thorough." I hoped he was thorough and looking at several people as suspects and not only me.

"I've always thought he was," Jack said.

I decided it was time to change the subject before it became obvious how curious I was about the murder. "So how do you know the bride and groom?"

"I grew up here. Analesa's dad and mine were best friends, second cousins or something."

Wait, Jack? My eyes zeroed onto his face as I considered, comparing him to the image of the little boy I knew. "Not the Jack who's a few years older than Analesa and me, who used to torment the girls at the pool during the summer?"

A chuckled. "Guilty as charged. Should I know you?"

Only if you remember being bested by a couple of younger girls, I thought. "I doubt it. I was a bit of a mouse." Holy terror, that's what he'd been. And boys like him so seldom grew up to be anything but bullies. I supposed that explained his attitude. This destroyed any interest I might otherwise have had in him—if I'd been interested, which I wasn't—and I turned to cut more slices.

Honey came over. "Tess, everyone's raving about your cake. Can I have another piece of the chocolate?"

"Wait a minute," Jack said as I handed a plate to Honey. He looked at her, then back at me. "Tess and Honey. What mouse?" he asked, putting his now-empty plate on the table. "You were no mouse—more like a spitfire. The two of you ganged up on me at the pool."

"That's still one of my favorite memories." Honey's words were wistful. "You so deserved it."

I flashed a grin at him, then turned to Honey. "We went too easy on him."

She nodded. "Good thing you grew up okay. I'm taking credit for that. Well, joint credit with Tess here. If we hadn't

51

straightened you out at such a young age, who knows what might have happened?"

Jack laughed, surprising me. "Well, I'll remember to keep out of your way. I don't need a whole lot more lessons like that one." He focused on me. "Thanks for the cake. It was delicious." He waved at both of us and moved back into the crowd.

Honey smiled knowingly at me. I glared back at her. "Forget it. He's a self-righteous, condescending jerk." Who just happened to be extremely handsome and had a decent personality when he wasn't being prickly. He'd helped me with my timeline, hadn't he—even if he didn't realize it. "Now Shawn Plumber, on the other hand—he's very nice, hunky and we have a date tomorrow night."

"Wow. Good job on getting back into the dating pool so fast, but," Honey's brow furrowed. "Shawn Plumber? Scrawny Shawn?"

"Not scrawny anymore. Where've you been?" I turned and pointed him out in the crowd. He was chatting up a woman. Another cousin, I wondered, or someone else? Then I decided it didn't matter either way. I was the one with the date for the next night, after all, and it wasn't like he would be around all that long, anyway.

"Oh, not scrawny Shawn at all," she agreed after a long look. "Dish."

"Nothing much to say. We flirted a bit, and he asked me out. I'll call him tomorrow and set something up. He had his business card in the inside pocket of his tux." I met her gaze. "Player?"

"Yeah, player. But hey, it doesn't mean you can't have fun with him tomorrow night." She wiggled her eyebrows at me.

"My thoughts exactly." I made another long two-inch-wide slab in the bottom cake tier, then flipped it on its side for slicing into smaller pieces.

Honey forked up another bite from her plate. "So what else have you learned?"

52

I brought up the conversations with Millie and Jeff, the tidbits I'd gleaned from Shawn—I hadn't asked Shawn much about Friday, actually. I'd gotten a little caught up in his dancing eyes. But I didn't need to pump everyone tonight, right? There was time to worry about it tomorrow. And as we had a date, there would be plenty of opportunities.

"Tad's sister agreed they finished their girls' night around eleven," Honey reported. "She said no one left early, as far as she remembered, and they all headed for bed, but if the murder happened after that, it wouldn't matter anyway."

"Right. So that's a bust as far as alibis go." We were getting nowhere fast.

"And we're more or less back at square one."

"Dang it." I eyed the chocolate cake, then reminded myself that I had the extra filling and cake tops at home, and it was totally unprofessional for me to eat at the party.

"Oh, I spoke to Nadine Frost, from the city council. She said they approved your business license in their Friday meeting." Honey did a little celebration wiggle. "You'll be getting the paperwork in the mail on Monday or Tuesday."

It felt good that she was so excited I was really sticking around. I knew I'd need her support. "Well, good. I officially had a business license before I brought the brownies here on Friday. Now if my tax ID number and equipment will arrive, I can get moving for real." The thought still gave me major butterflies, but I was starting to get used to the idea, however terrifying it might be.

Honey finished her slice, and disappeared back into the crowd to mingle again. Neither of us learned anything more that night, but as I toted all of my equipment out to my SUV, I knew there was still another day ahead of us. And lots of possibilities.

Chapter 7

I still needed to go back into Prescott and see if I could find a good stand mixer and bowls.

And I needed to return to Chicago to take care of things there. I was not looking forward to clearing out my condo. It could take a while to sell, and while I was in town, I had the feeling I'd end up dealing with Bronson, who had sent several nasty messages about leaving him high and dry.

I did have one more cake I should return to decorate. The Goulds had booked the hotel because I worked there. My design had been the breaking point between the DeMille Hotel and the Four Seasons, and the Goulds had been such good customers in the past. I knew Lenny, my assistant, could probably handle it without me, but I'd take care of it myself anyway.

I'd have to call Bronson again before long. But I'd let him stew over what to do for another day or two before making arrangements to return to tie up loose ends. I figured I deserved that extra bit of retribution.

I set the pen down and picked up my phone, along with the business card Shawn had given me the previous evening. I could use his help to move things out of the kitchen.

His cell phone only rang twice before he answered. "This is Shawn."

"Hey, this is Tess. How're you doing?"

"Great. I hoped you'd call, and that you weren't feeding me a line last night." His voice switched from professional to soft, maybe a bit smooth. If he'd had a drawl, I had the feeling it would have thickened.

I smiled despite myself. It had been a while since I'd played this game. Bronson and I never went through this stage, we'd known each other so well before we started dating. Well, I'd thought I knew him. "I always keep my promises."

"So what time works for you tonight? Could I pick you up, say around six?"

"Six works for me." I considered everything on my to-do list, but figured there would be time to clean before getting ready for the date. "I wondered, though, do you have a little free time in the next hour or two, and a friend or three who could help move some equipment around here? I need to get the grill out of the way so I can bring in my new oven when it arrives in a couple of days." And as long as I had muscles available, maybe I'd have them do a little extra work.

"Sure. Hold on." I heard a muffled voice, as if he'd covered the receiver. A moment later he came back. "I'll bring Jeff with me. We can take care of it. Half an hour good for you?"

"Perfect." I touched my hair. I definitely needed to do something about my appearance before he arrived. The morning had been busy already. We said goodbye as I made my way to the bathroom to primp.

The guys were prompt and both were dressed to work. Shawn and Jeff looked almost as good in T-shirts and jeans as they had in tuxes—not something just anyone can say. "Thanks, guys, I really appreciate this." I told them which equipment to move where and grabbed some metal shelving, pulling it into the customer area. The whole restaurant needed a good scrubbing and a fresh coat of paint. Upstairs too, come to think of it, but there wasn't time for that right now. I'd have to take a trip to the hardware store and look at paint samples, I decided, and made a mental note to squeeze it into my schedule.

"I expected you to be back in Prescott by now," I said to Jeff. Though it was 'out of town,' I didn't think the police would freak out about him returning to work when it was only eighteen miles away—in Chicago that was barely across town.

"I took an extra day off, thinking I'd do some hiking, but with the change of the wedding, things didn't work out quite like I expected. I have to head back tonight." He looked around. "So you're going to turn this into some high-class bakery, huh?"

"Yeah. Honey insists business will be good, and I'd love to give it a shot. I've been working for other people for too long." Way too long, no matter how overwhelmed starting my own business made me feel.

It was time to poke a little more, see if I could learn anything new from the guys. "So you're going to go home, dive back into work and won't have to worry about Valerie's dirty tactics, right?"

Jeff smiled. "There is that one little upside to all this. Though I really am sorry it happened to her. No one deserves that."

"Of course not. I heard she died between twelve and one a.m. Do you have any idea why she'd be running around the hotel then? Seems late to be getting back from her date. And why was she in the conference room? I'd have gone straight to bed." I tried not to let on how big of a wimp I was as I lifted the old microwave from the counter and hauled it to one of the benches in the other room. The ancient appliance was way too heavy.

"No idea," Shawn said. "Seems odd to me, too."

"Maybe she was meeting someone there," Jeff suggested as he and Shawn hefted the old grill, sliding it through the door without having to remove one of the jams—barely—and setting it in the dining area. "I mean, she must have run into someone down there. Maybe it was planned."

"A liaison?" I suggested. Was the theft an afterthought? Had she met a guy for a make-out session and ended up meeting with the wrong person? The front desk clerk hadn't seen anyone, but did that mean anything? Maybe he'd stepped away from the desk for a while, or the guy could have come in the back way, like Honey and I hypothesized.

"Wouldn't be the first time she had more than one date in a day," Shawn agreed. "She had this thing about juggling several guys at once. I remember Millie and Ana talking about it."

"Hmmm. Millie seemed a little jealous when she mentioned Valerie's success in the dating department." I tried to pretend I was only mildly curious, but since the topic had come up twice now, it had me searching for possibilities.

"She would be." Shawn grabbed one of the paper towels sitting on the counter and wiped his hands. "From what I understand, Millie was dead gone on some guy in college. Valerie knew it, but chased after him anyway. Maybe she chased him *because* Millie was interested in him. There's no way to know, but Millie seemed to think so. I don't think she ever forgave Valerie."

That didn't jive at all with the way Millie had spoken the previous night about her *close friend* Valerie's death. I decided to keep that tidbit to myself. "Huh. Doesn't sound like Valerie was a very popular gal. Anyone else hate her?"

"Everyone on the planet?" Jeff suggested as they moved to the grill. "You'd barely met her and she insulted you, didn't she? It took what, fifteen seconds?"

"Maybe seventeen," I corrected. He flashed a grin at me. "Point taken, though. To be fair, as much as I'd have liked to knock her on the head with one of Roscoe's dinner rolls, that might have been painful, but would hardly have been fatal. Someone else had a little more serious damage on their mind."

"Depressing topic, if you ask me," Shawn said. "I'd way rather talk about the Suns' chances of making it to the finals."

When Jeff took to the conversation change with alacrity, I figured they'd rather leave the not-so-pretty past where it was. That was fine; I had another angle to follow now. I wondered why Millie pretended she and Valerie were best buds.

Chapter 8

After that, I decided some baking was in order. Baking had become a form of stress relief for me over the years—yet one more reason I should bake for others, since I could only eat so many pastries before I started to look like a whale. While I had a few extra pounds on my hips, I loathed working out, so it was imperative that someone else eat most of my creations.

I decided to work on the adjustments to the chocolate cheesecake recipe I'd been tweaking and made a run to the store for ingredients.

Humming, I started with my favorite shortbread crust, mixing, then spreading it in the pan to bake while I beat the filling.

The temperature needed to be nice and steady, so I checked the preheating oven, then whipped the cream cheese and sugar.

It had been a full two days since I found the body, and I didn't feel like Honey and I had made much headway. Apparently, neither had the police, and I was certain they were devoting a great deal of time to the problem.

I finished mixing in the softened cream cheese and slowly stirred in the sugar, vanilla and eggs, one at a time. I took a break to make notes and conjectures about each of the players in this little drama, letting the KitchenAid do its job. I melted the bittersweet chocolate, cooled it and whipped it in with the cream. I added the two mixtures, and beat the whole thing until it was light and fluffy.

After I'd poured it all into my grandma's old spring-form pan, I put the pan in a water bath in the oven and set the timer.

I had more than an hour before the cheesecake would be done. Time for a ramble.

I decided to take a closer look at downtown Silver Springs and headed out. In the past couple of years, I hadn't made it back to town as much as I did prior to Grandma's death. A clothing boutique had closed, a pet store opened and the craft store had gotten a face lift—which was well overdue. Half a block down the road, I turned to my own storefront and considered it.

The building was on a corner lot, all brick and two stories. The large window beside the glass front door had a circular top— perfect for my planned vinyl-lettering sign. The upstairs windows were tall and let in a lot of evening sunlight during the summer.

The back side of the building had a quaint little courtyard, and the kitchen stuck out next to it. It had a flat roof and shingles down the sides that curved up at the bottom—very charming and European. A set of stairs led up onto the roof above this portion of the apartment, and I remember many July Fourths sitting up there to watch city fireworks. Thankfully, all the businesses shared a large parking lot out back, where we stashed the Dumpsters out of sight and where I entered the upstairs apartment.

Despite the quaint European feel to the exterior, the interior was more like an old mom-and-pop restaurant. After continuing down the road for a few blocks to see what else was new, I headed back to my place. When I drew close, I saw a woman and child approaching and realized it was Valerie's sister and daughter. Though they'd come to my table for cake Sunday night, there had been no chance for me to ask her any questions. I crossed the street and headed for Lidia.

"Hi, Lidia, isn't it?" I asked when I got close. I looked at Dahlia and saw her sad, sad eyes and pinched face. Sympathy swelled inside me.

The fair-skinned woman with almond eyes and black hair

like her sister's looked at me, the little girl's hand clasped in hers. "Yes, it's Tess, right?"

"Yes. How are you doing? Are you enjoying the nice weather?" I studied the woman's face. She looked worn out. Not surprising, considering everything she had to deal with.

She nodded. "Yes, it's pretty here." She seemed lethargic, and a bit wary.

"How are things going?" I asked. "You said you live in California?"

"Yes. My husband and I have a home in Long Beach. It's a long drive. I didn't get here until Saturday evening."

"And when do you think you'll be able to go home?"

She pressed her lips together for a moment, then shot a glance at the little girl by her side. "The police say I should be able to, um, arrange transport in the next day or so. We'll have the funeral in Prescott on Saturday evening. I think Valerie would have liked a sunset service."

"It sounds nice." You know, if a funeral for a thirty-ish woman can ever be considered a *nice* event. "Are you making all the arrangements?"

"Yes. Our father passed years ago and Mom followed a few years back." She dabbed at her left eye with the back of her hand and her voice hitched slightly as she spoke.

"This must be a terrible time for you. I'm sorry." I understood what she was going through, as I'd had to plan my grandma's funeral alone. Thank goodness for Honey. I looked at Dahlia. "It must be hard for both of you." I knew Valerie had been a single mom to this little girl, which now left Dahlia all alone. I stuck out my hand. "Hi, Dahlia, I'm Tess. I'm pleased to see you again. Do you remember meeting me last night?"

She took my hand and gave it a shake, her pitiful eyes turned toward me. "My momma died."

"I know, honey. I'm sorry. That's a hard thing." I crouched

down. "You know what? My momma died too. I was a lot older than you, but it was still hard."

That perked her interest. "How did your momma die?"

"My mom and dad *both* died in an accident. They were on a train and it went off the tracks. Lots of people died that day." So many families destroyed in an instant.

"I don't have a daddy, just a momma." The hand she had tucked in Lidia's moved, and I realized she held on so tight that her knuckles were white. Poor baby.

My heart broke for her. She was too young to be so alone. "I'm sorry, honey. But I bet it was special to have time alone with your momma."

"That's enough, Dahlia," Lidia said. "Mustn't spread rumors."

I rose and looked at Lidia. "Don't worry, I'm not a gossip." I only collect it. I'm not much for spreading it. "So will you get custody?"

"Yes. There's no one else. Tad and Analesa have been wonderful, though, offering to do whatever they can. Tad even offered to help arrange care if I had trouble swinging it, but I can't imagine having someone else babysit her during the days. She's been left alone at daycare too much already." She put a hand on Dahlia's head and smoothed her hair back. It glistened in the sun with deep red highlights. The gesture was familiar, easy and loving. That reassured me. Lidia would love and take good care of this little girl. "My job is flexible, anyway. I run my massage business out of my house, so I can schedule appointments while she's in school or arrange play dates here and there."

"Tad and Analesa's offer was very generous." Much more than I would have expected from Analesa, who had been more self-absorbed than most brides. "I'm sorry you have to stay here for so long."

She shrugged. "It can't be helped, but I'm moving into Valerie's apartment tomorrow until I get everything settled. Thanks for your kind words. If you don't mind, I think we're ready for some dinner. I promised Dahlia pizza."

"Yes, sorry if I kept you. Gregorio's Pizza is delicious—and I've been living in Chicago for years now, so that's high praise." I moved on, letting them go, but after a moment, I looked back over my shoulder at them. The little girl's slumped form strengthened my resolved to find out what really happened.

Chocolate Cheesecake

For a 9" springform pan.

Preheat oven 350 degrees—It's best to bake this with the springform sitting inside a large pan of water so the cheesecake bakes evenly. For consistent oven temperatures, you should preheat the oven for at least an hour before baking the crust with the filling. This can be done while baking the crust and preparing the filling.

Crust:
1 cup flour
1 tsp cornstartch
1/4 tsp salt
1/2 cup butter at room temperature
1/3 cup sugar
2 extra-large egg yolks
2 tsp vanilla

Butter the pan bottom and sides, and wrap the outside with aluminum foil across the bottom and up the sides.

Mix flour, cornstarch and salt. In another bowl mix butter and sugar until creamy, add egg yolks and vanilla, and beat until blended, then lower the speed and mix in the flour mixture. Mix the dough with your hands until it forms a ball when you squeeze it. Chill for thirty minutes if you have time.

Flour your hands and press the ball into the center of the pan working it up to the edges of the pan and up 1 1/2 inches up the side. Prick the crust with a fork, then bake until just golden and set, about 15 minutes. Don't let it over-bake. Set on a wire rack to cool. Leave the oven on for the cheesecake.

Filling:
4 8-oz packages cream cheese at room temperature (use full fat, not reduced-fat varieties)
1 2/3 cups sugar
¼ cup cornstarch
1 Tbsp vanilla
2 extra-large eggs
¾ cup heavy or whipping cream
1 tsp almond extract
½ lb semi-sweet chocolate, chopped
1 tsp ground nutmeg

Put one package of cream cheese, 1/3 cup sugar and the cornstarch into a bowl and beat until creamy. Then add the other packages of cream cheese, one block at a time until mixed in. Scrape down the sides as needed. Increase the speed of the mixer and add the rest of the sugar, the vanilla, almond extract, and nutmeg. Then beat in the eggs one at a time, mixing well.

In a pan melt the chocolate on low heat. Cool a little so it's still warm to the touch, then whip in cream. Add the chocolate cream mixture to the cream cheese mixture, blending just until mixed, but don't over mix.

Spoon batter into the prepared crust. Place springform pan into a larger, shallow pan containing hot water that comes about 1 inch up the sides of the springform pan. Bake about 1 ¼ hours or until set. Remove the cheesecake from the water bath and place on a wire rack to cool for two hours, then cover loosely with plastic wrap and place in the refrigerator until cold, at least four hours. Overnight is better.

Honey likes more almond in her cheesecake, so I double it when I make it for her, but Marge likes it when I cut up a small bottle of maraschino cherries and put them on the crust before pouring the batter on top.

Chapter 9

Shawn picked me up at straight-up six o'clock. I liked a guy who was punctual, so it earned him points in my book.

Not that I was keeping track of points. Obviously I wasn't interested in a real relationship. This was a harmless flirtation, a distraction from real life. I kept telling myself that, hoping it would keep me from forgetting.

"You look great," he said when he took in my black skirt and long-sleeved red blouse.

"Thank you. You look pretty terrific yourself." He wore a sports jacket over a button-up shirt and a pair of tan chinos. I think this man would look good in rags.

His answer was to grin, and maneuver to help me into my leather jacket. What a gentleman. How did he get a sister like Analesa again? I felt a slight shiver of excitement when his fingers brushed my neck as he settled the coat on my shoulders, then slid his hands along my shoulders.

Shawn took me to the hotel for dinner. Not that there weren't oodles of other places to eat, I thought, but the little restaurant was quaint, quiet and leaned toward romantic. This man was no socially inept teen, no matter what Analesa thought. I was going to enjoy that fact immensely.

We ordered and I glanced over as another couple was seated nearby. Tad and Analesa. "Looks like they decided to emerge from their room for a little while," I noted. I hadn't had a chance to ask her about the argument I'd overheard between herself and Valerie on Friday night. Of course, Millie told me what the argument had been about—assuming her information was accurate.

"Yeah. I thought they might. Analesa loves Tad, but she *needs* social interaction." Shawn twisted his glass on the tabletop.

"Even on her honeymoon? I'd have thought Tad would be oodles of social interaction for her."

Shawn laughed. "I think she's still fuming that they had to cancel their trip. The police weren't happy about them traveling to Florida for their honeymoon with the investigation still ongoing."

I hadn't thought about that. They'd told me not to go anywhere, but I didn't expect the bride and groom to be stuck in town, too. Had they made everyone stay? "Is one of them a suspect?"

"I think at this point just about everyone is," Shawn said. "Probably even me, and I have an in with the detective."

"Well, that makes me feel a little better. I thought I was being picked on." I took a sip from my water glass, letting my eyes linger on him. "Why would they think you killed her?"

Shawn leaned forward and lowered his voice. I followed suit, as if this was a deep dark secret. "I dated her for about ten minutes when I was eighteen. I must have a broken heart."

He didn't appear the least heartbroken. "The evil wench. What happened?"

"We went out, had some very nice goodnight kisses and I went home. She returned to college and a couple weeks later, I started dating Carla."

It sounded about right for teenage romance, but oddly made me feel a little jealous. "Apparently your sister never heard about it. She seemed to think Valerie flirted with you Friday night, and that she'd chew you up and spit you out."

He threw his head back for a laugh. "I grew immune to

Valerie long ago. Still, she was fun for a little light banter at the rehearsal." He took a sip of his drink. "Am I supposed to be a soft touch?"

"Tender-hearted was the way Millie described it."

"Unbelievable." He leaned forward in his chair again, took my hand on the tabletop and wiggled his brows. "I could be a soft touch for you, if you're interested."

I was glad the appetizers arrived then, as it took me a while to readjust my thinking. Was he serious, or a player? Perhaps he and Valerie had some common ground . . . the thought didn't please me. "So what were you up to that night?"

"I played pool with some buddies—including the detective— early in the evening, and was tucked in bed long before midnight. My life is super exciting." His smile was infectious, making me return the expression. Or maybe it was knowing he hadn't been with her that evening, and wasn't trying to fake an alibi. Wouldn't the guilty person make sure they could claim something? Or was that only in movies?

We were digging into our food when Analesa seemed to notice us for the first time. She yanked on Tad's sleeve, and they came over to speak with us. "What are the two of you doing here together?" she asked. When she looked at me, her gaze held accusation, as if she thought I was taking advantage of her baby brother.

"Looks like dinner to me, honey," Tad soothed.

"Just two old friends, becoming reacquainted." Shawn leaned back in his chair again and picked up his drink.

"I didn't realize you were such good friends." Analesa lifted her brows at him, crossing her arms over her chest. I couldn't see her foot, but wondered if she was tapping it.

"Settle, sis. It's a friendly meal. You don't need to worry that she's going to take advantage of me." He popped a mushroom cap in his mouth.

I felt my cheeks flush, so I was glad for the dim lighting. "You never know. I already had you hauling around equipment for me today. I might make you help me move the new stuff in."

His dimple reappeared. "Let me know when. I'll be there if I'm still in town. Here, try this. It's really good." He lifted another stuffed mushroom cap to my lips.

I ate it from his fingers, which was surprisingly intimate and disconcerting. He was right, though, it was extremely tasty. The flirting made me nervous, even more than normal because I could feel Analesa's irate eyes on me. What was her deal? I turned to look at her. "So, I hear your honeymoon plans were changed."

"Yeah." She put her hands on her hips. "The detective told us we can't leave town for a while. I mean, seriously, it's our honeymoon. Isn't it bad enough our wedding was pushed back? What's wrong with him? And why hasn't he caught the killer yet? The incompetence is unbelievable."

Right, because it had been a full thirty hours and there wasn't a single, clear motive for Valerie's murder. "What does he have on you? I mean, I thought only suspects would be asked to stay. Neither of you could have a reason."

Analesa waved her hand. "He's all upset about my argument with Valerie on Friday night. I said, you can't expect me not to watch out for my own family, can you? He's like, family is a good reason to take drastic measures." She lowered her voice to imitate the detective's. "I've never even hit someone before, and he thinks I killed her because she acted indecorous?"

"Lay off of Tingey, he's doing his job." Shawn's voice was calm but there was a definite edge of irritation in his eyes.

I turned to Tad, who looked mighty uncomfortable at the moment. Was it the topic of conversation, or did he have something to hide? "And you—are you stuck here by default, or did he say something silly about you too?" I asked.

70

"Him?" Analesa laughed as if the suggestion were ludicrous. "My Tad is clean as a whistle. He doesn't even speed." She snuck an arm through his and looked up at him, admiration all but glowing off her. "He's going to be a senator someday, maybe even president." The look was sickening. I supposed it was appropriate for their honeymoon, and counted myself lucky if it was the worst display of public affection I saw from them.

Tad chuckled lightly—nervously—I thought—at Analesa's words. "I'm no saint, sweetheart. Perhaps we ought to return to our seats. They'll be bringing dinner soon, and I'm sure we're interfering with Shawn's date."

Though Analesa looked as though she might not *mind* interfering in her brother's love life, I was glad when they left, if only because her gaze on me was accusing.

I turned to Shawn and realized he still held my hand. "Do you suppose I'm taking advantage of you, me being the older woman?" After all, he was probably the tender age of twenty-nine.

His brows lifted and his voice turned husky. "Do you want to take advantage of me?"

I met his teasing eyes. "Is it taking advantage if I invite you back to my apartment for chocolate cheesecake? I'm tweaking a recipe and could use a second opinion."

"For one of your sweets? I have the feeling I'd always be up for that."

"It's only dessert," I warned him when his grin turned almost feral. "That's all you're getting out of me."

He lifted his glass and took a sip, not looking away the whole time. "We'll see."

The chocolate cheesecake *was* a hit, as I knew it would be. I decided the slight hint of nutmeg in the batter was exactly what it needed.

"So do you always offer your dates dessert?" Shawn asked as he lifted his coffee mug after finishing off his slice.

"Not always. I had this handy. And you were around." I felt relaxed and happy. It had been a great evening, fun, flirty, with no pressure. I felt a tingle of excitement when he gave me a look over the top of his coffee cup that said he thought my mouth might taste as good as the dessert.

I was considering letting him kiss me—which I hardly ever allowed on a first date, but hey, sometimes you had to live dangerously. The question was how much of this reckless attitude came from leftover hurt. Was it all about the rebound relationship? I didn't think that Shawn was a naïve fool or anything, but he didn't deserve to be taken advantage of, either.

"Lucky me," he said. "If I took you out again, would you be willing to make dessert again?"

"I might, if things went well." And if I could find the time. I had far too much to do this week, and tracking down a killer was only part of my load. "Are you saying you want to go out again?"

"Definitely."

We lingered for a while longer before he rose, claiming he needed to get out of my way before I grew tired of his company. I doubted that would be likely.

At the door he turned to me. "What are you doing tomorrow?"

"Painting my kitchen downstairs. If you decide you're bored, feel free to come help." I really hoped he would. He brightened my mood and made me forget the darker pockets of my life.

He leaned in, tipping my head up toward him with his hand on my cheek. "I might."

Tingles zoomed through me as he carried out a slow, careful assault on my senses with his kisses. When he left, I felt a bit lightheaded, and couldn't help but hope we managed another date before he returned to his post in Nogales.

Chapter 10

The next morning, I decided a trip back to the hotel was in order. I hadn't remembered to swing by to talk with the manager on Saturday, and he'd been out of the office on Sunday—go figure. Since I wanted to chat with him about a possible business arrangement, and I also wanted to pick the brains of some of his employees to see if there were any details I missed on the scene, I decided I could kill two birds with one stone.

Because I'm efficient like that.

Before running to the hotel, I decided to go to the diner for breakfast. I usually cooked for myself—most of the time my own food was best—but I was in the mood for a big omelet stuffed with everything, and a side of greasy hash browns. If I could get a couple slices of almost-burned bacon as well, I would be in heaven. When I went out to get in the Outlander, I saw my tires were flat. "You've got to be kidding me!"

At first I thought it was just the front passenger's tire that was flat, then I walked around and realized it was all of them. They were slashed, not accidentally flattened. In a town where the crime rate was usually miniscule, this couldn't be random, could it? I sighed and went back inside to call the police department and a tow truck.

Officer Lambert, a little man with a thin mustache, came to the house and took the report. "We can check to see if anyone saw anything strange, but the chances that we'll catch the perp aren't good." He studied all the tires and took a couple fibers off one wheel, but it was impossible to know when they had gotten there.

The tow guy didn't arrive until after the officer had been gone for twenty minutes. He hauled the car up onto his flatbed truck and said they'd return the vehicle to me when they finished it. In the meantime, he took my AAA information, my insurance paperwork for the damage and my credit card information for the deductable. There are some advantages to small towns. In the city, I would have had to park my tush in a chair at the tire shop while I waited—which would have added insult to injury.

Still, this was so not what I needed. I went back inside to call my insurance company to start the paperwork.

Several hours passed while I tried to clean downstairs and waited impatiently for the guys at the garage to return my wheels.

As I'd anticipated, the hotel offices were located down a long hall on the far end of the building. The front desk clerk, a perky-looking girl with huge blue eyes, directed me where to go. I found Jet Larsen in his office, speaking on the telephone. I had to wait several minutes for him to finish the call, and he asked me to sit while he made a note or two. This gave me time to check out his degree in hotel management, his mounted fish—was it a swordfish? It was enormous—and his family pictures.

Finally, he turned my way. "Didn't I see you around this weekend?" he asked before recognition crossed his face. "Tess, aren't you? The cake lady?"

I loved that he already knew who I was. It smoothed things a bit. "That would be me. I'm impressed with your hotel."

"Thanks—we're trying to fill a need for the community, and

I think we're doing it well. The murder has put a major cramp in our bookings, though." He leaned in and lowered his voice, as if someone might have his office bugged, wanting to know his company secrets. "We've even had a number of cancellations, which is never good."

I nodded and gave him sympathetic looks. "I am sorry about that. Hopefully the police will be able to wrap it up soon. Having worked in a hotel for years, I know sometimes crazy things can throw off bookings."

"Yes, but I'm sure that's not why you came to me today. I saw your work on that cake, and I'd love to have someone with your abilities on staff, but I hope you know we can't afford to hire a pastry chef full time." He slid a pen through his fingers.

All the better for me. "I understand that, of course, but I thought we could consider a mutually beneficial arrangement. I'm opening my own business. Maybe we could arrange a sort of partnership."

He set the pen down and crossed his arms in front of him on the desk, leaning in. "What did you have in mind?"

When I left his office twenty minutes later, we'd thrown around numbers, plans and ideas, and I promised to get back to him with some basic prices. He agreed to have a contract written up. If there were no bumps along the way, I'd become the exclusive provider of the more elaborate occasion cakes. I'd be happy to leave the everyday desserts to his restaurant staff.

As I headed down the hall, I came across the laundry room. The door was open and three women were in there with a large laundry cart, filling washing machines. The familiar hum of dryers, the slosh of front-loading washers and the babble of women's voices was so familiar. I never worked in the laundry department, but over the years I made lots of trips there to collect clean towels for the kitchen.

"Hey, did any of you work on the wedding this weekend?" I asked when they noticed my presence.

A sandy-haired young woman with a bright smile turned, and I recognized a server from Sunday night. "I did. You made that gorgeous cake, didn't you? Can you believe the murder? It, like, totally freaked me out."

I stepped into the room. "I know, crazy, wasn't it? I've worked a lot of celebrations, and seen a lot of insane things, including a number of fights, but I've never found a body before. Did you see anything strange that day?" I leaned back against the folding counter, allowing my shock to leak onto my face. "I ask because I'm still trying to figure it out. Friday night she was there, eating my brownies, and Saturday she was dead."

"Spooky," the forty-something redhead across the room agreed. "I wasn't sure if I should come back to work after that. What if the hotel is cursed or something now?"

The third woman, a short Latina in her fifties, crossed herself and muttered something in Spanish.

That kind of thinking was exactly what we didn't need, not if the hotel was going to get lots of bookings and send me scads of new clients. "Are you kidding? A murder gives the place character. What's a hotel without a little juicy story here and there? Lots of high-class resorts are proud of their history, even the bad stuff. Besides, this could end up being interesting, don't you think? Was it a lovers' quarrel? A dispute over work? Maybe an illicit deal gone wrong? It's practically a made-for-TV movie."

The Latina moved a pile of towels off the folding table onto a set of shelves, and I sat in the empty space.

"Yeah, and the psycho could still be hanging around here, waiting to off another one of us," the redhead said.

I hoped it was something personal against Valerie and not some new serial killer, but I wasn't going to even think about that possibility. I didn't have to feign a shudder at her suggestion. "Was there anything . . . off or unusual going on? Anything you remember?"

The Latina woman approached, opened a dryer and pulled out a gleaming white towel, starting to fold. "Dere was da tableclot."

"Tablecloth?" I hadn't heard anything about this yet.

"Yeah," the younger woman piped up. "All the tables were covered with the centerpieces and everything Friday night when dinner finished up. But when we came in again the next day, one of the tables—one close to where the brownies had been set up—didn't have the tablecloth anymore. The centerpiece had been moved to another table, and there was no sign of the cloth. And someone forgot to take away the leftover brownies the previous night—what few were left. I had to haul them off before the wedding party started coming down."

She started up a washer at the end of the row and turned to help fold the fresh towels. "Anyway, we thought someone had stolen the cloth, so we pulled another one from the closet. Sunday morning, though, when we were cleaning, they found it stuck under the stairs in the corner exit. It had blood all over it, like they'd used it to clean up the floor in there—though polyester would be my last choice for that kind of job. I heard the detective say he thought that was what happened. They said someone, like, cleaned up the original mess because they found traces of blood smeared all over the floor." She looked a bit sick when she added this.

I didn't blame her, as I felt a bit sick myself. "That's awful. I wonder why they didn't stash the cloth with the body?" It seemed odd that the killer had carried the cloth anywhere when someone might have seen him or her with it. If they had the presence of mind to cover up the crime by hiding the body and cleaning the floor, why would they wander around with the tablecloth?

"Maybe they didn't want it to be obvious that they'd moved the body. Someone didn't want her to be found, I think. At least not until after the wedding." The redhead started stuffing sheets into an open washing machine in the middle of the row.

"I'm sure Analesa would have thrown a fit about her maid of honor disappearing, but the ceremony would have gone on without Valerie if I hadn't found her." That was an angle I hadn't considered. Did the killer want the wedding to happen before the body was found? That would make it who? Analesa herself? Her parents? Tad's family? So many options, so little apparent motive for the murder. They all seemed like petty complaints to me.

Except no one but the married couples seemed to have alibis, and who trusted the spouse's word, anyway? "Did any of you see or hear anything else odd?"

"Nope." The young woman looked around her; the other ladies shook their heads as well. That was it, then.

"All right, thanks. Never a dull moment around here, is there?" I hopped off the counter.

They agreed and I said goodbye, hoping they thought I was just curious and that they wouldn't make a big deal out of my visit.

Now I had to look more closely at all the people who had a stake in getting the wedding out of the way before the body was found. Who would want to kill Valerie, but hide her until the end of the day? One of the parents? A member of the wedding party? They had already been on my list, with few exceptions, as it was. Instead of leaving me with answers, the discussion only created more questions.

Chapter 11

I spent hours that afternoon taping off the windows and fixtures in the kitchen. Singing off-key—the only way I could sing—as I prepared to paint, I took extra care with the natural gas lines that stuck out of the wall, and the lever that kept the gas turned off until it was hooked to my new oven. I had gotten a call from someone who was interested in the grill, which thrilled me no end. The money would come in handy in stocking my kitchen without having to dip into my savings for it.

I moved to the front window, where customers would be able to watch me decorating cakes, building flowers, frosting and check out the fun and flashy projects I imagined in my future. The purple tape—I love it you can buy painting tape in every color under the sun—contrasted nicely against the yellowed once-white paint. I bobbed my head to the tune coming through my headphones when Detective Tingey came to stand in front of me on the other side of the glass. I paused as he pointed to the door and I nodded. Great. What did he want this time? To arrest me?

As I turned, I bumped one of my razor blades into the crack in the middle of the ordering counter. The blade was pointed down, and it was wedged in there. I tried pulling on it, but decided I'd deal with it when the cabinets came out. I made a mental note to cover it with tape later so I didn't cut myself on it.

I unlocked the front door and let the detective in. "Miss

Crawford, sorry to bother you again. I wondered if you'd thought of anything more that might be helpful from Saturday morning."

I could have told him about the things I'd picked up from poking around, but there wasn't anything concrete, so I kept my conjectures to myself and stuck to the facts. "Not really. I've been trying to remember more but haven't come up with much."

He nodded. "I did have one other thing I'd like you to do. Could you go get fingerprinted?"

I took a step back at his request as my heart began to race. I'd known he was considering me, but the request still took me by surprise. "So you *do* think I did it?"

"It's a formality. We found prints on the murder weapon, but they don't match anything in the database. We're asking everyone we know who had access to the room to please come forward and be printed so we can eliminate suspects."

Cold washed down my back. He said it so casually, as if it was an unimportant request, and not the serious expectation I read in his eyes. "But I already told you I touched that vase."

"Yes. I wouldn't worry about it too much. I don't know why you'd have been wandering around the hotel at that hour." He leaned against the counter and studied the dining area. "Looks like this place is going to keep you busy."

"Yes, there's lots of work to do before I open." I pressed my lips together as a frisson of fear rushed through me. "I can go have the fingerprinting done." What difference would it make? I definitely wanted to appear cooperative, and he could always get a court order. I gripped the tape roll in my left hand until the cardboard center left impressions in my fingers. "I'll be in as soon as I finish taping off this window."

I had no real choice, unless I wanted to go on the lam in some country that wouldn't extradite for capital punishment. Besides, he had to have better suspects than me. Hadn't Jeff

80

suggested that everyone had motive to kill Valerie? Still, I felt a bead of sweat trickle down my back and had to feign indifference to worry.

"I appreciate that." He tucked his notebook back in his pocket and headed out. Before he closed the door, he reminded me to lock up behind him. After all, there was a killer on the loose.

I gave the lock a vicious twist. Thanks for the reassurance, detective.

Getting fingerprinted wasn't nearly the ordeal I'd expected. The officer at the precinct was friendly, chatting with me about the weather, asked about any hiking trails I'd been on. He sounded interested in the business when I opened it and asked what kind of daily offerings I would have for purchase. I admit, I had expected something out of a hard-boiled detective show with gruff jailers and hard stares pinning the guilt for everything on my shoulders. I'd seen way too much television, I guess.

I left there grateful that the detour had been quick and that it was over with, then popped by the hardware store to order the paint for my building.

Chapter 12

Painting, I decided, was not my strong suit. It only took me twenty minutes before I realized I'd gotten in over my head. Maybe renting a sprayer would have been better after all, I thought as I dipped my roller in the paint yet again. I ended up with drips on the newspaper I'd spread across the floor and a lopsided application to the wall.

I was nearly ready to throw the roller when the bell over the front door rang. I poked my head around the corner to find Shawn standing there in clothes that had seen better days. "Hi. What are you doing here?" I asked.

His dimple popped into existence with his grin. "You said you were painting this afternoon. I thought maybe you could use a hand."

"You're on vacation and you've come over to help me haul around large appliances and paint? What kind of saint are you?"

"Saint, me? Not hardly." He walked through to see what I was doing and pressed his lips together, as though trying not to smile. His dimple gave him away, though.

I nudged him with my elbow, not the least amused. "I've never done this before. I thought, hey, it looks simple. How hard could it be?"

"It is simple; you just need a little direction." He took the roller from my hand and put it back in the tray on the floor. "First, you want to cut in the edges with a brush." He lifted the three-inch brush I'd purchased and painted in the edges along the ceiling and outlets. "Then you roll over the edges. That way, you don't leave as many brush strokes on the wall, and it makes it easier later." He loaded the roller with paint now, coating it evenly and slid it up and down the wall. "It's better to put on a little extra up front, and roll it smooth, than to be stingy and realize you have to do another coat because you can see through it. Here, you try it."

I felt like a complete idiot. Was I really too stupid to figure out painting on my own? Still, this was my business and I wanted to do everything I could myself, so I took the roller from him. Shawn set his hand over mine on the handle and helped me maneuver the implement. He stood behind me so his breath feathered against my ear and I felt the heat of his chest on my back. He talked to me as we rolled on the paint. His free hand found its way to rest at my waist.

His lips brushed against my ear. "Like this. How's that?"

"Better. Thanks for the lesson." I tried to keep my voice level, calm, but could hear the shakiness in it. I knew he must be gloating at his effect on me, but I was a little too mesmerized to care.

"No problem. Does my help get me another date with you?" I felt his minty breath fan across my cheek.

I smiled despite myself. "Well, I suppose it might." I turned my head so I looked into his face, inches from my own. "What did you have in mind?"

His lips curved, and the bell rang over the front door as someone entered.

"What do you think you're doing? Who is that?" The voice from across the room was all too familiar.

I almost dropped the paint roller, but Shawn kept his hand tightly wrapped around mine even as he straightened, shifting his torso a few inches away from mine.

I didn't have to look at the intruder. I'd know Bronson's voice anywhere. What was he doing in Silver Springs? It's not like it was only an afternoon drive from Chicago. I turned to face him. As usual, he was decked out in his suit and carrying his laptop bag. As mad and hurt as I was over what happened, I still sucked in a little breath when I saw how terrific he looked. Then I clenched my jaw—I was not going there again.

Shawn released my hand, but not my waist, nor did he move away.

"Bronson, what are you doing here?" I stared at him.

He approached, his actions indicating he thought he had a right to intrude. "I came to talk some sense into you. What is *he* doing here?" He gestured to Shawn.

"He came to help me paint. There's a lot to do before I can open this place for business." The warmth of Shawn's hand on my waist grew scalding, but I didn't shake him off. It felt good having someone behind me, supporting me as I faced down Bronson. And I was amazed he hadn't stepped forward to interfere. No way would Bronson have let me handle a confrontation without thinking he had to be the big tough man in charge.

"Who's the suit?" Shawn asked.

"I'm her fiancé, Bronson DeMille the third." As always, his introduction was self-important. Usually his attitude just made me roll my eyes, even if only on the inside, but right now I found it more than a minor irritation.

Shawn let go and moved away from me, as if I were suddenly contagious. "You're engaged?"

"No, he's my *ex*-fiancé, who became my *ex* when I caught him cheating on me." I missed having Shawn's hand on my hip, but decided it was as well. I turned my attention back to the jerk I once thought I would marry. "What do you want, Bronson?"

Shawn's defection seemed to give Bronson courage and he walked over, taking my free hand. "Sweetheart, that was all a misunderstanding. You know how much I love you."

Okay, this was an approach I hadn't anticipated. But I hadn't expected to see him at all, so I supposed I shouldn't have expectations about how he would act. "Really? So I find you sucking face with Karen—made all the worse by the fact that I hate her—and I'm supposed to know that it's not important, that you still love me? After all, it's just one of those things that sometimes happens before a guy gets married." I let the sarcasm ooze and drip.

He took the paint roller and set it in the tray, then moved to take my other hand. I snatched both hands out of his reach and stepped back, closer to Shawn. Bronson looked hurt. "Tess, it was a mistake—a major one—but I promise it won't happen again. You belong in Chicago, not in this backwater town making cupcakes and brownies for school children." There was more than a little sneer in his voice.

"*Gourmet* cupcakes and brownies, and it won't only be for children. I'm going to enjoy what I do here, having my own space, doing things my way." Even if I am terrified of the paperwork and taxes and balancing the books. "I already have a few clients and am working out an agreement to do wedding cakes for the new hotel in town."

"Don't be silly, Tess. You're too right-brained. You can't handle running your own business." His voice had turned from wheedling to condescending. Jerk.

"I wouldn't be so sure of that," Shawn broke in, setting a supportive hand on the small of my back. It was a little gesture Bronson might not have noticed, but I couldn't help but give my full attention. "She seems to be making a great go of it. Business license, tax ID number, new name, new equipment. It looks to me like she's plenty capable."

I flushed from his praise. Such a difference from Bronson, who tended to put me down in business instead of letting me prove myself. Not that I wanted the position he'd given to

Karen, but it would have been nice if he'd acted like he thought I was capable of doing it.

"It won't last six months. Besides, you have commitments in Chicago. The Goulds are threatening to sue the hotel, me *and* you if you don't take care of their wedding cake and pastries. They say the biggest reason they booked with us was because of your talent. And the Tanners are right behind them."

I should have called him back. Or answered one of his calls. If he'd known I planned to come back and handle the Goulds' wedding, he might not have shown up here. Still, I didn't say anything yet, just gave him a steady look. I was rewarded when sweat beaded on his upper lip. This was all too easy, and surprisingly entertaining. I'd forgotten I had such a mean streak. I usually manage to keep it in check.

"Why don't you get rid of him," he gave Shawn a nasty look, "and we can work this out."

"Actually, Shawn is here to help me paint, and I need to get the kitchen done today. How about if he stays and I'll meet you tonight to discuss specific clients."

Shawn said, "Are you sure you want to meet with him?" while Bronson's response was, "You're picking him? And who is he, anyway?"

I counted to ten. Seriously, men drove me crazy sometimes. I turned back to Shawn. "I do need to work things out for the Goulds' cake, at least. I realized that a couple of days ago. Even though I'm mad at him, I do still care about the clients. I have to go back to Chicago and clean out my condo, anyway. When I left Chicago I hadn't intended to stay here permanently."

Bronson let out a relieved breath even as Shawn's brows winged up. "I knew you'd come to your senses," Bronson said. "But why didn't you answer one of my calls so we could work this out over the phone?"

I turned back to my ex. "I enjoyed letting you sweat for a

change. And I'm not coming back to work for you—I'm coming back for a little while to do those two cakes and clear out my condo while details finalize here. So I really need to finish painting today." I gave him a pointed look.

"All right. We'll discuss it over dinner. Is there somewhere decent to eat around here?"

It only took me a moment to decide where I wanted to go. "Paul's Burger Shack on Center Street and Gilla Lane. Six o'clock."

"When I said somewhere decent, I meant somewhere nice." He looked down his nose at me, as if disgusted. Had I never noticed what a snob he was? Had I become that bad while we dated?

"If you want to talk to me, you'll buy me a burger. I've been too busy to eat there since I made it back home, and they have great food. Take it or leave it."

"This is not your home," Bronson insisted. "Chicago is your home." He tried claiming my hand again, but I picked up the paint roller from the counter and held it between us and he backed off.

I slid my empty hand into my back pocket where he couldn't reach it. "Since I've moved here permanently, I say this is home. Now if you'll let me get back to work?"

He scowled at me, at Shawn and turned on his heel. "Six sharp," he called over his shoulder before heading out the door.

I waited for the door to close and the ringing bell to go silent before turning back to Shawn, who grinned at me. "What?" I asked.

"You're feisty! I had no idea. I mean, I have a couple of vague memories from when we were little, but you seem so buttoned down and cool now."

"Well, you know some things never change. I'm just harder to rile than I used to be." I leaned over and picked up the paintbrush he'd set down and handed it back to him. "You're tall—do the high spots."

He went to work with enthusiasm. A moment passed before he started talking again. "He cheated on you?"

"Yep." No good, lousy jerk.

He slid me a sideways glance that held more than a hint of appreciation. "Is he crazy? Why would any man cheat on a gorgeous, feisty woman like you?"

I blushed and averted my eyes as I started laying down the paint. "You flatter me."

"Not at all. And I think I'd be afraid to cross you." He tugged on a lock of my hair and I turned to face him.

"No need. I didn't hurt him, or Karen. I even left the engagement ring, though on second thought, it would have bought me an awesome cookie roller. Maybe I'll ask for it back so I can hawk it." I wouldn't do any such thing, unfortunately. Beyond being unethical, it would give Bronson hope, and I was going to have a hard enough time getting rid of him as it was. Apparently.

"Ouch." But there was amusement in Shawn's voice, so I wasn't fooling him.

I decided we'd talked too much about my relationship with Bronson, and turned the conversation to memories from my visits to Silver Springs as a kid. Shawn didn't protest the change of subject.

We finished the kitchen, the buyer came for the grill and Shawn helped him load it. Finally we shifted everything back to the kitchen or clustered it in the middle of the room so I could paint the dining room. I still wasn't sure if I wanted to use part of this space for storage or displays, but I figured there would be time to consider that later. When Shawn left me at four-thirty, it was with a kiss, and a date for lunch the next day—a meal I was definitely looking forward to, as compared to that night's meeting with Bronson.

Chapter 13

Paul's Burger Shack was one of those great old places with a display of Coca-Cola memorabilia and pictures on the wall of all of the celebrities who had stopped in to eat. The restaurant even smelled like it should—sweetness from the ice cream and soda machine, grease from the fryer, the lingering hint of bacon. Childhood memories practically surrounded me as soon as I walked in the door. I ordered, then joined Bronson at the table.

"So what was up with that guy today?" Bronson asked almost the moment I sat down.

"He's a friend." I chose not to elaborate, if only to drive Bronson crazy.

"A friend. *Really?* Because the way he touched you looked more than friendly to me." His beautiful mouth was set in a firm line. I used to love kissing that mouth. Now when I saw it, I could only think about whom else had enjoyed it.

I did my best to look unconcerned. "Sorry, you lost your right to be jealous when I caught you with Karen."

His eyes narrowed and he rested his hands on each other on the tabletop. "I don't remember you mentioning anyone named Shawn before."

"I didn't talk about everyone I knew from here. I haven't seen him in years. Get over it." I glanced at the menu board, not wanting to discuss my flirtation with Shawn. They announced my shake—that's what I call super-fast service—and I jumped up to get it.

When I reached the front counter, I looked over my shoulder at Bronson. It was strange—I'd never felt so empowered when I dated him. Most of the time he made demands, and I agreed to what he wanted—not because he was mean or controlling so much as the fact that he was a bit of a whiner, and it was irritating dealing with him if he didn't get his way. There were benefits to letting him have his way though, since a happy Bronson was so easy-going and fun to be with. Generous, articulate and I did mention something about him being a good kisser, right?

I waited until my order was ready: a burger and onion rings—some of the best on the planet—while I enjoyed my thick chocolate Oreo shake. My favorite. Of course, I'd be taking long power walks every day for weeks to work off the fat and calories, but I'd been pretty good lately. Or maybe not, I realized as I remembered the éclairs. And the brownies. And the cheesecake. I paused for a second to add up the calories. But it had been a stressful weekend, I finally decided, so I was entitled.

"You know that's going to make you feel like a bloated sow," Bronson pointed out when we were seated again at our table.

Tact was not one of his strong points—not in his personal relationships, anyway. "Not your problem anymore." I took a large bite of the thick, juicy hamburger and almost purred in pleasure. It had been way too long since I'd eaten here.

"Fine." He held up his hands as if I had yelled at him.

Well, maybe I had snapped a little. Who would blame me?

After a long moment passed and he was halfway through his own burger, he started talking. "So you actually like it here? I mean, I know you enjoy visiting, but to live in Silver Springs full time?" He looked around, as if unimpressed by anything he saw.

I became even more defensive. "Yes. It's charming and friendly and I love it."

He snorted, like he knew me so well. "You aren't going to get bored?"

"Prescott is only twenty minutes away, and there's plenty going on there. Phoenix is less than an hour, and there are tons of shows and restaurants there. But I doubt there'll be much free time." I knew enough about running a business to be certain I wouldn't get days off or be able to take time to relax with any regularity.

"You already know how I feel about that. Not everyone is suited to be their own boss." This time the words were soft, cajoling, as if he was trying to break an unfortunate truth to me.

"Yes, I know," I said, putting ice in my voice. "And you've made it clear you think I can't do it, so there's no need to tell me again." I hated that his words hit the mark. I'd never done anything like this. What if he was right and the bakery tanked?

I was grateful he didn't seem to have an answer to that, or continue pounding on my already fragile ego. I decided it was time to turn the conversation to something less personal.

"We might as well get down to business," I said when I'd finished swallowing a bite of onion ring. "The Goulds' wedding is first, and the Tanners' is mid-week, what—four days later?" I pulled out my notebook with the sketches and details. "While I'm there, I can make the flowers for the Fosters' and McKennas' events as well. Then my replacement only has to do the cake itself, and that should be no problem." If he or she wasn't a moron. I should probably have faith in Bronson to pick someone decent to fill my shoes, but then, he'd hired Karen, so his track record was far from sterling.

His hand covered mine and I pulled away, moving on. "Lenny can handle the rest of the cakes for the following month if he has to. He has my cell number, so remind him that he should feel free to call me with questions."

He grabbed my hand and held on when I tried pulling it away again. "Tess, are you sure this is what you want? You're not doing this because you're upset with me?"

I looked him in the eye. "I'm absolutely sure about this." Not. I was surprised that I managed to keep my gaze steady even as I again mourned what I'd thought I had with this man, and learned that I didn't. I remembered the good times with him—they weren't that far in the past, after all.

I'd loved Bronson, or had it just been what he represented that I loved? I wasn't sure anymore. All I knew is that I deserved someone who didn't think Karen was a valid substitute for me—for any length of time. Had it been my fault? I pushed that thought away. The worry had bothered me from the first, but didn't deserve attention. Now if I could wipe out the doubts completely.

Having Shawn around took the edge off the pain because another man valued me for myself without consideration for whether it affected his business—and how sad and pathetic was that? But I needed to believe Bronson's cheating wasn't my fault, so Shawn's attention was a balm to my ego.

When Bronson didn't release my hand, I tried to tug away, but he held on tighter. I reached over and used the self-defense move I'd learned as a teen. Push the right pressure points and anyone will be forced to let go.

"Hey, what was that for?" Bronson asked, shaking his hand when he released me.

"I don't like being manhandled," I told him evenly.

His brows lifted. "Since when?"

I narrowed my eyes at him. "Do I need to try out some of my other self-defense moves on you?"

He lifted his hands palms forward, though he looked unrepentant. "Sorry."

I turned and saw Lidia and Dahlia, who were coming in the door. I waved, and they came over.

"We've gotten the official word now," Lidia told me. "The medical examiner will be releasing her tomorrow, so the funeral will be held in Prescott on Saturday."

"I'm glad you'll be able to get everything settled. Did you enjoy the pizza place yesterday?"

"Yes, it was terrific. Is this as good?" Lidia slid Dahlia into the bench across the aisle from us.

"Oh, yeah. The ice cream is fabulous. You have to at least get a cone." I ducked my head around Lidia and wiggled my fingers at Dahlia, who gave me a shy smile and wave back. "What are you doing in Silver Springs? Aren't you staying in Prescott at Valerie's apartment?"

Bronson interrupted the conversation. "Hello, I'm Bronson, Tess's fiancé."

"*Ex*-fiance. *Ex*," I corrected.

Lidia's brows lifted and Bronson shrugged. "She keeps saying that. I'm hoping to convince her otherwise."

I rolled my eyes. I was about to say something concerning his delusions when Tad and Analesa entered. "What is this? The newlyweds come out of seclusion again?"

Lidia turned and waved and Dahlia climbed off the bench and ran over, wrapping her arms around Tad's legs. He grabbed and lifted her so she was taller than him before setting the giggling girl on his hip.

"That's why we're here, to meet them for dinner," Lidia said. "Aren't they cute together?" Her eyes were on Tad and Dahlia.

Analesa had walked away from her new husband and was close enough to overhear. "Adorable." Her voice was dry, her expression not amused. It made me wonder what her issue was.

"I didn't expect to see you again so soon," I told Analesa.

"It's not turning out to be much of a honeymoon, with everything that's going on." She turned to Bronson, studied him for a moment and I saw him open his mouth to introduce himself. I hurried to cut him off and give the right introductions as Tad and Dahlia approached. "This is Bronson, my old boss from Chicago. He's come to town to discuss arrangements for a few of my bigger clients."

He offered his hand to Tad for a shake. "We're engaged."

"*Were* engaged," I corrected. "I wouldn't be moving here if I had any intention of marrying you now." Seriously, did the man never let up?

He gave that suave smile that said no, he wouldn't.

Analesa seemed to like him immediately—not that I found that surprising. Bronson could be charming; he was good looking, and wore a suit well. Add to that the fact that he wasn't Shawn, and I figured there was every reason for Analesa to be thrilled I was eating dinner with Bronson. I was tempted to mention my lunch date with her brother the next day just to tick her off, but it really wasn't any of her business and I didn't need the hassle.

Tad held Dahlia on one side and they both smiled, though Dahlia still looked sad. "It's good to meet you, Bronson, even if she is holding out on you." The guys shook hands.

Holding out on him? Did Tad really say that, because I'd actually liked him until five seconds ago. I didn't respond, though—it was bound to egg the guys on. Instead, I fisted my hands at my sides and counted to ten. I was doing that a lot today.

"She insists she's not coming back, but a guy can always hope." Bronson threw me his most charming smile. It didn't work on me anymore. Much.

I bit my tongue on the response that wanted to fly from my lips and narrowed my eyes at them both.

Tad held onto Dahlia, took their requests and went up front to order. After they finished, Dahlia sat across from him. Since Bronson and I had completed our business transaction as far as I was concerned, and I didn't want things to get personal, I started asking him about mutual friends and coworkers—even though it had been less than two weeks wince I'd left. I'd been a little distracted with things like cakes, my business and murder to keep up with everyone online. I told him so.

"Murder? What do you mean?"

So I filled him in. If anything, it convinced him that I was not safe in this backwater town, but I refused to listen to his complaints. Instead, I tuned into the conversation at the table across from us.

"Of course we'd like to help any way we can," Tad said to Lidia as he handed Dahlia another one of his fries.

"Yes. Of course," Analesa echoed, though with far less conviction. "Valerie was a close friend of mine, after all, and we do love Dahlia."

"I appreciate that, but as we live in different states, I don't know what you're going to be able to do," Lidia protested. "Besides, Don and I have wanted to have children for a long time. Dahlia will be a welcome addition to our home." She smiled at her niece, the love practically vibrating from her.

"I know we're just married," Tad said when Dahlia had jumped down to get more ketchup, "but I feel responsible for the position you and Dahlia are in." He reached for his wife's hand. "I think Ana and I are more than ready to help out, maybe take her for vacations to give you a break."

"Though perhaps we ought to discuss this first." Analesa removed her hand from his, making it clear she had no intention of parenting her dead best friend's child.

I couldn't really blame her; a child, at any age, was a major commitment—even for a week or two of vacation. I thought Tad was being a little too Dudley Do-Right and overeager.

"Thank you for the offer," Lidia said, "but I couldn't. Really. It's my responsibility as a member of the family."

His mouth firmed in a grim line.

Dahlia came running back with the ketchup in her hands. "I found it."

"So you did, bug. Now, are you all set?" Tad asked.

"Earth to Tess. I am still sitting here, you know?" Bronson said, nudging my arm.

My eyes snapped back to his face and I ate the onion ring dangling between my fingers. "Sorry, I've had a lot on my mind. I've been trying to figure out this murder and—"

"Why are you getting involved in that?" Bronson asked. "That's for the cops. Leave it alone."

"I can't leave it alone. I'm one of the suspects," I hissed back at him. As soon as the words were out of my mouth, I knew I'd made a mistake. If Bronson knew that, he was going to throw a fit. I was right, of course.

"Tess, what do you mean?"

"It's nothing, really. I think the police suspect everyone right now. I had a little run in with the victim. Actually, she said *Roscoe Marks* was a better pastry chef than me." Stupidly, I expected him to understand my disgust with that.

He looked at me for a moment. "Who?"

"The pastry chef I competed against in that bake-off competition last year," I reminded him. Roscoe and I'd had faced off several times over the years. When the reference didn't seem to ring a bell with Bronson, I narrowed my eyes at him. I know I'd discussed the competition, and Roscoe, numerous times. Hadn't he been listening? I decided to let it go. "Anyway, the police seem to think I'd kill Valerie because she made nasty comments about my brownies. Several other people had better access and much better reason to want her dead, though."

96

Bronson seemed to realize I was smoothing over the seriousness of the issue. He started shooting questions at me and wouldn't let up.

I couldn't wait to leave.

Chapter 14

I called Honey to come over after I left Paul's Burger Shack, since it was only seven-thirty. There was still too much to do to go to bed. "The kids have been hellions all day," she said as she flopped onto the sofa nearly an hour later. "I was glad to get your call, since the kids are 'in bed'—meaning they'll be out again ten times in the next hour—and George is working on his ship-in-a-bottle." She rolled her eyes.

George had started building his ship-in-a-bottle about a year earlier, and still hadn't finished it. I'd caught a glimpse of it when I was at their house the previous week, and it wasn't the most promising sight. Still, we all need hobbies, and considering others out there, it could be worse.

"I'm glad you could stop by." I filled her in on all the things I'd learned that day.

Honey nodded and picked at the fruit platter I'd put together with an easy fruit dip while I waited for her arrival. "I ran into Lidia and Dahlia at the grocery store. Cute girl. Other than the coloring, she doesn't look much like her mom, though, does she?"

"No. Did you notice the green eyes? Gorgeous. And so, so sad."

"I know. I can't even imagine what it must be like for her." She selected a slice of kiwi and popped it in her mouth. "Kinda reinforces the desire to find our killer, doesn't it?"

"Yeah." I paused, considered where the investigation needed to go next. "I've been thinking about how Shawn said

Millie and Valerie were serious enemies, but Millie kept pretending they were best buddies. It bothers me. You want to go check up on her, see how she's doing?" I glanced at my watch. "It's not even nine yet."

Honey grinned. "Sure. Let's go find her." She popped to her feet and I slid the fruit tray back into the fridge, then snatched up my car keys.

When we arrived at the hotel, we had the front desk clerk ring up to Millie's room, but no one answered.

"Maybe she's out to dinner," I suggested.

"Where?" Honey asked. "Nothing's open at this time except the bar and the Taco Shack." She checked her phone. "And the shack closes in ten minutes."

I chuckled, remembering where I was again. "Right. My mistake. In that case, how about if we hang out here for a bit and see if she comes in?"

"Fine by me." Honey plopped into one of the sofas in the hotel foyer. "It means I can rest a little longer before I have to go home and deal with dishes and laundry."

"I didn't realize that was such a chore." I was amused by Honey's martyr's attitude.

"I never thought it was that big of a deal, but with three kids, I'm doing a couple loads a day to try to keep up, and the dishes—they never end."

I could understand her feelings about dishes—not my favorite part of the job, and I wasn't going to have anyone around to clean up after me in my bakery. I sighed. "I bet I'll be doing more washing up than you every day—at least, if the business does well."

"True." That seemed to brighten her attitude.

Before I could change the subject, Millie entered the room, speaking with Caroline and her husband, Craig. The Richardsons were dressed up, as if they were on a fancy date, but it appeared they had come from a quiet dinner together. Strange, but rather sweet. Millie, on the other hand, was in a T-shirt and jeans, and looked like her evening plans had leaned more toward a burger and a movie than champagne and dancing.

"Hello," I greeted the three of them. Honey echoed me.

"Hello, ladies, how are you tonight?" Mr. Richardson asked. "I didn't expect to see you here. Can't get enough of this hotel?"

"We wanted to chat with Millie," I said.

"And is your business keeping you busy?" he asked. "You must be so excited about starting something new and fresh."

"I am," I told him. "I've been busy today getting my store cleared out, among other projects." Said projects being picking everyone's brains about the murder. "Have you been out to eat?"

"Yes, we ate at a little café between here and Prescott," Craig said. "And we ran into Millie in the parking lot."

"The beauty of a small town—you run into everyone you know the moment you leave your house," Honey said. "I didn't expect you to still be in town."

"The police won't let us leave yet," Caroline said with a sniff. "They've told everyone to stay for a few days. Well, except for Jeff and those guys, since they live close by." She glanced at her perfectly manicured nails. "I have committees, projects, commitments at home and we're stuck here."

"Now, darling." Craig set his hand over the one looped through his elbow. "I know it's inconvenient, but it's important that the police have time to check everything out. We want Valerie's killer to be caught, don't we?"

Her lips pressed together in a mild pout, but she nodded. "Of course, sweetheart. You're right. I've been stressed about this whole thing. I'm sure it will be taken care of soon." She looked up at her husband's face and smiled, her company expression back in use.

"Speaking of the police. Have you heard any news from

them?" I asked, though I doubted Detective Tingey was being more forthcoming with them than he was with me.

"They're working on fingerprints, and the pathologist was supposed to be, ah, taking care of his job this morning, I guess, so Lidia is supposed to be able to hold the funeral this weekend," Caroline said. "It's such a terrible shame that she's having to deal with this—and with her husband out of the country."

"Poor woman, and poor child," Millie said with a shake of her head. "I still can't believe Valerie's gone." She put a hand over her mouth, as if trying to hold back the sobs. Pathetic insincere attempt, I thought, even though I hadn't thought her words insincere only two nights earlier.

I decided now was as good a time as any to broach the issue that bothered me. "You know, it's funny how you talk about what great friends you were, how close you've always been, but I heard that you and Valerie had a big fight when you were in college. What happened?" Once the words were out, I wondered if I should have been a bit more tactful, but it was too late.

Millie stuttered for a minute and Caroline spoke up, stepping slightly in front of Millie, as if to shield her from the interrogation. "I don't see why you're asking these questions. It's all water under the bridge now. If Millie wants to remember the good times instead of the petty misunderstandings, how is that your problem?"

"It's not my problem, but I am concerned that the police are looking at me as a suspect." I stared them both down. "I'm not taking the blame for something I didn't do."

Honey tugged on my sleeve, her move surreptitious, a reminder to tread lighter. "Don't overreact, Tess. You know you're not a serious suspect."

I didn't know it, but the reminder was good and I pulled myself back.

"Calm down," Caroline said, tightening the filmy silk scarf around her bare arms. "There's no use getting excited about a petty slight. In trouble like this, cool heads must prevail."

"Did you call it a petty slight?" Millie turned to look at Caroline, incredulous. "Petty? Her stealing my boyfriend when we had begun talking about marriage was *petty*?" Apparently she was still quite bitter about it.

I had to agree with Millie, since my own wounds were pretty raw. I kept my voice light. "Doesn't sound too petty to me. People have killed over less."

Horror filled Millie's face and she stepped back. "I did *not* kill her. I can't believe you'd suggest that." She flipped the hair back from her face.

"I didn't accuse you of anything," I said, thinking maybe even my not-so-casual observation had gone too far—especially if I wanted her to talk to us.

Caroline studied me for a long moment. "Still, you need to be careful about what you say and how you say it. Such a comment can be misinterpreted."

"Now, dear," Craig said, patting his wife's hand. "You're tired and overwrought. Let's go back to our room and rest. I'm sure you all understand." He said this last to the rest of us, and of course, we agreed.

It was a well-bred way to extricate themselves from the conversation, I thought, and admired Craig's deft handling. Caroline nodded to us. "It was nice seeing you again, Honey, Tess." She gave Millie a hug. Because they were that close, or to show us where her loyalties lay? I wasn't sure.

Her words were insincere, but I smiled, accustomed to playing the politeness game with clients. I wish I could manage to apply some of my own social training to this situation. What was wrong with me, anyway?

The Richardsons turned and walked off, and Honey and I

fell into step alongside Millie as she turned in that direction as well. They took the elevator up, and we waited at the bottom.

"So where are you headed?" Millie asked.

"We wanted to chat with you," Honey said. "It must be so hard for you right now. Even if you and Valerie weren't really best buddies, it must be traumatic for you. I mean, Analesa is a little busy with Tad right now, so she's not around to talk it out."

Another set of elevator doors opened and the three of us entered. Millie took an emotion-studded breath, as if she were trying to hold back tears. "That's so kind of you." She pushed the button for her floor and the doors closed. "We lived with each other so long, even if I didn't like her much at the end, she was still my friend once. This is all so shocking."

We stepped into the hall and walked toward Millie's room.

"It's always hard when something like that happens to someone we know," I agreed. "I remember when a kid in high school died in a car accident; it shook everyone up, even people who didn't really know him well."

A moment later we were in Millie's room.

She walked to the box of facial tissues and grabbed a sheet, touching it to her dry eyes. Her hand moved to slide a magazine to the side on the nightstand, and I caught a flash of color before it was hidden by the smiling starlet on the glossy cover.

If I had antenna, they would have started quivering. Still, I tried not to appear too interested. Since Millie was on the far side of the bed, I couldn't see the magazine well, so I walked over to grab myself a tissue. "Even now, thinking about my schoolmate's too-early death is difficult." Which was a true statement, but I wasn't thinking about him—I was wondering if I'd seen what I thought I'd seen.

Honey sat beside Millie and set a hand on her arm. "You can talk to us, you know. What happened that night?"

I pulled out a tissue, then bumped the magazine as I retracted my hand. The sparkle of gems flashed again in the light of the table lamp, which she'd left on earlier. "Wow." I pulled the necklace out so it was completely revealed. "Isn't this Valerie's?" I kept my voice curious and surprised, but inside, my thought was *gotcha.*

"Do you think it looks like hers?" Millie asked, her voice rising in pitch. "Valerie and I must have similar taste in jewelry. She did have good fashion sense."

"Yes, she did, but she told me, an ex-boyfriend had commissioned the earrings, necklace and bracelet for her for their first anniversary. There isn't another set like it out there." This was a bluff on my part. Millie hadn't been in the room to know what we'd discussed.

Millie's gaze slid away from me, and she clasped her hands together nervously. "Maybe you're wrong."

"Come on," Honey said with a derisive look. "You can't expect us to believe that. We know you had problems with Valerie. You might as well come clean."

"Fine. You want to know the truth?" Millie slumped. "Valerie used people, you know? Lance wasn't the first guy I liked that she'd made a play for—but she kept borrowing money, charging things on the phone bill, promising to pay me back. She owed me close to two thousand dollars by the time school finished, and I ended our friendship. She never paid me."

Millie sighed. "She left the necklace in Ana's room that evening before she went out for her date, probably because the clasp is broken. I saw it sitting on the table when I went in to do my nails, and slid it into my pocket. If she forgot about it, all the better. I figured it was fair payback."

"You had it all evening? No one else realized she'd left it behind and asked about it?" I asked. I didn't think I believed it, but at the same time, I couldn't be sure the story wasn't true. When I picked up the necklace and checked it, the clasp *was* broken. "So why didn't she put on something different before she went out? She's not the kind of person to go out un-accessorized."

Millie shrugged. "I don't know. Maybe she was running late for her date when she finished talking with Ana." Though she made the pretense of being helpful, there was a stubborn glint in Millie's eyes that said she was done answering questions.

Honey and I looked at each other. "That makes sense." If you think I'm an idiot. "We need to head out now. It's getting late."

When Honey and I stepped into the hotel parking lot a few minutes later, we started rehashing the conversation.

"I don't know. Do you believe her?" Honey asked.

"It seems kind of far-fetched, and I've seen her lie and be insincere before. She could be dangerous, but I'd rather turn that issue over to the cops to figure out."

"I know. I think it's true Valerie owed her money, but she went about collecting it all wrong. Besides, that's what I call loan-shark interest—her necklace was worth more than two grand."

"I know. I'll have to deal with it later, though. I'm tired, after the long day of painting." I hoped I would be able to sleep once my head hit the pillow despite it not even being ten yet. My mind was full of everything I'd learned that day.

Chapter 15

I waved goodbye to Honey at the back entrance of my home. I thought again of the conversation with Bronson. He had all the answers I was willing to give, but I had the feeling it wouldn't be enough. He wasn't going anywhere in the morning. Drat.

The sky was moonless, so the parking lot was dark, lit only by a flickering lamp in the middle of the block. I made a mental note to contact the city in the morning and see if we could get the lamp fixed. I grabbed some garbage from my car on the way to the back door, then leaned to toss it in the Dumpster. There was a rustling noise just as something pounded on my shoulder, knocking me off balance.

My arms wheeled to break my fall as I went down, hitting the Dumpster and then my knees. A second blow hit me in the back of the head, pushing me forward so my hands landed hard on the rocks and my crown banged against the garbage receptacle. I tried to get my balance and decide if the reason I saw nothing but blackness was because of the blow to my head or because it was dark out. I heard quick footsteps like the heels of athletic shoes slapping against the blacktop, running away from me. A car passed on the road thirty feet off, but in a different direction from the one my assailant had taken.

My head spun and my stomach lurched. My knees and the palms of my hands felt like they were on fire as the old, uneven blacktop dug into them. The air had been knocked out of my lungs and I sucked in oxygen a little at a time until I felt like they were filling again. I groaned as I rolled off my knees, my back to the Dumpster so I could see what was going on around me—or I would have been able to, if there had been more light. The attacker was long gone now, but I studied the shadows as I recovered. Passing cars, barking dogs and the heavy bass of a rock song blared for a moment. After a long while I dragged myself to my feet again and hobbled inside.

When I was in my apartment with the door locked tight behind me, I took inventory: my favorite pair of jeans had a rip in one knee now—not the fashionable kind—and I had scrapes and light bleeding on both knees. My hands were scraped from the Dumpster, and one had a long, shallow cut along the side from rubbing on something sharp—the lid, I guessed. This gave me visions of tetanus and hepatitis, and had me scampering for the first aid kit Grandma had always kept in the bathroom. I had abrasions all over my palms from the rocks as well. My right shoulder blade hurt like the dickens—I was going to have a serious bruise there—and my head pounded.

I struggled out of my clothes and into a pair of soft, cut-off sweats and a T-shirt before calling the police. Through it all, I kept thinking: who would have done that to me? And why did someone hurt me? Could it have been kids playing games?

I didn't know. If this incident had been isolated, I might have thought it could be kids or a random attack. In concert with the slashed tires, though, it seemed a little more ominous. Was someone trying to stop my investigation?

When I decided the bleeding on the back of my head wasn't serious, I padded across the living room in my stocking feet and picked up the phone to call in the attack.

The officer who came to my house was young and familiar. A glance at his name tag told me he was one of the Mitchell boys, which was good enough for me. "Hello, Tess. Can you tell me what happened?" he asked when I opened the door.

Before I could invite him in, I heard sirens outside and I

saw an ambulance pull up beside the squad car. I groaned. "I'm fine, really. No need for EMTs."

"It's just a precaution. We'll have them take a look. It's been slow tonight. I'm sure they'll be glad to have something to do." He moved past me into the room.

I bit back a sigh when I saw Jack hop out of the ambulance, a huge yellow case in one hand, an oxygen tank in the other. "It had to be Jack's night, didn't it?"

"What?" Officer Mitchell asked, scrunching up his freckled face.

"Never mind." I invited him to sit. Footsteps on the stairs announced the paramedics' arrival and I let them in. Jack looked worried, and his eyes scanned me. "Are you the one who was hurt?"

"Yes, but I'm fine. I don't need help." *Just a Lortab or two for my headache.*

He tipped his head. "You look like you'll live, but how about if we check you out while the officer takes the report."

I wondered what he would do if I said no. When I hesitated, he added, "There's no charge unless you ride with us to the hospital, so you ought to at least let us take a blood pressure and make sure everything's okay."

I could tell he wouldn't leave, so I may as well give in. "Fine. No needles, though."

"Scouts' honor." I think he would have saluted, except his hands were full of equipment. His partner came up the stairs behind him.

"You were a Scout?" I asked as I stood back and let the two guys in.

"Sure. Go ahead and sit next to Zach there." He pointed to the sofa where Officer Mitchell sat.

I was tired and I hurt, so I did as I was told. When I sat, I realized how disheveled I must look and was embarrassed to have Jack see me like this. Then I wondered why I cared what he thought of me. He was disagreeable in the best of circumstances.

"Okay, start from the beginning," Officer Mitchell prompted. "When you pulled into the parking lot. What happened?"

I told him about returning from dinner—I didn't say where or with whom—and being accosted. The paramedics went to work running their gizmos and interrupting my tale to ask about medications I'd taken, if I hit my head when I fell, etc.

"Can you think of any reason that someone might want to hurt you?" Officer Mitchell asked when I finished talking.

I hesitated. Was I jumping the gun by admitting it could be because I was looking into the murder? I decided I might as well be honest.

Footsteps pounded up the stairwell and the door flew open. Bronson stood at the top of the stairs, his chest heaving, his eyes wild. His gaze fell on me and he hurried to my side. "Are you okay? I drove past and saw the ambulance." He knelt in the space between Jack and the officer. "I don't know what I'd do if something happened to you." He took my hand in his, studying my face.

"Right. What would you tell the Goulds?" I didn't want him in my home, and my humor and patience were long gone.

Bronson sputtered in response. "This is about *you*, not the Goulds."

"Who's this?" Jack asked, jabbing a thumb at Bronson.

"I'm her—"

"Don't you say it, Bronson, unless you want my fist up your nose." I balled up my hand and shook it at him. "I am *not* marrying you!"

Jack's eyes widened. "Well, Bronson, was it? Could you back off while we finish up here? She's got some scrapes and bruises, but seems fine overall." His voice held so much authority that, miracle of miracles, Bronson complied. Jack turned back to me. "You said whatever it was hit your shoulder?"

"Yeah. The first blow hit my shoulder, the second one hit me in the back of the head. It was really hard."

Bronson gasped. "Someone attacked you?"

"No, I needed the company so I thought I'd take up these guys' valuable time." I slanted a glare at him, then looked back at the officer.

Jack got up and walked around behind the sofa, which was stationed between the television and the piano, dividing the room. "Lean forward. I'm going to check your spine. Tell me if there's any tenderness or bruising anywhere I touch."

While he checked, the officer asked me again, "Can you think of any reason someone might want to hurt you?"

I winced as Jack reached the area where my shoulder blade was and I sucked in a breath.

"There?" Jack asked.

"It's the shoulder blade, not the spine. Whoever it was hit me pretty hard. And the only reason I can think that someone would hurt me is—" I hissed as he pressed his fingers into my shoulder, even if his touch was light.

"You ought to have an x-ray," Jack said.

Like that was going to happen. "I don't have insurance anymore."

"Sure you do," Bronson interjected. "They took it out of your paycheck on Friday. They might throw fits that you're in another state, but I'll take care of it."

I ground my teeth together. "Great."

"The only reason someone would want to hurt you is?" Officer Mitchell prompted again.

"Right. Because of the murder last weekend. I've been asking questions. But Detective Tingey has been asking questions too, and I doubt anyone tried to knock him out."

110

"Have some sense, Tess, and leave the investigating to the professionals." Jack started probing around in my hair on the back of my head. "You're still bleeding back here, but it's sluggish. It doesn't look like a very big gash. Check her eyes."

The last part must have been to his partner, because the man pulled a penlight from the pocket on the side of his thigh. "Close your eyes for a minute, will you?"

Jack put a hand on my shoulder. "I'm going to look at this shoulder blade, then we'll load you up."

"I'm not going into the ER in the ambulance," I protested.

"Sure, sure. Lean forward." He shifted the pillow I'd been leaning against.

The other paramedic had me open and close my eyes while his light added to the pain beating against my skull. Jack pulled up my shirt in the back to expose the injury. I was glad the shirt was oversized so it still covered me fine in front. "Some scratching, minor abrasions on the surface, but you'll have a whopper of a bruise. You said he knocked the wind out of you?"

"Yeah."

"Hey, quit touching her!" Bronson protested as Jack felt the damaged area with his fingertips. Jack's touch was all very clinical, but Bronson didn't seem to realize that.

"Jack's a paramedic, you idiot," I said with a grimace as he pushed an especially tender spot further down my back. "He's doing his job." The pain shot through my body. "Is that really necessary? I hurt, okay?"

"Oh, so it's *Jack*. Is he an old friend as well?" Bronson asked. "How many *old friends* do you have in this town?"

"No, he's not my friend. More like my new nemesis." I winced as he lightly pressed around the edges of the bone. "Aren't you done yet?"

"I think you have a concussion," the partner said.

"I'm done." Jack put my shirt down and came around to the front. "Now, about going in for that x-ray?"

111

I noticed that Officer Mitchell had given up on asking questions, but he appeared to be patient. I supposed he was used to sitting back and waiting for the paramedics to do their jobs before moving in for the kill. Might as well let them make me miserable first. Concussion. Now that was something I didn't want to deal with. I wondered how serious it was.

"I can drive myself," I said through clenched teeth. No one was going to strap me onto a gurney and wheel me into the hospital.

"No, you can't drive yourself. You have a concussion," Bronson protested. "I'll take you."

"Listen to the guy you're not going to marry," Jack said as he put things back into his yellow supply case. "If you won't go in with us, let him drive. It'll be easier on you if you do. Unless you're considering getting a restraining order against him for not taking no for an answer, in which case, I'll be happy to call Honey for you."

I glared at Jack for a moment before I decided he had a point. "Call Honey."

Bronson let out an exasperated huff. "Tess, don't be foolish. I'm going to the hospital either way. I'm not leaving you alone like this."

"Your blood pressure has gone up since we arrived," the second paramedic announced as the air left the cuff again. He started pulling it off. The Velcro made a loud ripping noise that caused me to jump in surprise.

"You think? I wonder why that might be." I couldn't help the sarcasm; Bronson was reason enough to raise my blood pressure. The thought of going to the hospital wasn't helping. I'd never been a fan, but after watching my grandma slowly die in one, I had no great love for the facilities.

Bronson folded his arms over his chest and stared at me. I decided I could get some really wonderful pain medications at the hospital, and sighed. "Fine, I'll go in with Bronson." I shot a glare at Jack. "Satisfied?"

"Very. Take care of yourself." Jack stood and picked up the equipment he'd brought in. "I'll see you around. My daughter is excited about your shop. If that cake was typical of your baking skills, I think I might be excited too." He exited the room.

Was that a civil conversation I just had with Jack? Odd. And he liked my baking, even if he hadn't mentioned it before. Hmmm. Wait, did he say daughter? Honey had mentioned he was divorced, but she hadn't said anything about a daughter.

Officer Mitchell stood. "I'll lead you out to the hospital. We can finish this discussion there."

"Let me find you some shoes and a jacket," Bronson said as he also stood and headed for the hall.

"Room on the right." I supposed I was going to have to sort through Grandma's stuff since I would want her bigger closet. I'd worry about that next week.

A minute later, Bronson brought a pair of shoes, socks and a jacket. He'd dug through my closet. Great. He pulled on my shoes and socks, kneeling at my feet, then helped me stand, slid the jacket over my shoulders, locked the apartment behind us and led me out to his car. He did all of this without a word of complaint or reproach, making me feel like he really did care about me. It felt kind of nice having him coddle me. It didn't happen very often, but I rarely allowed him to coddle me, either. On the few occasions when I had felt under the weather or needed his support, I remembered Bronson had always been there for me. Always. How had I forgotten that?

As we pulled out of the parking lot behind Officer Mitchell, I thought my life couldn't possibly get any more complicated.

Chapter 16

Of course, one always thinks things are going to get better instead of worse, and I admit, I was relieved to learn that my shoulder blade was only majorly bruised instead of broken—I can't imagine the kind of cast that would take. I was also happy about the pain killer samples they sent home with me, along with a prescription for more.

Officer Mitchell took the full report, admonished me to leave the detecting to the police and to add a security system—complete with floodlights—to the back of my building. I promised I'd make the call in the morning. He deserted me with a worried Bronson hovering over my shoulder. No matter how many times I told Bronson to sit in the waiting room, he was back again in minutes, checking to see if I needed a drink, a snack from the vending machine—as if we hadn't eaten a huge dinner—Was I too hot or cold? He was driving me nuts.

When we reached my apartment, he followed me in, despite my best efforts to make it clear that he wasn't invited. "Are you going to be okay? The doctor said you have a concussion," he said.

"I'll be fine," I told him, as I had done a dozen times already.

"The doctor said you shouldn't be alone tonight, that you should have someone waking you up every few hours. Maybe I ought to stay." He rubbed his hands up and down my arms, studying my face.

"You are not staying over here."

"You have another bedroom," he pointed out. "You don't need the second bed for yourself."

I ground my teeth together. "It's my grandmother's room. No one else has stayed there since she died, and the sheets haven't been changed since the funeral, if not before that."

"I can make a bed. I've been known to do it before." He touched my cheek, using a finger under my jaw to lift my face until I was looking him in the eye.

I pulled out of his grasp. "Forget it. You have a hotel room."

"Someone needs to check on you."

He was right. The doctor had said I needed someone to make sure I was okay every hour. I hate doctors. "You have my cell phone number. Call me. Now get out of here so I can collapse into bed."

"Tess, sweetie—"

"No, Bronson. You're not staying here. End of story. Call and wake me up if you must."

"Fine. If you don't answer, I'm getting the ambulance back here, though, so don't even think about turning the ringer off."

In my head, I grumbled about bossy men. "All right. Get lost. I need my sleep if you're going to wake me up constantly."

With a look that said he wasn't pleased with my choice, he headed out the door, saying good night over his shoulder. I wasn't even settled properly into sleep when the phone rang the first time. He called me dutifully every hour on the hour after that.

Though I wanted to throttle him half the time, part of me was grateful to see he cared. He'd never acted so sweet and considerate before—or, not recently. It was almost enough to have me thinking maybe there was a way to put things back together for us. Almost.

Chapter 17

My whole body ached the next morning, including several muscles I'd never realized existed. Though it took time to manage my morning routine and the stairs, I eventually made it to the restaurant. I came through the back door to grab the notebook off the front counter when my eyes were draw to the big picture window. On it in red spray paint, heavy with drips at the bottoms of the letters, was a message, the mirror image of "Leave it alone."

As if the pain all over my body wasn't plenty for me to deal with. My stomach tightened in a knot. *Leave it alone.* My neck and arms broke out in goose bumps as my breath caught. This hadn't been there the previous night when we got home from the hospital. I knew it hadn't, because we'd driven right past it and I would have noticed.

I didn't move, frozen at the thought that someone had defaced my building. Well, my window anyway. I hoped that was all. I hurried to the front door and flipped the lock open, then stepped onto the sidewalk and studied the message, reading it again. I checked the brick for splatters, but was relieved to see that the paint was only on the window. It would be a pain to remove, but it would come off fine—which was good, because I didn't have the money to replace the custom window or hassle with getting the paint off the bricks right now.

A black-and-white pulled up while I studied the vandalism, and Detective Tingey emerged from the front seat. "Do you know what that message is about?" he asked as he came over to stand beside me.

I shot him a look, but returned my gaze to the window. "I guess it's about the murder."

"Someone left you a message to leave the murder alone? What are you doing?" He crossed his arms over his chest, as all cops seem to do out of habit, even though he wore a blazer, rather than a uniform with the belt packed with cop paraphernalia.

Should I admit it? Jack had called me stupid the night before for trying to figure out what happened. Was he right? I wasn't sure. "I've been curious about the murder, and talking to people about it."

Detective Tingey's irritated expression indicated he wasn't happy with my answer, but perhaps wasn't surprised, either. "Learn anything?"

I knew I should bring up the issue with Millie and the necklace, but wanted to feel out the conversation first. "Yeah, it sounds like half the people who knew Valerie had a reason to want her out of the way. Even the bride was upset about the way Valerie acted at the wedding rehearsal. It seems like the only people who didn't have a grudge against her were her little girl and Tad's family, and I'm not sure that's true."

"Why are you asking questions, though? Don't you think I'm doing a thorough job of checking into it? You can't think I'm actually working on anything else right now—not when we have a murder, which hardly ever happens around here."

I studied him. He seemed to be competent, but I still didn't know if I trusted him to find the truth, rather than going with the easiest answer. I thought of Dahlia again, of the way she sobbed into Tad's shoulder as he carried her away from the murder scene, and knew I couldn't let it go. "And have you learned anything interesting?" I knew he wouldn't tell me—the cops in detective shows never shared any of the juicy information.

"I think pretty much everyone has a grudge against her. Yours seems to be a mild one compared to some of the others, which puzzles me."

Considering I had spoken with the woman for no more than a few seconds, I didn't understand why he was confused. Shouldn't my grudge have been mild? "What do you mean?"

He unfolded his arms and set a hand on each hip. "If you don't have much of a reason to have wanted her dead, and all this bad stuff is happening to you because you're poking your nose where it doesn't belong, why is it that yours are the *only* fingerprints on the murder weapon?"

I felt the blood rush out of my head and had to put a hand on the building to steady myself. "What? How? That can't be." If I could get my mind to work at all, it would have been racing to try to understand. There ought to be the prints of the hotel staff, at least.

"You okay?" He reached out and touched my shoulder.

"Yeah. Yeah, I'm fine. Really. Maybe." I shifted and leaned back against the building as my head swam. "How come the murderer's prints aren't on the vase? Not even the shard in her chest?"

"I'm going to have to ask you to come down to the station."

"Are you arresting me?" I thought of everything I needed to do, and the likelihood that I'd spend the next twenty-five years rotting in prison. No way would I be allowed to participate in the regional cake show next year, in that case.

"No, I'm not arresting you. Not yet, anyway. I just want to talk to you in a more formal setting."

I understood what he meant was that he wanted me in a more *intimidating* setting, even if he was trying to act nice about it now. "Would you take a report about the graffiti first?" I asked.

"How about if you get into the back seat of my car before you keel over from shock, and I'll snap some pictures. I'll take your statement while we're at the station."

I knew the reason he wanted me in his car: I'd be locked in the back seat, where he wouldn't have to worry about me running away. I wanted to protest, but I wasn't feeling too strong and could use a long moment to sit down. Could things get any worse? "I need to lock both the restaurant and my place upstairs. I only popped down here for a second."

The detective must not have thought I was much of a threat, despite the fact that he saw me as a murder suspect, because he didn't cuff me or anything. He followed me back into the building, locking everything behind him as we retraced my earlier steps.

I snatched up the notebook with my to-do list as we walked through. The walls looked beautiful with the new coat of paint, though the ceiling and trim hadn't been done yet. I wondered what it would cost to replace the tables and chairs with something a little less dated and made a mental note to check restaurant auctions.

My mind should have been on the upcoming horrors of the interrogation room, the possibility of being locked up forever, but it wasn't. This made me think I was either in shock, or there was something seriously wrong with me. Maybe the concussion had been worse than the doctor thought.

We finished locking up the building and Detective Tingey took me to his car, opening the door for me. I was grateful he didn't handcuff me, but I still felt trapped in the back seat between two locked doors and a metal grate separating me from the front. I leaned my head against the seat, still tired from the previous night's multiple interruptions, which left me groggy. Bronson had taken his job a little too seriously.

The detective seemed to dawdle over snapping pictures, studying the sidewalk for any evidence and disappearing around

the side of the building for a while. He returned empty handed—
or at least it looked that way.

"Any clues?" I asked when he sat behind the wheel.

"Nothing useful, but it could be tied to the murder
investigation. I'll have someone check into it." He started the car
and pulled onto the road.

"Great." I settled into the seat and paid attention to how we
got to the police station. If I ever needed to come here when I
wasn't a suspect, I wanted to know where it was.

In the interrogation room, we started with my movements
of the previous evening, prior to the attack, then continued
through bedtime and this morning when he found me studying
the new artwork.

"Are you sure you didn't hear anything?" he asked, a pen
scratching at his notepad.

"Nothing. I use a white-noise machine to drown out traffic,
so they would've had to be really loud to wake me."

"All right, we'll see if anything turns up. Now, I want you to
go back to Friday night and tell me what you remember from
the moment you arrived at the hotel until the next morning
when police got there."

He took me through that scenario twice, despite the fact
that he had already grilled me on Saturday and had my three-
page written statement. I thought about my near-run-in with Jeff.
"As I was leaving Friday night after I set everything up, Jeff and I
almost collided in the doorway. I moved out of the way and
bumped the pedestal with the vase of flowers. I remember I
dropped my box and grabbed the vase, managing to catch it
before it fell. Jeff apologized, we introduced ourselves and he let
me pass him."

The detective wrote something in his notebook. He looked
up at me without tipping his head up. "You didn't have plastic
gloves on when you'd been working with food?"

Right, because I wear them everywhere I go. "I had them on earlier, but I took them off when I finished. I'm sure if you ask him about it, Jeff will remember what happened."

"Was anyone else in the room when you bumped into the vase? Anyone who would have seen you touching it?"

"You think Jeff won't remember?" I supposed he had been distracted. Maybe it hadn't made an impression on him. Doubtful, but possible.

Detective Tingey shrugged. "Either that, or maybe someone else saw you pick it up, and decided your prints might distract the investigator."

That was a new thought—one that gave me chills. "You think someone tried to pin it on me?" I was nobody. Who would dislike me enough to frame me? Or was I just convenient?

"It's possible. We're still processing evidence." He tapped the end of his pen on the top edge of the notebook. "I'm considering all the options."

I thought about it and tried to remember who else had been in the room. "I think Analesa and Caroline were in the corner talking. Tad had already walked out; he was sent after Jeff and Valerie, and I don't remember seeing him in the foyer as I left, but I can't be sure. For that matter, Valerie might have been headed back and seen it as well." I searched my mind. "I don't know if Millie or anyone else was there—I wasn't paying attention—but I know someone else was going to bring the rest of the family and friends in for dinner." I shook my head. "I wish I was more help."

"You did fine." He crossed his arms on the table. "And now, you said you've been poking into the murder. Tell me what you've picked up, and maybe we can figure out who attacked you last night."

I studied his expressionless face and wondered if he was prying for information to pin this on me, or if he believed me. I couldn't tell. "I've talked to nearly everyone in the past few days. All the Plumbers, the Richardsons, Jeff, Millie, Lidia and Dahlia—that little girl is so adorable."

"Yes, it's unfortunate she's an orphan now. Either no one knows who her father is, or they're not telling. No one can find the birth certificate. Dahlia's aunt seems more than willing to take custody, though, so that's good." He lowered the notebook to the table. "Anyone say anything that stood out to you, seemed off?"

"Not really, but I did learn something interesting last night." I filled him in about the necklace and how Millie said she'd gotten it. He wrote several things, but didn't change his expression.

"You also said almost everyone had a grudge against the victim. I'm sure I've heard it all, but can you tell me what you know?"

"Let's see—Valerie stole Millie's college boyfriend when she said they had been getting serious. Though of course, if he was filchable, it probably wasn't as serious on his end as on Millie's. And Valerie owed Millie a big chunk of cash." I started counting on my fingers. "Analesa had been upset with Valerie for being an attention hog, and because she thought Valerie was focusing too much on her baby brother, Shawn, who couldn't care less about her."

"Okay, who else?"

He'd made a couple of notes, as if there were a few tidbits he'd been missing, or maybe something I said sparked his memory, but most of the time he watched me. Was he looking for an indication that I was making this all up? Did he think I was trying to deflect the blame from myself? "I'm sure you know about her professional rivalry with Jeff. According to him, she fabricated evidence for a recent lawsuit between their clients, which had cost him some personal pride, if nothing else. They were going head-to-head again on another issue soon." I studied him for a moment. "But you knew that already."

He nodded. "Yes, I did. Jeff's part, anyway. So the Richardsons, the older generation and Tad's sister, don't have a reason? No motives or grudges hiding in their past?"

"Aren't those enough people to check out?" I looked at him, but he stared me down. "No, I don't have anything on the Richardsons or the older Plumbers. If there's anything to learn, I haven't heard a whisper."

He flipped his notebook closed. "And you're going to stop looking for answers right now. Someone has it in for you, Miss Crawford, whether it's related to your search or something else. You need to let yourself heal and keep yourself safe if someone is after you." A hard glint entered his eyes.

I felt a chill go down my spine, but I suppose that was what he wanted.

Chapter 18

Detective Tingey dropped me back in front of my bakery two hours after he picked me up. I still hadn't eaten breakfast. Painkillers and a long, hot soak in the tub to calm my aches and bruises were in order. I was not amused to enter my little courtyard and find Bronson standing at the door to my apartment, apparently willing to wait until I either came home or stepped outside to deal with him. He did look surprised to see me approaching from the parking lot, though, so I had that small grain of enjoyment.

I pulled out my keys. "If you don't get out of here and leave me alone, I'm going to apply for that restraining order Jack mentioned."

"I don't have that long here before I have to go back to work." He walked over, lifting a hand as if to push the hair back from my face—something he'd started doing as soon as we'd begun dating. I shifted away and he dropped his hand instead. "Come on, Tess, have a heart. I don't want you to be alone after the attack, and now you've got graffiti on your front window—have you seen it?" When I nodded, he continued, "I'm worried about your safety. You know I love you."

I didn't know any such thing, but my options at the moment were to let him in or to shut him out, knowing he'd probably still be there when I left again in three hours. "Fine, be my guest. Just stay in the living room, and keep your feet off the furniture."

"I've never put my feet on the furniture," he protested as he followed me in.

"You keep acting as though this town makes you nervous, like you think it's going to wear off on you and you'll lose some of your city polish. I wanted to let you know what's off limits, in case you've forgotten." I moved to the kitchen, ignoring his continuing arguments.

The doorbell rang and I groaned. It better be Honey, I thought. If it wasn't, I might strangle whomever was bothering me when I was tired, hungry and in pain. Or maybe I'd recruit them to help me kill Bronson. Then I could be prosecuted for a murder I *did* commit.

It wasn't Honey. Instead, Shawn's voice was the one questioning Bronson's presence in my home.

I rubbed my face and stepped back in the living room in time to hear Bronson's response. "She's my fiancé, and I love her. What else do you expect me to do when she's been attacked?"

"Attacked?" Shawn's eyes zeroed in on me. "What happened?"

When Bronson started answering for me and Shawn turned to listen, I decided my presence was unnecessary and returned to the kitchen to do something about breakfast—a few hours late.

"Hey, where are you going?" Bronson asked.

I ground my teeth, but made an effort at pleasantness. "You didn't seem to need me, as you've already decided you know how I am—even though we haven't discussed it this morning. I thought I'd leave you to the explanations."

"Sweetheart, I'm sorry. Don't get like that." He came up behind me, placing a hand on my back and rubbing it.

I shifted away, wincing as he rubbed over my sore spot. If he was trying to give comfort, he was failing. Irritation, on the other hand . . . "Don't you 'sweetheart' me. We're not engaged

125

anymore." He reached toward me, and I winced again as pain lanced through my shoulder when I brushed his hand back. Determined not to give into it, I opened my fridge. "Are either of you hungry?" As long as I was cooking, I might as well feed them. As much as I'd rather not, good manners dictated that I ask. I really wanted to curl up in a ball and block everyone and everything out until I felt better.

"You know me, I can always eat," Bronson said. "Especially if you're cooking."

"I thought we were going out for lunch," Shawn reminded me as he approached.

I sighed. "I'm sorry. I forgot, I've had so much going on since I saw you last. Forgive me?" Now I was acting like a jerk.

"Of course." He brushed a kiss over the bruise on my forehead in a possessive move. "I'm sorry you had such a rough night. Tell me what happened." He looked into my eyes, studying my face.

The doorbell rang again and made me want to cry. This time it had better be Honey or I might be the one leaving this apartment. How long did it take her to respond to an SOS text anyway? Thankfully, it was Honey, and she'd brought her adorable toddler, Zoey. I'd been told that at two, Zoey wasn't considered a baby anymore, but it was close enough in my book.

I called Honey back into the kitchen to chat. The testosterone circling around me was stifling. Bronson had made it clear he had no intention of being faithful to me and Shawn would go home in a few days, so why were they both flexing their man muscles?

"What happened to your face?" Honey asked as soon as she saw me.

"I was attacked last night." I filled her and Shawn in on what happened.

Shawn swore low under his breath and Honey covered

Zoey's ears so she wouldn't hear, but her eyes said if the child hadn't been there, she would have vented as well. "Are you okay? You should have called me," she said as she brushed the hair back from my forehead to get a better look at the bruise.

"You should have called *me*," Shawn said. "I can't believe someone wants to hurt you." He took my hand and gave it a squeeze.

"Bronson was there." When he gave a superior look, I added with a scowl, "Whether I wanted him to be or not." I returned my gaze to Shawn and Honey. "It was late and there was nothing either of you could do. I figured I'd fill you in today."

"Next time, call me." Honey gave me a hard-eyed stare. "That's what best friends are for."

I chuckled. "I hope there isn't a next time. The last thing I need is to be attacked again." I took her darling brown-haired girl, ignoring the pain in my shoulder, and changed the subject. "I can't get over how much this little one looks like you." I leaned in, nose to nose with Zoey, and crooned. "Yeah, you have your mommy's eyes. And where did this cute little button nose come from?" I touched the nose in question and she giggled and grabbed my finger. I used my other hand to feather over the tight dark curls on her head. She would probably hate her hair all of her life, but I thought it was adorable.

"According to pictures, the nose came from Great-aunt Martha," Honey said.

I turned and gave her a questioning look. "Great-aunt Martha?"

"Yes, sorry. Chance's class has been studying family trees at school and they've talked about how heredity works. He thought it was so cool, he's been analyzing everyone's features against family photos. He's decided to turn it into his science project, so he'll probably hit you up for photos from your family soon." She pulled a hair elastic from the front pocket of her jeans and used it to pull back her cornrows.

"That sounds like fun. Tell him I'd be happy to help him out." I opened the fridge and grabbed the milk, shooing the guys back to the kitchen doorway. The room was too small for four of us. "I'm working on a recipe for cheese blintzes. Care for some?"

The guys both agreed with alacrity.

"Are you kidding?" Honey asked. "Have you seen my hips? Do you think I ever say no to good food? Of course I want some! Who could turn down your blintzes?"

I eyed said hips and ignored her comment. She was so not fat, it wasn't even funny. She was well formed, curvy like a real woman. I didn't get the whole fascination people had with being so skinny you looked like a twelve-year-old boy, and that had never been a problem for her anyway. "This version is somewhat less fattening than many recipes, but they're still delicious."

"Do you ever make anything that isn't delicious?" She opened cupboards and pulled out flour, salt, sugar and the butter from the fridge. "I'm assuming we start with your famous crepes."

"We sure do." I shifted the baby to one hip and retrieved the rest of the ingredients, checking in my personal recipe file to verify that my memory was correct.

"We miss having your recipes around," Bronson said.

"That's too bad. I'm sure your new pastry chef will have his or her own recipes to share with you."

Again, he slid into the voice that had always given me pleasant goose bumps. "It would be easier if you came back to us."

"Not happening." He was starting to sound like a broken record, and since he was almost never this persistent about anything, I had to wonder why he had chosen now to start. Could he really feel that bad about what happened? The image of him kissing Karen flashed through my mind again, and I sloughed off the thought of his remorse. "Honey, you said you had a chat with Caroline yesterday?" I passed over the baby and cracked the eggs into my mixer the poured in the milk and oil.

"Yeah. She came into the store to pick up a pint of Ben & Jerry's and we stopped to talk for a bit. She mentioned the big fight Jeff and Valerie had on Friday. One of the hotel staff told her they were worried they'd have to break it up because they were in each other's faces about their work." She dug into the cupboard and pulled out a half-empty box of crackers. "Apparently, Jeff accused Valerie of tampering with evidence, and she denied it. Then he questioned whether her amorous pursuits had extended into the judicial realm. He said he wouldn't let her ruin any more cases for him."

My jaw dropped. "Are you serious? He accused her of sleeping with the judge?"

Honey shrugged. "Who knows if the story is accurate? It's possible the staff member misunderstood or filled in the blanks. Or Caroline might have heard the bits the staff remembered and figured out the rest. According to Analesa, her mother-in-law has never been a big fan of Valerie's."

I added flour, salt and baking soda to the bowl, and the mixer whipped them in. "I can vouch for that. Caroline came into the reception room on Saturday morning looking for Valerie, wondering what happened to her. She made a comment about what a better choice Millie would have been as maid of honor." I used a rubber spatula to scrape the sides of my bowl, and mixed the crepe batter a moment longer before setting it aside.

"I've heard her mention it several times—and that was while I was still in Nogales, so she definitely wasn't keeping it a secret," Shawn said, standing beside Bronson at the kitchen door.

I pulled out the cream cheese, cottage cheese, sour cream, and put them in a second mixing bowl. "I wonder if Caroline or the staff member at the hotel bothered to share this info with Detective Tingey." Not that he wasn't aware there was an issue between Valerie and Jeff, but the argument might provide some extra clues.

"I could put a bug in his ear," Shawn suggested. "I've known Tingey for years. It would be no problem. I gotta tell you, though—Jeff doesn't seem like the type to kill a competitor. He's pretty straight and narrow when it comes to his job. Tad says he doesn't play dirty, even if he does dig for loopholes."

"Well, maybe it's time we found out a little more about Jeff, asked a few more people who've worked with or against him and see if you're right." I tested the pan on the stove to see if it was hot enough, added a swirl of butter to the bottom. When it bubbled, I poured a thin layer of crepe batter into it.

"No way," Bronson said, stepping into the kitchen again. "The officer last night told you to leave the investigation to the police."

I sent him a poisonous look that didn't make him back off at all. "Yes, and this morning not only did I wake up to a threatening message on my window, but Detective Tingey took me in for questioning. He has my fingerprints on the murder weapon, Bronson. I could go to prison for something I didn't do, and I'm not going to back down."

"After what happened to you last night, Tingey thinks you're involved?" Shawn looked incredulous.

I shrugged, though I agreed the suspicion was ridiculous. "He talked like he believed me, but he brought me in for questioning, so what does that tell you?"

"I think Bronson's right," Shawn said. He reached out, grabbing a small lock of my hair and tugging lightly. "Your safety is important."

"So says the gun-toting lawman." I didn't bother to keep the sarcasm out of my voice, but neither did I pull away as I had when Bronson had tried to touch my hair.

"Yeah, I am that, and I know how dangerous this can get." His finger brushed my jaw. "I don't want you to get hurt. You should stay out of it."

I lifted a brow. "You don't have useful information about the suspects that might help? No changes or relationship stuff?"

He sighed and released my hair, then leaned back against the cupboards. "Fine. I asked questions yesterday, naturally. I am a cop. It seems you've learned everything relevant that I've found out on my own. There's nothing much to add unless you think it's important that Ana was whining because Tad wants to arrange visits with Dahlia to give Lidia a break. Ana doesn't want to be a mom yet, and though she and Valerie were best friends, she doesn't want to take responsibility for someone else's kid—not even part time."

"I can't blame her," I said. Everyone gave me curious looks.

I was going to continue, but Bronson piped up first. "I thought you wanted kids. We talked about it, about you scaling back so we could start a family. Was that a lie?"

"No, it wasn't a lie, but we talked about waiting a year or two to have some time alone, then starting with a baby, not with someone else's half-grown, traumatized little girl." I held up my hands when they all continued to stare at me. "I'm not saying I wouldn't take in a close friend's kid if I was the best choice—I'm saying there is another option here. Lidia seems to love Dahlia, and she's family, so it's not like Dahlia's going to end up in foster care or something." When that comment seemed to calm their scandalized feelings, I turned back to the pan. "I admit, I was surprised at how close Dahlia and Tad are. They're very comfortable with each other."

"That's the thing," Shawn said. "Lidia lives in California, so she's rarely seen Dahlia—a few times per year at most. On the other hand, Tad and Ana have spent a lot of time with Valerie and her daughter, so she does know them a lot better than her own aunt. It's kind of sad, but it doesn't change anything."

Sad didn't even begin to describe it. But what did I know? I didn't have any siblings, so I may have felt that stronger than most people. Growing up, I always wished for a brother or sister.

"Where were you this morning?" Bronson asked. "I sat here for over an hour. I thought you were just ignoring me. I was about to call the police, afraid something bad had happened because of the concussion."

"I'm fine." I decided not to mention that ignoring him would have been my first choice.

"You need to take it easy, sweetie," Bronson said. "Someone has it in for you."

Shawn elbowed Bronson, who had come to stand at his side. They crowded into the space, stealing my air. Shawn put his hands on my shoulders and turned me to face him. His hand touched my cheek, tipped my head up to meet his gaze. "Are you sure you're okay? A concussion can have effects that last for months."

I covered his hand on my cheek, both out of appreciation for his gentle concern and to spear Bronson's ego. I'm not ashamed that I can give into pettiness. Besides, his touch was sweet and comforting—something I appreciated after everything I'd been through. "I'm fine. Thanks. A little bruised, but I'll survive." I studied his face. "You hadn't heard about the attack before you came today?"

"I drove by and saw the vandalism. I knew the front window would upset you and thought I'd check to make sure you were okay, even though I was a little early for our date."

Bronson crossed his arms over his chest, all but tapping his toe in irritation. The kitchen was feeling very crowded. "What date? And will you stop touching her?"

I glared at him. "I thought we decided that I'm the one who gets to decide who touches me." And because I was irritated with Bronson, I turned and laid a kiss on Shawn, which he reciprocated without hesitation.

When Bronson growled and stomped into the other room, I backed away. "See how you like it," I called out at the top of my lungs.

Shawn dropped his hands and crossed his arms over his wide chest, his muscles bunching. "I like you, Tess, don't get me wrong, and the kiss was great, but I don't like being used as a pawn."

I felt my stomach lurch. Had I done that? Oh yes, I had. But so had he, I realized. "You're one to talk. Like you haven't been trying to establish your territory."

He stared at me for a moment, then nodded as if to say I had a point.

"Besides," Honey said as she slid another crepe out of the pan, "I didn't see you putting up a fight when she kissed you. In fact, you looked pretty in to the whole thing."

"What can I say? I enjoy kissing a pretty woman." He brushed his hand down my arm. "But maybe from here on out, we can *not* use each other as weapons."

"I suppose I might be able to do that." I did feel a little guilt, but not enough to apologize.

"And that goes double for me," Bronson called from the living room.

"Trust me," I muttered under my breath as I started filling the crepes, "I'm more than happy to oblige in your case."

"I don't even know why you're talking to him," Bronson shot back. "You know we belong together."

"Oh, yes, and when Karen said the two of you had been seeing each other for a while, and it was about time the truth came out, that was because you love me so much." I dropped the spatula into the bowl of cheese filling and walked over, drilling my finger into his chest. "Well, guess what? I'm not some weak-willed idiot who's okay with letting you play around behind my back. I don't even know why you bothered to come here."

He stepped back, probably so I would stop bruising him with my finger. "What happened with Karen wasn't important, Tess. It was a mistake."

"Oh, yes, it was a mistake, but I'm not so stupid that I'd take you back." I felt tears rise behind my eyes and whirled away so he couldn't see them, only to almost run into Shawn. "Get out, Bronson. I don't want to talk to you."

"But, Tess—"

"You heard her," Shawn said, staring Bronson down.

"You don't think I'm afraid of you, do you? You can't move in on my girl like this."

I laughed, though there was no mirth in it. "Don't make me laugh; Shawn would break you in half. Get out. Maybe I'll be ready to talk later." Like in three years.

A glance over my shoulder told me that Shawn stood between us, intractable. Bronson huffed, but apparently decided I was right about Shawn and exited with a few expletives and a promise to call me later.

Honey drew me back to the stove, sliding an arm around my shoulders as the first tear fell. "Hey, he's a jerk. Don't worry about it." With her free hand, she picked up the strawberry sauce and poured some over a couple of crepes. "Have some of this. It's bound to make you feel better."

I gave her a quick hug and wiped the tears away before Shawn could see them. "Thanks. You finish the crepes while I fill a few more." I passed the plate to Shawn, who looked uncertain about what to do after that scene.

I grinned at him, patting his cheek. "Thanks. Now take a seat and enjoy those. We'll join you in a minute."

He smiled at me. "You're some strong kind of woman, Tempest."

"You better believe it." I winked at him, then turned back to the stove. I needed a minute to finish pulling myself together. The day had already been long, and it was barely lunchtime. I reached inside for a little of that strength and decided I could hang on until I had time alone. Tonight when I was in bed with the light out would be soon enough to break down.

Cheese Blintzes

Crepe batter
2 Tbsp melted margarine
1 Tbsp sugar
2 eggs
2 C milk
$\frac{1}{2}$ tsp baking powder
$\frac{1}{2}$ tsp salt
$\frac{1}{2}$ tsp vanilla
1 $\frac{1}{2}$ C flour

Mix butter, sugar, eggs and milk, then add baking powder, salt and vanilla until well mixed. Add the flour and mix. Should make a thin batter. Preheat a frying pan on medium or medium-low. Use a dab of butter, or spray oil between each batch to make it simple to remove. Pour a thin layer of batter (about 2 tablespoons) into the bottom of the hot pan and swirl it around. When the sides begin to curl away, turn it over and lightly fry on the other side for only a few seconds, then place on a plate. Repeat until all of the batter is used up.

Filling recipe
8 oz cream cheese, softened
1 egg
2 Cups cottage cheese
3-4 tablespoons sugar
1 tablespoon grated lemon peel (or $\frac{1}{2}$ tsp lemon juice)
1/2 teaspoon vanilla extract
extra-virgin olive oil (or other vegetable oil) for frying

Mix filling ingredients together. Put 2-3 teaspoons in each blintz on the more-fried side (depending upon size), fold the sides in and roll up like an envelope. Before serving: Fry the prepared blintzes very carefully in butter or spread melted butter on top and heat in oven. Top with any of the following: a dollop of sour cream, powder sugar, a drizzle of chocolate syrup, fresh fruit, or drizzled jam melted in the microwave.

Honey's kids don't like the cottage cheese filling, so they ask for pudding or a little jam instead.

Chapter 19

After we ate, Honey left to swing by the store to take care of a few things, and I said goodbye to Shawn. My new commercial gas oven and cook top were delivered shortly thereafter, an event that caused me much joy. The delivery man dropped them in the kitchen near where they would be installed. I'd have to make a phone call to set that up right away. "You used one of these before?" he asked as he looked at his clipboard.

"Yes, they're similar to what I used at my last job."

"Great. Sign here."

I did, and he handed me my copy of the paperwork. "Have a good day, ma'am."

"You too!" I waited until he pulled out of the back parking lot before I started uncrating the equipment—I wouldn't be able to move it with all of my aches and pains, or even take it off the pallet, but at least I could get a look at it. Excitement buzzed through my blood with anticipation.

My wimpy screwdriver wasn't long enough or strong enough to pry the boards apart, so I ran out to my car and dug in the back, letting out a crow of excitement when I found my lug wrench—it had one end that looked like a pry-bar. It was awkward wielding the tool, but the top boards came loose pretty easy once I got the edge between the layers. The sides took a little more work, but after some squeaky nails, they too released, exposing their cargo.

It was so pretty, all chrome and glass and fancy new dials

with numbers that hadn't worn down to near illegibility yet. I unwrapped the wire shelves and slid them inside, then ran a hand along the top and down the side and smiled with joy.

After I was done admiring that toy, I began unboxing the rest of the stuff from my trip with Honey into Prescott. It was slow going, but I made steady progress, setting aside the bowls, spoons, whisks and other kitchen staples, along with the emergency candles I'd purchased for my apartment.

That's how Honey found me, midway through unpacking.

"I told you this was where you belonged," she said as she entered with Zoey on her hip. "I can see it on your face. You were stifled by that job in Chicago."

I wasn't going to correct her, even though I enjoyed my job there, and the prestige I doubted I would earn here. Still, I thought I could make a nice life for myself in Silver Springs, and I had already begun to feel like part of the community. I'd been stopped in the street a few times by people asking if I was really opening a bakery.

"I guess I hadn't realized I could be as happy here as I was in Chicago, but assuming we get through this murder issue without me ending up in the slammer, I think it's good to be good for me," I teased.

I pulled the box from my new stand mixer and squealed at all the glittering chrome and extra attachments. "Okay, so maybe I'm a little more excited about this than I'm letting on. But that may just be because I get to buy all these shiny new toys."

"I know how you like shiny things." She shifted Zoey to the other hip. "So what are you going to bake first?"

"Snickers cookie bars. But we'll have to take them upstairs to bake, because I don't have the oven hooked up yet."

While the cookie bars were in the oven, Honey and I

139

started a planning session. "What do we do next?" I asked. "Detective Tingey will look into Millie and the jewels. It sounds like we need to research Jeff better, and I wonder if Lidia has more information about Valerie. Jeff said he didn't think Valerie made a lot of money, but she sure had some expensive designer clothes and bling."

"And not costume stuff, either," Honey noted.

"And Jimmy Choos aren't exactly available at your local K-mart."

"Right."

"If she's got student loans and all these expenses, how does she afford the designer clothes and fancy car?" I scribbled in my notebook, hoping it would make more sense once it was on paper.

"And childcare—you have no idea what that costs. It's unreal, even if Dahlia is only in daycare for a few hours a day after school, and I'd bet with Valerie's ambition, Dahlia was there a lot."

"Lidia did mention that Valerie had Dahlia in daycare almost all the time. So how do we check into that?" I tapped my fingers on the tabletop.

Honey stood, sliding her purse strap over her shoulder again. "Maybe we need to talk to Lidia."

We found Lidia and Dahlia on the playground of Valerie's apartment complex.

"Hi, Lidia," Honey greeted her. "How are things going?"

"Could be better." She sighed, rubbing her eyes. "Sorry, I know you both like it here, but it drives me crazy. I need theaters and a Nordstrom, not Paul's Burger Shack and the dollar store. I need to go home. It's been a tough week."

"No problem, we're not offended. It can take some

adjusting. Do you have any idea how irritating it is that I'll either have to special order or travel almost an hour to Phoenix for some of my baking supplies? And the equipment . . . it's going to drive me nuts." I looked down at my designer jeans. "Okay, and I'm going to miss the shops too, but I'll deal with that." I was exaggerating a little. I figured Honey would forgive me if it got us more answers.

"You didn't say you didn't like it here." Honey looked a bit wounded.

"I love it here—it's just . . . not the city." How was that for a massive understatement?

"I can't argue with that." Despite her words, Honey still appeared a little disappointed. She turned back to Lidia. "Anyway, that's not why we came to see you. First, if you'd like, I'd be glad to have Dahlia over to play with my daughter when school gets out this afternoon. Dahlia's about the same age as Madison, and I know they'd have fun together."

"I'd like that. Thanks. I'm sure she'll enjoy it."

"You can probably stand a break after so many days of full-time childcare," I said, seeing the exhaustion in her eyes.

"I love Dahlia, and I'm totally excited to have her come live with me, but it's going to be a major adjustment, you know? And it's not so much the childcare as that on top of everything else I have to do."

"I understand Tad and Analesa have offered to, um, lend a hand with Dahlia." I watched her for a response, saw her jaws tighten, her lips firm.

"Yeah. I know Dahlia's more familiar with them than with me, but it seems so strange, them offering to take her on. Especially since they're newlyweds. And while Tad's very gung ho about it, I don't think Analesa's quite so enthusiastic."

I wasn't going to tell her that she was right. "Analesa can be

141

a bit standoffish," I said instead. "And keeping Dahlia with family is important, don't you think?"

"Absolutely. I'm Valerie's sister, so I'm the closest family Dahlia has. She belongs with me." Though she nodded as if it was settled, she still looked worried.

It seemed almost wrong to badger Lidia about Valerie's finances and other problems when she was already tired and a little broken down, but we didn't have time to spare. Everyone would be allowed to go home soon, and unless Detective Tingey found more evidence against Millie than just possessing the necklace, I was still in prime position to be charged with murder. I took a seat across the picnic table from Lidia. "We wondered if you could tell us anything else about Valerie. Anything that might explain why someone would kill her."

"I've been over this so many times. I know she tended to tick people off a lot. I mean, she was pretty self-absorbed and inconsiderate. Honestly," she lowered her voice, looking across the playground at Dahlia. "I didn't think she'd keep Dahlia. I mean, she's more the type to get an abortion, or give her child up for adoption rather than taking on the responsibility. No one was more surprised than me when she brought Dahlia home."

"That must have been difficult as a single parent with a demanding career," Honey said. "It's hard for me working part-time, and I have a husband and in-laws who help out a lot."

"I'm sure there were compensations, though. Dahlia's a sweetheart." I watched her as she swung higher, her face turned to the sun, filled with determination as she pumped her legs.

Lidia picked at her fingernail. "I know Tad wants to help, but I look at Analesa and know I can't leave Dahlia in her hands. Not if she doesn't love my niece. She and Valerie are a little too similar for that."

"Childcare must have been really expensive." I brought the conversation back around to what we needed to know.

"I'm not sure how that all worked out," Lidia said.

142

"It's obvious Valerie liked to spend big, but Jeff said she probably didn't make much as a grunt at the law firm," Honey said.

Lidia tugged on her jacket, smoothing the wrinkles and, sliding her pink Prada clutch under her arm "No matter how big she talked, she was a glorified law clerk with plenty of bills. The win against Jeff last month was pretty huge for her. A few more wins like that, and she would be moving up the ranks pretty fast." She pushed the hair back from her face, strain showing around her eyes and mouth.

"But if she didn't make that much, and childcare is expensive, where did she get the money for designer suits and fancy jewelry? Did she have massive amounts of debt?" Honey asked. "That'll be a mess to untangle."

Lidia shrugged and looked a little mystified.

"Where do you start with something like that?" I asked.

Though she appeared for a long moment to wonder if she should speak, Lidia eventually opened up. "This morning I had a friend who does home loans pull Valerie's credit for me so I could see what her debts look like," she admitted. "The sooner I can start working to straighten that out, the better, but she doesn't have much debt. She loves designer everything, but she also had a thing about not having anyone own her—including the credit card companies. She used to say that the only way to live was to own someone else."

"Own someone else?" I played that back through my head and tried to figure out how to ask without making Lidia defensive. "Did she mean like having a sugar daddy who helped pay the bills?"

Lidia stood and picked up a twig from the ground, twirling it in her fingers. "I don't know. It wouldn't surprise me. She was good at manipulating people, and she always had a way with men."

"It would explain a lot." Honey stood as well, and I joined

them as we began walking the sidewalk around the playground, always staying where Lidia could keep Dahlia in sight. "We'll have to ask Analesa if she knew anything."

"Do you have access to her bank account?" I asked. Seeing the pattern of deposits and her spending habits would give a pretty good indication. There had to be more than one account if the statement Honey had found in the hotel room was typical for that account. Once we knew that, we could decide whether this was an angle worth pursuing. Yes, we had her account numbers, and I knew someone who could hack in, but I didn't want to push my luck if there was a better option.

Lidia shook her head. "Not yet. The paperwork takes ages."

"I know someone who might be able to help us." I pulled out my cell phone and grabbed the information Honey had written down when we'd gone through Valerie's hotel room.

"I don't know," Lidia said. "Maybe we shouldn't, I mean, it's Valerie's privacy we're talking about here."

"It's murder we're talking about here," I reminded her. As I found the number I needed in my contacts list, I walked far enough away that Lidia wouldn't be able to overhear the conversation.

"Hey, Lenny," I greeted him when he answered his cell. "What are you up to?"

"Not much. I have tonight off. How are you doing? The rumor is you caught the boss with Karen and kicked him to the curb." As he had been my assistant until I quit, he was well informed on all hotel gossip. I'm surprised he hadn't heard the jerk was cheating before I found out. If Lenny had known though, he would have said something.

I heard a thud through the phone, and could imagine him sitting back on his sofa and propping his booted feet on the table. The image made me smile, even though I felt uncomfortable about the subject of my defunct engagement. "Yeah. The idiot showed up here a few days back. Do you think

144

you can cause a problem so he'll have to rush back there and take care of it?"

His laugh was deep and throaty—the result of too much smoking for too many years, despite the fact that he was only twenty-eight. "I'll see what I can do." He added a few comments about Bronson that were unrepeatable and more than a little on the salty side. For once, I didn't argue, or try to defend Bronson.

"I do have a real favor to ask, though. I need some info about a couple of bank accounts. Do you think you could use your special skills?" I knew he'd gotten into hacking as a teen, and spent some time in juvie. He swore his time "on the inside" was for boosting cars, and any hacking was all for fun. I wasn't sure "for fun" rather than "for mischief" made it any better, but I decided to ignore that detail for the moment. I filled him in on what we needed and rattled off the account numbers and banks they went with.

"You gonna tell me what this is all about?" he asked when he had time to write it all down.

"Ever heard of plausible deniability?" I tried.

"Yeah. Pretty sure it doesn't fit here, though, since I'm the one committing the felony for you. Can you do better?"

"You're not going to get caught if you help me out, will you?"

"Nah, I have some crazy wicked safeguards. I'm the best."

I hesitated, afraid he'd leak it to others at the restaurant. But he was pretty good with secrets. "Between you and me only, okay?"

"Fine."

So I filled him in, giving him the extremely abbreviated version, aware of Honey and Lidia standing nearby, even if they were out of earshot.

He whistled. "That sounds interesting. You sure you're in

that Po-dunk town and not somewhere with more people than cows?"

"Come on, Lenny. Will you do it?"

"Sure. Give me some time and I'll email you the FPT site where you can download it."

"You're the best!"

"Of course I am." He hung up.

"With any luck we should have answers this afternoon, the evening at the latest. You want to meet back at my place?" I asked Lidia. "It'll give you some time to get things together."

"I'll be there."

Snickers Cookie Bars

Preheat oven to 300 degrees.
1/2 cup butter, softened
1/3 cup granulated sugar
1/2 cup brown sugar
1 egg, slightly whipped
1/2 tsp vanilla
1/2 tsp salt
1/2 tsp baking soda
1-3.4 oz package vanilla pudding (4-serving size)
1 3/4 cup flour
1/2 cup raw Spanish peanuts
1 cup chocolate chips
1 cup caramel bits (you can buy them in bits in some stores, but if you can't find it, you can chop up caramels into pea-sized pieces)

Grease and flour a 9x13 pan; I like to use spray oil like Pam and then flour the pan. Mix butter, granulated sugar and brown sugar until smooth. Add the egg and vanilla, mix. Add one cup of the flour along with the salt, baking soda and vanilla pudding. Mix well and add the rest of the flour. Mix in peanuts and chocolate chips and press into prepared 9x13 pan. Press the caramel bits into the top of the pan. Bake for about 35 minutes or until slightly brown on the edges.

Chapter 20

Lidia, Honey and I reconvened at my apartment and settled Dahlia in front of PBS. To my surprise, in the hour since my call, Lenny had already sent data from one account. The man was a wonder. He attached the information I needed as jpegs.

The first account appeared to be where Valerie's paychecks went. It showed regular withdrawals by the childcare center, the housing company where she rented, her car payment and the utilities. The woman had everything set up on direct withdrawal, and the other purchases—all by debit card—appeared to be meals and gas. The savings account associated with her checking held three thousand—enough to cover most emergency expenditures.

It took a little longer before he sent me a text message saying that he'd emailed the rest of the data. The second bank account had a different pattern altogether. It showed irregular deposits of twenty to thirty thousand dollars every three months or so with charges to clothing stores, expensive meals, jewelers, hotels, plane tickets, shows—all the kinds of things one used discretionary income to buy.

There were a few charges here and there for kids' clothes and other things for Dahlia, but by and large, this money seemed to be play money for Valerie alone. Unfortunately, there was no way to track where the money came from, as it all appeared to be deposited in cash or cashier's check rather than transfers from any accounts at other banks. The account was down to thirty-two dollars and fifty-seven cents.

"Look at this. It can't be some guy helping her with expenses. These payments look more like hush money," Honey said, peering over my shoulder. There had been a few stores we didn't recognize, and with a few clicks of the mouse, she had been able to find the businesses. She was also the one who recognized the names of the children's clothing and toy stores, since she shopped at many of the same places for her own kids. "Other than stocks or something that paid quarterly dividends, I don't know how she could have come up with the extra cash to invest, unless there was a major inheritance."

"Not that I know of. It could be work bonuses," Lidia suggested. "Maybe a case that went well?" She was a little pale, as if uncomfortable with looking at the accounts.

"Or Dahlia's father might be making lump child support payments," Honey said.

"Some child support," I said, thinking most families could survive on half the 'support' payments, if that were the case.

"It can't be from work." Honey pointed at the latest major deposit. "See how it wasn't transferred from another account like her work paychecks? A lot of employers can split your direct deposit checks to two accounts, or to a savings and checking in the same account, but it has to be set up to do that automatically. It's not something you change as the mood hits you. And if it were, you would still see her employer's name listed on the deposit like they are for the other account."

"It really looks like hush money, doesn't it?" I asked, almost afraid to voice the question.

"That's how it feels to me," Honey said. "Regular cashier's checks with that kind of balance. It definitely feels off."

When I looked at Lidia, she shook her head. "I think you're right about the sugar daddy. Or she was blackmailing a client. She wasn't exactly known for her ethics."

I wasn't sure I understood where this was all going. So now

we knew she could have been blackmailing someone. The question was, who and why? And could that person have been the one responsible for killing her? Someone thought I was heading in the right direction or they wouldn't have hurt me. I told myself this because I needed to believe there was a positive reason for my aches and pains.

"Does anyone know who she met Friday night?" I asked after we all sat in silence for a long moment.

"I have no idea. She said something about dancing," Lidia said.

"Not in Silver Springs, then," I said. That left things pretty wide open, as I had no idea how many dance hotspots there were in the greater Prescott area. With a population over a hundred thousand, there could be several.

"Actually, you've been away for a while," Honey said. "There's a cowboy bar, the Silver Spur, on the edge of town that has dancing at night. I know the guy who runs it."

"Valerie? Country dancing?" That was a twist I didn't expect. Valerie didn't seem like the type to listen to country, never mind dance to it.

"Maybe she didn't know it was country music. Either way, if she was there, Joe's bound to have noticed her. He'll have heard about the murder, so he'll remember." Honey scratched a couple notes in the book we'd been keeping and I closed the bank account documents Lenny sent me.

"Let's go see what we can see, shall we?" I asked.

"I'm going to have to beg off," Lidia said. "I need to head into Prescott to make arrangements for the funeral, then I'll pop by your house to drop off Dahlia, if that works for you." She looked at Honey for confirmation.

"That'll be great." Honey shut down the laptop and gathered Zoey and her diaper bag. "Let's go have a chat with Joe."

150

The bar was already smoky and a number of patrons were scattered around the large room. Music poured from the speakers a little louder than a Learjet at takeoff. After a quick scan of the room, Honey led me to the sandy-haired man in his forties standing behind the bar. "Hey," I greeted him when we got close enough to be heard—which meant leaning over the bar and raising our voices.

"Hey, Joe, how are things going?" Honey asked, sliding onto a bar stool. We'd stopped by her in-laws to drop off Zoey, since she was a *little* underage for bar hopping. I settled into the seat next to Honey.

"Been steady. Weekends are starting to pick up again. Can I get you ladies anything?"

"Not right now. So the dancing's been a hit? That's great. I'll have to drag George in one of these days."

"You came to my bar, but don't want a drink?" He looked puzzled. I doubted he'd got that response before.

"We have a couple questions for you," I told him.

"I heard the murder victim Valerie Crofts came in here with a date Friday night, probably with a local guy. Do you remember seeing her?" Honey asked.

"Yeah. She was in here earlier that evening. Tiny little red dress, lots of glitters. Looked like she was out of place, too classy for a honky tonk." He lifted a finger of acknowledgement to someone behind us and moved a couple feet to pull a beer.

"Do you know who she was with?" I tried to sound mildly curious, instead of anxious. This was what we needed.

"She had a beer with Lars Taylor."

The wrinkle on Honey's brow indicated she didn't know the name.

Joe continued, "She danced a few slow dances with him,

then they took off. Not sure what time. Wasn't payin' attention. Why you askin'?"

Honey fielded the next question. "We're trying to clear up a couple things. Do you know where Lars works?"

"Try the feed store." Joe came around the front of the bar with the two beers he'd poured and headed for a table.

I realized what he'd said a moment before. "One last question," I said as I trailed after him. "You mentioned Valerie wore a lot of glitter?"

He shot a disgusted look at me over his shoulder, and looked forward again as he set the drinks on the table and collected their money. When he turned, he said, "Flashy earrings, necklace, bracelet with dangling stuff on it. It was more out of place than the dress."

"Did the necklace have a big sparkly pendant on it?" I asked.

"Yeah. Are you done yet?"

"Yeah. Thanks, Joe. I appreciate it," Honey said as she hopped from her stool.

"You're welcome, and hope to see you two in here again sometime. As *customers*."

I smiled. "I'd really like that. I'll have to fit it into my schedule." It had been years since I did any country dancing, but maybe I could nudge Shawn to bring me in before he returned to Nogales on Saturday.

When we got out of the bar and into the parking lot, Honey looked at me. "Millie was lying. She didn't find the necklace in Analesa's room before Valerie's date."

"Nope. How about if we have another chat with her after we talk to Lars?"

"Sounds good. I'm up for a quick trip to Prescott."

The feed store was one of those big-box stores—country style. Local farmers and ranchers, as well as people who just wanted to raise a few goats, horses, or chickens all used the store, which had live chicks and turkeys for sale along with everything one could need to raise them. After asking employees for directions twice, we found Lars hefting fifty-pound bags of horse supplements into the back of a truck.

"You Lars?" I asked, then wondered where my English had gone. Had the hours alone working in my bakery already sapped away half of my vocabulary? I made a vow to myself not to start talking to the walls if no one came to buy cakes from me.

"Yeah." He dropped the next bag in the truck bed and turned, lifting the front of his cowboy hat to wipe his forehead, despite the cool breeze. I could see what would pull Valerie toward this guy. He had a face fit for Hollywood and the build of a rodeo star—all thin, wiry goodness. He scanned us. "Who wants to know?"

Honey stepped forward. "We're working with Valerie's sister, Lidia. We heard you had a date with Valerie Friday night."

"Yes, but I don't know nothing about murder. I dropped her back at the hotel before midnight, like she wanted, as if that sweet little red dress might turn to rags if she stayed out later." He huffed. "Never saw her again."

"Before midnight?"

"Yep, just a little before that. I'd thought we might stretch the evening out, make a night of it. She said she had business to take care of, and the wedding in the morning. That's all I know. Except, what kind of business does a woman like her have in the middle of the night?"

"That's a really good question," Honey said.

If we could figure that out, we'd have the murder solved.

Chapter 21

When Millie answered her apartment door, she didn't look happy to see us. "Hey. What's going on?" She didn't invite us in.

"We had a couple more questions about Friday night," I said.

"You're not the police, and I don't have to put up with this harassment." She tried to shut the door on us.

Honey stuck her foot in the doorway, blocking it open. "We know Valerie didn't leave her necklace in Analesa's room before her date. She was wearing it that evening."

Millie's lips thinned. "It's not what you think."

"Do you want us to have this discussion on your porch, where your neighbors might overhear?" I asked, afraid if we weren't inside when Detective Tingey arrived, he'd send us home and I wouldn't get to ask my questions. I wondered if calling him when we left the feed store had been a good idea—he hadn't been thrilled that we were heading to Millie's.

A moment passed while she appeared to be considering her options, then she opened the door further and let us in.

Her apartment was small—not exactly high class, but tastefully decorated, and not a thing out of place, unless her purse sitting on the floor beside the sofa counted. Japanese fans adorned the wall above her sofa, and three varieties of lucky bamboo sat in dishes on the black enamel Shaker coffee table. The sofa fabric had a Japanese design on it in black and white, and a nearby chair was covered with a black-and-white throw.

"So, what's this all about?" Millie asked, a façade of calm on her face, though her hands shook.

The doorbell rang and we all turned. Millie gave us an irritated look and stomped over to it. When she opened up, Detective Tingey stood on the other side. "Hello, I'd like to ask you a few questions, if you have a minute." His words were solicitous, but his manner suggested that even if she didn't have a few minutes, she'd be chatting with him anyway.

"Come on in, then. Might as well make a party of it. Sorry I don't have any good snacks." She practically growled out the words as she ushered him in.

Detective Tingey's forehead crinkled for a moment. Then he saw Honey and me. "I thought I told you not to come over here."

"We're just having a friendly chat," I offered with a smile. I pretended I wasn't intimidated, but wasn't sure if I succeeded.

His scowl said he wasn't fooled. "Really?"

"It's nothing," Millie said. Apparently getting in trouble wasn't on her to-do list that day, either. "What can I do for you, sir?"

"I came to ask you about a certain necklace you have in your possession."

Millie curled her fingers together in front of her. "What necklace would that be?" Her voice cracked.

"Don't play games with me. The one the victim wore the day she was murdered."

I became the recipient of Millie's accusing glare. "I don't know what you're talking about."

"Ma'am, it'll be much easier if you show it to me and explain yourself. I can get a warrant, but I won't be nearly as nice if I have to wait for it." He met my gaze. "Maybe you ladies should be going along. I'll be able to handle this just fine. You shouldn't interfere in police business."

155

I gave him my best "Who, me?" expression, but he didn't appear to buy it. "Okay, but I do have a question or two, which I'm sure you'd like to hear the answers to as well."

When I could see he was going to kick us out, I did my best to convince him. "We learned some new things, and if you haven't learned the same information yet, it could save you some time."

He sighed. "Fine. But keep it brief, then get out."

I wasn't about to try his patience, so I turned to Millie. "Valerie was wearing that necklace when she went on her date, but it was missing in the morning. You didn't pick it up in Analesa's room during the party. So how did you get the necklace, Millie?"

She looked at us, then at Detective Tingey, who crossed his arms over his chest and stared her down. Her fidgeting increased. "Look, I know what it seems like, but I didn't kill Valerie." Millie turned and started to pace. "Yes, okay, so I didn't find the necklace in Analesa's room. Valerie wore the jewelry that night. You can't imagine she'd go anywhere without the proper accessories, after all." Her voice held scorn.

"I admit, it did seem out of character," I said. "So if you didn't kill her, how did you end up with the glitters?"

Millie turned and looked at me. "I had a chocolate craving. I kept thinking about your awesome brownies and the fact that there had been some left after we finished dinner. It was late, almost one, and I knew the only other thing I'd find in that hole would be a candy bar from the machine in the hallway." She paced across the carpet, gesticulating as she spoke.

"Go on," the detective prompted when Millie stopped talking for a moment.

"I didn't notice anything wrong or out of place. Not really. It looked fine, except that the hotel staff had left the tray of

156

brownies out when they cleared everything else. I saw her purse there, sitting partway open and the flash of her necklace inside it. I didn't see her anywhere." Millie swallowed hard. "She was probably already under the table." She rubbed her hands up and down her arms. "The thought of that freaks me out."

"So you took the purse?" I asked.

She shook her head. "Just the necklace. I really hate Valerie. You have to understand—she ruined my life, stole the man I loved and left me in debt because she refused to pay back the money she owed me. Finances have been really tight lately, and she has all that expensive stuff. The jewelry was sitting there, and she wasn't.

"I didn't want to admit I had the necklace after you found the body because I figured I'd be blamed for her death." She turned to face us. "I swear, I didn't kill her."

"So if you took the necklace, where did the purse go?" I asked.

"I don't know," Millie said.

"The hotel staff turned it into the front desk. We have it," Detective Tingey said.

"So you stole the necklace because it was convenient?" I asked. Millie's story sounded great, but I wasn't convinced, and Tingey's expression said he wasn't, either.

"Spare me your Nancy Nice attitude. You'd have taken them too, if you were in my spot," Millie insisted.

I wouldn't have, and neither would Honey, but I decided Millie wouldn't believe me, even if I tried to convince her. I studied Tingey's stony expression, but he wasn't giving anything away, so I looked at Honey and lifted my brows. *What do you think?*

She pulled the face that said she thought it might be true.

Millie didn't seem much like the type to kill, and the story sounded reasonable to me, even if it made her sound like a total idiot. But I'd leave her in the "maybe" category for a while longer.

As if the silence made her nervous, she prattled on. "I keep wracking my brain. I mean, I heard her on the phone with her sister, Lidia, arguing about something that afternoon. And Jeff and Valerie were bitter work rivals. I actually thought they'd come to blows a couple of times during the rehearsal."

"I'd heard about that." And I was still considering it. The loss in court must have tweaked Jeff's ego, and I knew that a hurt ego was a great motivator—I was setting up business in Silver Springs largely because of my own, wasn't I?

"I don't know who else. It seemed like a lot of people didn't like her much. As I said, she was a user. I'm still not sure why she and Ana stayed such good friends over the years." She seemed to forget that she had been telling everyone how close she'd been to Valerie. I guess having bad taste in friends didn't sound as damning as being a murderer.

"Is that the end of your questions?" Detective Tingey asked us.

"Yeah, that's it." I clasped my hands in front of me.

"Then move along while I finish chatting with Miss Lawson."

Though I was dying to find out what other questions he had for her, I knew I was already pushing my luck. "Thanks."

Honey and I said goodbye and headed back to the car.

Chapter 22

We returned to Honey's place to figure out what to do next.

Lidia showed up at the door with Dahlia fifteen minutes after we arrived.

At the kitchen table, I sipped on the glass of sweet iced tea Honey had given me. "Well, we know when Valerie came back to the hotel. The question is what her business was about, and who was she meeting. It sounds like she planned to talk to someone that night, doesn't it?" I asked after we filled Lidia in on the conversations.

"Yeah. Strange that she said she had *business*. Could she have gone out again?" Honey asked.

"The hotel clerk said that she came in before midnight, and the police think she died in the following hour, so I doubt she went anywhere else."

Chance came over, waving a piece of paper. "Tess, can you get me pictures of your family for my science fair project?"

"I'd be happy to. I'll go through my pictures tonight and see what I can pull out." I wracked my brain, wondering what I had handy. There were plenty of pictures of me hanging on the walls from when I was growing up. I supposed I could always have color copies made for him.

"Do you look more like your mom or your dad?" he asked, studying my face.

"A little of both. I have my dad's hair and nose, but my eyes and a lot of my face look like my mom. Just like you have your dad's eyes and your mom's nose." I tweaked his nose between my knuckles and made a honking sound.

He didn't look amused. Note to self: apparently kids don't enjoy that anymore by the time they're eight. "I have my dad's eyes and chin," he said.

"True, but I still see your mom when I look at you." There was so much of her in his face. I didn't expect it to stay that way for long. In a few years, the testosterone would kick in and he'd start to fill out. The thought amazed me. I still remembered when he was a new baby. Eight seemed so old—the mental image of him as a man made me feel ancient.

"That's gross. She's a girl, I'm a boy," he protested. "I can't look more like her."

I held back a grin. "I see your dad in your face, too. Don't worry—in a few years you'll probably look way more like your dad than like your mom."

He scowled, not soothed by my words. Then he turned to Lidia. "You're Dahlia's aunt, right?"

"Yes."

"Do you have pictures of her mom and dad? Can I use them too?"

She looked a little surprised by his request—flustered even. "I'm sorry, I don't have any pictures with me, but I'll see if I can find some with Valerie from the wedding rehearsal. I should be able to get a few from the photographer. I'm told she took dozens of pictures there."

"Okay." He took off again and started working on the poster board laid out on the table at the other end of the room.

Lidia looked at her watch. "Honey, I appreciate you letting Dahlia stay here with you. There is so much to do still."

"No problem. We're glad to have her."

"I need to head home too." I turned to Lidia. "Would you mind giving me a ride?"

"No problem," Lidia said. "I wanted to see inside your restaurant. I heard you've been working hard to fix it up."

"Let me show you around."

Lidia gave Dahlia a kiss goodbye and we headed out to her Mercedes. Apparently her husband was doing well financially.

I slid onto the butter-soft leather seats and felt the warmer kick in. The interior was spotless—perfection that far exceeded anything my Outlander ever saw. I doubted she'd ever have to apologize for cracker crumbs and spare cereal bits on the seats. Her dash shone from treatments and her windows were spotless, holding only a parking permit and the sticker in the corner that indicated when it was time for the next oil change. Ever diligent, she'd had it done only the week before. The woman was an organizational menace, I thought, and smiled.

When we were on the road, I asked, "So what does your husband do?"

"He's a software consultant. He travels all over the world for big companies, troubleshooting and helping fix systems in trouble. Sometimes I travel with him, but right now he's in the Philippines, and two weeks there was more than enough for me." She firmed her lips in distaste.

"So is he's gone most of the time? That must be difficult."

"It is, yes, but it's always been like that, so we're used to it. When he was in France, I spent all day touring museums and eating crusty bread at little sidewalk cafes. It was lovely."

"So there are benefits." I grinned at her. "I love France. I spent a year there myself on internship, though I wasn't living in Paris. I managed a few trips into the city of love. I had to work out every morning to keep from gaining a hundred pounds while I was there. Lovely area, as long as you're careful about your pocketbook and what parts of Paris you wander into."

"But that's true everywhere," she agreed, tipping her head in my direction. "Good thing my masseuse training taught me so much about pressure points. It came in handy the one time I wandered into the wrong neighborhood." She smiled as she pulled into the back parking lot at my home. "So what are you calling this place?"

"Honey's going to get her way, of course." I chuckled because we'd gone back and forth on names in the week leading up to the wedding. She had mentioned this one at least three times a day. "It's the Sweet Bites Bakery."

"Catchy."

We got out of the car and I pulled out my keys to the back entrance. We walked through the narrow kitchen, past the freezer and walk-in fridge, past the empty spot in the wall where the oven would be installed the next week and along the stretch of stainless-steel countertops. Boxes of equipment and supplies were stacked everywhere.

"Purple, I see," she said as she looked at the walls. "It looks surprisingly great."

"I hope you're not the only one to think so." We passed through to the customer area of the business. Big cutouts in the wall would allow people to see me work—which had me a little uncomfortable, really—but they wouldn't be able to touch anything or get in the way. In the long run, I hoped it would create interest in my cakes and be a draw that sold goodies. "More purple in here. I'm not quite done, but I hope to finish up by the end of the week."

"Too bad about the ugly tables and benches," she said with a frown of distaste.

"Yeah, hideous, but orange and purple are complimentary colors, right?"

She lifted her brows and gave me a look that said I was stretching the Pollyanna attitude.

I tipped my head in acknowledgement. "I'm looking into replacing them with bistro-style tables soon. The sidewalk is wide enough that I thought I'd see if I could put a table or two out there when the weather's good."

"And what kind of drinks will you offer?" Lidia ran her fingers over the existing order counter.

"I'm bringing in a cappuccino machine, and I'll have a cooler with sodas and milk. I'm also replacing that hideous counter with a display case for cupcakes and cookies." I'd considered Italian sodas as well, but that wasn't high on my priority list.

"Good call." She turned to me, smiling. "Looks like you know what you're doing. I'm sure it'll be a success."

"I hope so." We exited through the kitchen again and I locked up. "Have a good evening." We waved goodbye before I headed up the stairs to my apartment.

Chapter 23

I had been home only ten minutes when Bronson knocked on my door. I knew it was him before I even lifted my attention from the photo album. He always does the same thing when he knocks on my door—the old 'shave and a haircut—two bits' routine. It was engraved in his personality. Funny how charming I'd found it only a few weeks earlier.

My eyes closed as I considered whether or not I wanted to answer. If I did, he would be in my face again about returning to Chicago, or freaked out that I'd been gone most of the day. I hadn't forgiven him for his bull-headed, testosterone-driven attitude earlier. At the same time, he'd been unusually considerate of late. The question was how long the penitence would last before he was back in Karen's arms. The thought made me grimace. Why was I torturing myself with the image of them wrapped up together in his office?

"Tess, your car's here, so I know you're in there. If you don't respond so I know you're all right, I'm going to get the police to break down this door."

I was still tempted to ignore him, but decided it would cause more hassle in the long run. Instead of standing, however, I called out, "I'm here. I'm fine. Go away."

"I have something for you. Can you open the door?" His voice was muffled, but the words were clear.

Though I thought—for about two seconds—about calling the police and asking to have him removed from my doorstep, I stood and set the photo album on the coffee table. Then I walked over, setting my foot in front of the door so it would only open a few inches, even if he tried to force it further.

I was greeted by a huge bouquet of wild flowers, something that sent my irritation into a quiver between melting and rising in force. He'd given me roses on many occasions, but mixed flowers, never. I had a soft spot for lots of color and texture in my bouquets. Had he been talking to Honey, or did he suddenly get much, much better at this romancing thing?

Don't get me wrong. I love a good bundle of roses as much as the next gal, but there are times when I'd like the guy to think outside the box, and he never had. Until now. Sort of. After all, if he'd really wanted to get back into my good graces, he would have given me a second stand mixer for the business. That kind of thinking was beyond him, though, and probably a bit unrealistic, darn it.

"They're lovely," I said, though I crossed my arms over my chest instead of taking them. The insanity that had come over me when I saw the petals had already fled. He couldn't seriously think he could buy me off with a bunch of flowers.

He nudged on the door, but it hit my foot and stopped. He lifted his brows in surprise. "Aren't you going to let me in?" Casual charm lit his face, a look that usually got him everything he wanted. Not today.

"No. Is there a reason I should? And shouldn't you be returning to Chicago? Don't you have a hotel to run?"

His face darkened for a moment, then he paused, as if considering what to say next. He blurted out, "I'll fire Karen."

That was intriguing. I'd like to see it happen even if I didn't work for him again. She may have been a good financial manager, but she made the entire kitchen staff miserable, which was bound to cause huge turnover—never a good thing in a restaurant with such a high reputation. It would be good for morale if he found a replacement. "Keep talking."

He gulped. "I'll give you Karen's job if you come back."

What a change from saying I was incapable of managerial-type duties. Still, I wasn't interested. "I don't want Karen's job, even though I'd like to see her gone, as would most of the kitchen staff. But you've always known how much I disliked her. Tell me, did you sleep with her?" I knew he'd deny it, and I had no intention of believing him, but I had to ask. I'd be able to see the truth in his face.

His eyes went wild, freaked out. Guilty. "No, no, it wasn't like that. We were friends. I swear, we only kissed once or twice."

I doubted that. Highly. Especially considering Karen's words. Of course, she may have exaggerated to upset me, but I still wasn't ready to take any chances. The fact that he'd gotten involved with her at all was what mattered. "You're lying."

"No, it's true. I wouldn't do that to you." He took my free hand and gave me a look of desperation. "You're the only woman for me."

"Oh? What happened to 'It's one of those things that happens before the wedding'? I still can't believe you said that." It was a good thing I could hear the phrase resonating in my mind; his charm had always managed to soften my anger or frustration in the past.

"It was a mistake. All of it, from beginning to end, but I promise, I never cheated on you before, and I won't do it again. You have my word."

This was getting redundant, so I decided it was time I got back to something productive. "Are you going to keep playing this broken record? Your word isn't worth much."

He reached down and lifted a large plastic bag with foam takeout containers in it. "Would you have dinner with me?"

"Why would I want to do that?" I asked. Now it was coming together—flowers, a romantic dinner. He thought he'd break me down, make me reconsider.

166

He rubbed his thumb over the hand he still held—why hadn't I snatched it back? I couldn't remember. "Come on. I promise not to push. We used to have great conversations." He lifted my hand to his mouth, brushed his lips across my fingers, his eyes focused on my face, intense. He was really very good at this move. Always had been. "We could do that again, start over."

I felt the edge of a sigh. You know, the sigh you get when a gorgeous man romances you and you want to give in, even if you know it's a mistake? I pulled my hand away instead. "We're never going to be able to be friends again, Bronson."

He looked sad. "I brought Italian from a restaurant on the interstate. It's supposed to be great, and I know how you love Italian."

That almost tempted me. "I don't think it's a good idea."

"I wish you'd give me a chance to make it up to you, Tess. You are the best thing that ever happened to me."

I felt a literal pain in my chest. It was too bad he didn't figure that out sooner—like before he even considered looking twice at Karen. Still, I managed to control myself and not say it. "Of course I am." I allowed my lips to curve.

"At least eat what I brought you, even if you won't eat with me." He set down the flowers and pulled out a big carton, and a smaller one. "I'll leave you the tiramisu as well."

I took the food and watched him pick up the flowers and bag with his meal to walk away.

Before I shut the door, I asked him, needing to know. "Would you really get rid of Karen if I asked?"

His gaze caught mine and his response was sincere. "Yes. I'll do anything you want. I know I screwed up big time, Tess, but I love you and I want you back. It's not too late to forget this whole business—you know it was an impulsive move, and you'd hate to realize in six months that you made a mistake. Please give it some thought." And he leaned in to kiss me. I stepped out of his reach.

When he backed away, I ignored the disappointment in his eyes and shut the door between us.

I was still trying to figure him out when I drifted off to sleep an hour later.

Chapter 24

I woke confused about all things Bronson, my feelings further complicated by dream-memories of good times with him. If he was willing to make changes, to try to be different, shouldn't I give him the chance? We had so much history, and I didn't want to jump into my life here without being sure the old one was unrecoverable.

But I loved this small town—even if it was irritating sometimes that I couldn't buy what I wanted around the corner. I'd already ordered and received new equipment, picked up my business license, got all the balls rolling. Could I walk away from this?

I decided to clear my mind. I needed to be certain, very certain, of my choice in a way I hadn't been when I impulsively told him I was starting the business here, staying forever. I couldn't go into this with doubts or it would never succeed.

After walking down the length of Main Street, I ended up at the little gift shop across from mine. The bell on the door rang, tinny, small and not nearly as obnoxious as my own. I'd have to consider getting a different one.

"Hello, Marge, how are you doing today?" I asked as I approached the old proprietor who had been one of my grandmother's best friends for decades. I had seen her around town and stopped to chat with her on the sidewalk the previous week, but I hadn't been into her store in several years.

"Glad you made it in," she said, giving me a warm hug. The

wrinkles in her face seemed to multiply when she smiled, even though the vivacity of it made me think she couldn't be as old as I knew her to be. "Looks like you've been having some trouble over there. Are you going to clean that window off or not?"

I laughed. "Yes. I'll do that. I was a little busy yesterday, but it's first on my list today, when I finish chatting with you." I took the chair she indicated and settled in for a gab session.

"It sure is nice that you're back here again, opening your grandma's old restaurant, even if you are doing something different with it," she said. "We need businesses on Main Street to keep people shopping in town. I often saw pictures of your cakes; you have real talent." Her nose was a bit beaky, her eyes bright, though tiny in her wrinkled face. It would have been an imposing or scary face, if she hadn't had the sweetest smile in all of the Southwest and used it often.

"It's a big job, but I'm excited. I've wanted to be in charge of my own life, and here's my chance." Now if I could be sure I'd made the right choice.

Marge laughed, a sound like gravel rubbing together. "You say that now, but running your own business is more like it owning *you* than the other way around. You'll end up working far more hours than before."

I doubted I'd be that busy in a town like Silver Springs, but with taxes and the books, she could be right. "That's a fact. Paperwork alone is making my head spin."

"Oh, you'll be fine with that, and if you love your work, it won't matter how many hours you put in. Starting my own business was the best thing I ever did, even if it meant that I had real tight times when I wasn't sure if I would weather the storm." She pulled out the tin of cookies she'd always hidden behind the counter for as long as I remembered, and offered me one.

"Thanks. I could use that reassurance." I picked out a small chocolate chip cookie. "So how are things going here?" I looked around, taking in the change of merchandise, noticing the displays.

"New products, fancy faddish things out all the time, but they sell well," Marge said.

My eyes caught a black circle poking out of one wall near the ceiling. "Is that a camera?" I looked up and verified the video camera would catch my every move.

"Sure is. Theft around here has increased. No one seems to have any respect for other people's property. I've been meaning to come over there and talk to you about that, in fact. You see that camera?" She pointed to one that took in the front displays, including the windows that faced the street.

"Yeah. Catch a few shop-lifters with it?"

"Not yet, but someday." She clicked the mouse on her computer and a screen with four video images popped up. "I've got the whole shop covered."

I looked at the screen and noticed how the cameras canvassed the small shop from counter to displays. I paused, stared at the square that covered the front window. I could see my own store. "Could I check your recording from a couple nights ago? The person who painted my window might be on it."

"That's what I wondered." Marge reached into a cabinet and fumbled for a minute, then pulled up the tape marked "Wednesday, Camera 3". "Do you have the equipment to play this?"

It was a small tape, the kind that fit my video camera, which had me grinning. "No problem. I'll return it as soon as possible. If the police need it as evidence, I'll replace it."

"Don't worry about it. I hope it helps you."

"If anything will, this will. Thanks." I took the tape. "And for that, I'm going to make a batch of cherry almond shorties and bring some over for you. We'll make it a party."

"That sounds right fine, dear. I'm sure I'll love anything you make."

I took the tape and said goodbye, heading back across the street to my place. It was time to see what I could find out about this vandal—and hope that whoever it was could be linked to Valerie's murder. I was ready to put this whole situation to bed.

The tape took a while to cue up, but my front window was clear on the screen, and the light of the street lamps helped, making it easy to see the front walk.

When the video came into focus and the person entered the screen, it took me a minute to decide it was really him. The vandalism occurred around midnight, less than an hour after I'd returned from the hospital. And I knew why I hadn't seen it before, because the person who caused the damage had been with me, and unable to deface my building while I was away. He waited until he said goodnight, pretended to care about me and then painted my window. I felt my mouth firm, even as the muscles along my shoulders tensed.

I wasn't sure at first, because I couldn't believe my eyes, and let's face it, the store front was quite a distance away. And the quality of the picture wasn't all that great. Still, I knew that gait. I'd been dating that sack of bones for two years; I knew every mannerism, every move he made. And I'd make certain that Bronson cleaned up his mess, and went packing back to Chicago within twenty-four hours. I wasn't sure if I was more hurt or angry at his actions, then decided on angry. It was safer.

The thing that really bothered me, though, was why he'd done it. I had every intention of finding out.

I reached into my pocket and pulled out my cell.

"Hey, Tess," he greeted me when he answered a few seconds later.

"Hi. You know, Bronson, I have this problem, and I think maybe you're the only person who can help me with it." I laid it on thick, making my voice a little bit breathy, worried.

"Really?" Oh, yeah—he'd lapped that right up.

"Yes. Can you come over now, or soon, anyway?" I knew he'd jump at the chance. He was here for me, after all, so what else did he have to do?

"Of course. I'll be right there."

When Bronson arrived ten minutes later, he looked disgustingly eager. I had turned the television off, though the DVD player and Camcorder were still cued and ready to go at the push of a button.

"I'm glad you called. I know you haven't wanted to ask me for help," he said when I opened the door.

"I'm sure you understand. It's been hard for me." I opened the door wider and gestured for him to enter.

"Yes, I know I'm the one to blame for our problems, and I'm sorry about that, but I'll do anything to make it up to you." He leaned in and brushed his lips over my cheek.

It was all I could do not to deck him.

I didn't plan to make it easy for him. "You said last night that you'd fire Karen."

He adjusted his shirt, straightening it, which was a sign that he was uncomfortable with the request. "Yes, I thought I made that clear."

"Good. I also want to help you pick her replacement. If I might work with the new head chef, I want to have some say on things. You could consider me the staff liaison." I kind of liked the sound of that title.

He nodded even as his fingers jerked again and grew fidgety. He hated the idea. "I think we could do that, so long as you understand that we do need to have someone competent in there, someone who is going to run the kitchen and keep the long tradition of excellence my grandparents started. But with you on the staff again, that's a given."

Now for the bombshell. "That's the thing. I'm still not sure

173

it's a good idea for me to come back to work for you. Maybe I should find a different job in another restaurant, or start my own business there instead of here."

Bronson's eyes grew wide, and desperation oozed from him. "No, you can't do that. You need to keep working for my hotel. It's important to me to have you nearby, to see your smiling face every day." The first part of his comment had been worried, hazy and upset, a little freaked out, but he seemed to catch himself. He took a deep breath and held my hand in his. "Of course, the most important thing of all is that we're together. We can work out the rest of it later."

"Do you think so? Because I have to wonder. For example, what were you thinking Wednesday night after you brought me back from the hospital?" I managed to keep my tone light despite the anger shooting through me. When I started the video, I expected panic.

Wariness entered his eyes. "What do you mean? I was worried about you. I wanted to make sure you were okay."

"Really? Is this how you show me how important I am to you?" I flicked the remote to turn on the television, then pushed play on the Camcorder when the picture came in all the way. A few seconds passed, and Bronson's figure walked onto the screen. He looked casual, unconcerned at first, then glanced around him, lifted his arm and began spraying words on my window.

The Bronson beside me was silent while he watched the footage, and I watched him. Stress, fear and finally calculation filled his expression. When the clip finished, he looked at me. "That should help the police find the culprit, don't you think? Or at least to have a body type to go on." He tried to sound calm and unworried, but his voice quavered, and his face had gone pale. "Too bad there's not a good shot of his face."

I threw the remote control at his head. Unfortunately, he

ducked and it missed him, slamming against the sofa instead and bouncing down to crash on the floor. "How big a fool do you think I am? I know your walk, your every gesture. Don't think for a *second* that I didn't recognize you because the picture's a little fuzzy."

"I can explain," he said, lifting his palms toward me in a calming motion. "It's not what it looked like."

"Funny, isn't that what you told me when I caught you kissing Karen? Guess what, I'm not buying it. And to think you had me doubting my decision to move here." As soon as the words left my mouth, I realized I shouldn't have admitted that. Too late now.

"I did?" He sounded too happy about that.

"A little, but you can forget it, because I wouldn't date you or work for you again if you doubled my salary and wore a chastity belt."

His brow furrowed. "Do they make them for men?"

Angered beyond reason, I socked him in the chest with my fist, which caused him to move away, a look of pain on his face. Similar aching ricocheted through my hand.

"Ow! Why did you do that?" He rubbed his chest.

"Why did you vandalize my building?" I tried not to show how much my hand hurt from hitting him. I extended all of my fingers, checking to make sure nothing was knocked out of joint despite the pain. All would be fine.

"I know it looks bad, but I need you to come back to work for me." He lifted his hands in front of him in placation, desperation on his face. "I'm glad you're going to fix things for the Goulds and Tanners, but I have other clients who only signed because of you. They'll back out; go somewhere else if you aren't there."

"And whose fault is that? You're a man—buck up and take it. I'm sure if you wheedle and up the pay, you'll find someone decent to take over for me. The clients may even be satisfied with their work." It tweaked my pride to say it, but there were plenty of other pastry chefs around who were capable of doing my job adequately.

He didn't appear mollified. "Yeah, but Grandma wants you."

I froze. His grandmother was a formidable woman. She held the purse strings for the hotel, did spot checks to make sure it was being run right and always, always used me for her parties and events. She'd long ago said she wouldn't eat someone else's pastries.

That was nonsense, of course. She'd eat anything she darned well pleased, but it was a nice little sop to my pride. She still loved my work when someone complained that the cake wasn't exactly what they wanted—whether or not they gave me a clear idea from the beginning—or some idiot like Valerie was feeling crabby and mean and chose to pick at me. I might not be the most even-tempered person on the planet, but I've never looked for minor problems with people's work so I could make them feel bad about themselves.

"So," I said when I had finished processing his words, my heart breaking. "This isn't about us at all, or, not about you loving and wanting me. This is about pleasing Grandma. What did she threaten you with if you didn't get me back, both as your fiancée, and as your employee?"

Silence filled the apartment like a heavy fog, but I refused to be the first to break it. Finally he swallowed. "If you don't come back, she'll replace me at the hotel and make me find somewhere else to work."

Sometimes I really loved that woman; her punishment was so much better than anything I could have done to him. "You'll have to tell your grandmother that I'm very sorry, but I've been in the city too long already and it's time for me to return to my roots. I love this town, Bronson. It's where I belong, and you are a major jerk." I pushed my hurt away and focused on what came next. Sucking in a breath, I crossed my arms over my chest. "I'm giving you two choices."

He moved to argue, but I held up my finger and spoke over him, "One: you can clean my window, every single scrap of the paint must be removed, and you can leave town tonight. Fly back to Chicago tomorrow and never bother me again. Or two: I'll turn this video over to Detective Tingey and press charges."

He sank onto the sofa as if his legs wouldn't hold him any longer. "Tess, come on, have a heart." He didn't look convinced that his words would make a difference this time.

I shook my head. "You *had* my heart, Bronson, and you threw it away. I was even starting to wonder if I had been too hasty. But this little trick," I pointed to the frozen frame of the vandalized window, "tells me it can't happen, that I didn't really know you at all. How could you do that to me, to my shop?"

He put his head in his hands. "I wanted you to stop searching before you got hurt again, and I wanted to spook you so you'd come home where you belong. Being attacked didn't scare you enough."

I really wanted to hit him again—in the nose this time, but I fisted my hands at my sides instead. My voice rose to a yell. "You are such a jerk! The man I thought I was going to marry would never have done something like that to me. There's nothing you could say that would make me trust you again."

"But you'll be wasted here. You need to go back to the city, where you belong and will be appreciated more."

"*This* is where I belong." And for the first time since my arrival, I really, truly believed it. Whatever else happened, this is where I needed to be for the foreseeable future. "I'll be back in Chicago in a couple of weeks. I'll take care of the two accounts I mentioned, and if you want help finding a replacement for me,

I'll be happy to look at applications and with interviews while I'm in town. I even plan to visit your grandmother. You know how much I like *her*."

He sat there, silent, though he nodded at my last sentence. I handed him the razor blade, bottle of glass cleaner and roll of paper towels I had gotten out while I waited for him to arrive. "Go take care of the window."

He stared at me for a long moment, then turned and headed for the door without protest. When he reached it, he looked over his shoulder at me. "You're not going to change your mind, are you?"

"No, I'm not."

He left. The storm door slammed closed behind him at the bottom of the stairs.

I should have felt vindicated, victorious, thrilled, but instead I felt the loss of my ideals all over again. I'd thought I'd known who and what he was. I thought he really loved me, but now I had to wonder if he'd only proposed because his grandma wanted it. Two weeks ago I would have sworn he could never do the things he'd done. Now I knew better. Was anything the way I thought it was?

Cherry Almond Shorties

1 Cup butter, softened

2 Cups flour

½ Cup sugar

¼ tsp salt

½ tsp almond extract

1 tsp cherry flavoring

¼ C chopped dried cherries

2 Tbsp slivered almonds, crushed into smaller pieces

Cream butter and sugar. Add almond and cherry flavorings and salt, mix. Mix while you add the flour one cup full at a time, then add the chopped cherries and slivered almonds. Chill the dough for at least half an hour to make it easier to work with. Roll out to ¼" thick on a lightly floured surface and either cut with a knife or use cookie cutters to cut out cookies. Chill for 15 minutes before adding to 350 degree oven and bake 8-10 minutes, or until lightly browned.

Bronson's grandmother loves shortbread, but is allergic to cherries. Instead I put in craisins and replaced the cherry flavoring with vanilla.

Chapter 25

Later that afternoon, I went to Honey's to drop off photocopies of my family pictures for Chance. "I think we need to find out who Valerie called before she died. I'm sure the police know, but maybe they missed something. You have the account information for her cell phone, don't you?"

"Yeah." Honey went to grab her purse, then fished around for the paper she'd written on. "Here it is, though I don't know what good it'll do you without the passwords. Oh wait, never mind—you know a guy, right?"

"You got it." I didn't want to risk Lenny getting caught, but he was our best bet right now. "I'll call him and see what he can scrape up."

"We're running out of options, aren't we?"

"For sure. Oh, and let me tell you what I learned about my little paint vandal." I filled her in on my discovery and the confrontation with Bronson. She was the only person in the world I could be totally honest with about my feelings. "Even after everything we've been through and what he's done to try to get me back, he didn't really care about our relationship—he was following Grandma's orders." I wondered how long that would make my chest ache and my eyes sting with unshed tears. Too long. He wasn't worth my pain and anger, but I knew it would take time anyway.

"That little weasel. If I see him again, I won't be nearly so diplomatic." Honey's face pinched until she looked meaner than I'd ever seen her.

I lifted my brows. "Really?" I couldn't imagine her laying into anyone; she was too polite for that. Then again, I remembered her whaling on her brother after he pulled a particularly nasty trick on us when we were thirteen. Maybe she still had it in her.

"Of course, really. You have to think that the moment you got back to Chicago with him he would start making eyes at some other woman. Maybe not Karen, but someone."

I slumped against the wall. "That's what kept holding me back. I couldn't take it again, and I don't want to try trusting him." I wouldn't mention that I had been softening toward him. It was too humiliating. What kind of masochist was I?

"You don't seem to have a problem trusting Shawn." Honey nudged me with her elbow "What was with that kiss?"

I felt my face heat and imagined I was roughly the color of a tomato. "Shawn's different." Oh, was Shawn ever different from Bronson.

"I see." Her grin was more than a little sly.

I hit her arm with the back of my hand. "No, I mean he's different because I'm not serious about him. We're just having fun together. If he turned around and started kissing some other woman I wouldn't love it, but I wouldn't feel betrayed." He was a good guy, and I was glad he was there for me, but I didn't see a real relationship in our future. If he lived closer I doubt I would have let things get so interesting. I wasn't ready to try trusting again.

"It's a shame he's working on the border, isn't it? But I guess I know what you mean. You're not looking for strings." She waggled her eyebrows. "Too bad, really. He's such a hottie!"

I decided to ignore that last comment and changed the subject. "I have to make a run to Prescott to pick up some supplies and thought I'd drop by Jeff's office to see what I can glean. You up for a run to the city?"

"Yeah. Meet you at your place in an hour. I'll bring Zoey. Your car or mine?"

"Mine. More room to stow stuff in the back." And as I needed to do some major shopping, space was important.

I headed out the door and almost reached my car before my phone rang again. This time it was a number I didn't recognize. "Hello?"

"Hey, it's Shawn. I have to leave tomorrow, but I wondered if you'd like to do something tonight."

I smiled. Yes, I was sorry he was leaving so soon. His call was welcome after the situation with Bronson. "How do you feel about dancing?"

"Are you talking about going to The Silver Spur, or did you want to go into Prescott for something a little more rock-ish?"

"The Silver Spur, of course."

He chuckled. "There's no 'of course' about it with you, Tess. You have so many layers—you're always surprising me. That sounds like fun. What time?"

Layers? He thinks I have layers? The thought that I intrigued him pleased me. "I'm not sure. Honey and I are going into Prescott to pick up some supplies. I'll call when I get back."

"Sounds great."

It had been a while since I'd spent any real time in Prescott. Either my memory was bad or there had been a lot of new construction. We'd already made two stops and I had purchased a plethora of cake pans, oodles of decorating equipment, heavy-bottomed pans, a double boiler and other supplies.

Piles of gleaming purchases were crammed in the back of my Outlander, and I couldn't wait to unpack them all and revel in their shiny newness. I was already thinking about stacking them away on their shelves and cupboards.

Jeff's law office was in a large brick building, but didn't

appear to share space with any other companies. My first impression was of success and opulence as we crossed thick carpeting and passed mahogany furniture to the reception desk, where a man spoke to someone on his headset and typed at the same time. He glanced up, lifting a finger to indicate we should wait.

He finished the phone call a minute or so later and made a few final clicks on his computer before turning his brown eyes on us. "Hello, ladies. What can I do for you?"

"We wondered if Jeff Calhoon is available for a few minutes."

"Let me check." He pushed one of the dozens of buttons on his phone and paused. "There are some clients in the front office who'd like to speak with Mr. Calhoon. Does he have a few minutes?" After another pause he looked at me. "She said you can go on through. Do you know the way?"

"No. I've never been here before, actually."

He told us which route to take and we thanked him. We rode an elevator to the next floor and I was surprised to find the second level as polished and lovely as the first. I had convinced myself that it wouldn't be, that lower-rung attorneys, like Jeff would have to make do with less fancy digs, but it appeared that the bosses at Marks, Marks, & Walton liked outward signs of success.

A woman in her fifties wearing a blue dress suit and bifocals greeted us. I realized as I entered the reception area, she appeared to be the secretary for several attorneys as I could see three doors with names on them going down the hall, as well as a small conference room with the door wide open to my right. "Hello. Are you here to see Mr. Calhoon?"

"Yes. Does he have a minute?"

"Let me make sure he's not on the phone. What were your

names?" She stood gracefully and I realized she was quite tall. She had several inches on me, in any case.

We gave her our names, and she entered the second door after a brief knock. Perhaps thirty seconds passed before she came back. "He said he'll see you now." She gestured to the open door.

Jeff sat behind an enormous table, not a desk, which surprised me, but a credenza and several legal file drawers ranged behind him. The table held only a lamp, his laptop, a stack of files and a can of pens in various colors. The main phone was behind him. He stood when we walked in. "Ladies, what can I do for you?" He studied me. "Do you need business advice already?"

I hoped I never needed *that* kind of advice. "No. Actually, we have a few questions, if you can spare a minute."

"What about?" He gestured to the overstuffed chairs across from him and took one of them. Honey set Zoey on her lap and handed the gabby toddler a toy.

I was glad he was being direct. It made it much easier for me to be the same. "It's about Valerie. I know you didn't get along well, but I wondered if there was more you can tell me about her."

His expression was inscrutable. "I thought after you were attacked that you'd stop poking around."

I grew alert. The gossip had made its way to him here? How did he know about that? "You heard?'

He steepled his fingers on his lap. "Yes, I spoke with Shawn yesterday. He's worried about you."

Of course he'd spoken with Shawn; they had spent a lot of time together this week. "That's very sweet of him, and of you, but I'm fine. I don't think my attacker wanted me dead, just to scare me." Of course, I was still sore and the bruises and scrapes would take a while yet to heal completely, but who was I to quibble?

"Apparently it didn't work." He leaned forward in his chair, making him look earnest. "I really wish you'd leave it to the authorities. Once the person has killed, there's nothing to stop him or her from doing it again." His face held worry—for me, I thought. I'd hoped to see an indication that he was guilty, but saw no hint that he was concealing anything.

"I'll be more careful. Thanks for your concern."

His mouth thinned, as if my answer didn't please him. "Back to the murder, since I really don't have much time," he said. "You're still looking for the killer, and you wonder if it's me." He picked up a pen and flipped it end over end, seeming to consider for a long moment. "You can take me off your list because I wasn't alone that night."

That was a surprise. "I thought you didn't have an alibi." Why hadn't he mentioned it earlier?

His eyes skittered away from mine, settling on his hands. "Yeah, well, there's a reason the police haven't been poking at me, don't you think? I had more reason to want her dead than you did." He set the pen back on the table as his cell phone rang. He glanced at it, pushed a button to silence it and put it aside again.

"True. But if you weren't at the hotel, where were you?"

He cleared his throat. "I was at the hotel, just not in my own room. I was with someone." He said it as if he were ashamed, like he'd picked up some random woman on the corner, which I totally didn't buy. He wouldn't have kept it a secret if there wasn't a good reason.

"You were?" I tried to make it sound like I didn't believe him, and maybe I didn't.

His gaze slid between Honey and myself. "You have to promise not to tell, because we haven't told anyone about our relationship yet. But I was with Janice."

I felt my eyes bug out. "Janice, Tad's sister? Have you been together long?" I let my innate curiosity get the best of me. I'd paid attention to both of them during the reception, or so I'd thought, and hadn't noticed a single indication that there was anything between them—a scowl, maybe. Of course, I wasn't looking for those kinds of signals.

"A while. Anyway, that's why Detective Tingey left me alone." He lifted his hands in dismissal.

"Thanks for telling us." I looked at Honey for confirmation of what I was about to say. "You can count on us to be discreet."

"Oh, of course," Honey said, though I could tell she was bursting to dissect it with me. "We'll let the two of you bring that up when you're ready."

"Thanks, I appreciate it." His cell phone started to ring again. "Is there anything else?"

"No, I guess that's all that we need. Thanks." I stood and Honey followed suit. We hurried out to the SUV and slid inside.

"I can't believe he was with Janice," Honey said as soon as she had the baby buckled in and had taken her own seat.

"I know—they're so different. Seriously, she's kind of flaky, and he's..."

"Very together. Maybe they complement each other?" She put on her seatbelt.

"I guess." I put the car into gear. "So that's a dead end. Now what?"

"Home to check on the kids and a strategy session."

Since I had an interesting date planned with Shawn, I decided her suggestion was spot on.

Chapter 26

We arrived back at Honey's in time to meet Lidia and Dahlia, who had come by for another play date.

"How's everything going?" I asked Lidia when she had released her niece into the fray. Honey's girls pulled Dahlia into their games right away.

Lidia pushed the hair back from her eyes, which had dark circles under them despite her makeup. "Good. I'm starting to make headway on clearing out Valerie's apartment. I'm not sure if I'm going to get through it all before the funeral, and my husband is supposed to be home from the Philippines next week. I'm anxious for him and Dahlia to get to know each other better."

"How does he feel about gaining a daughter?" Honey asked. I could tell she was choosing her words with care.

A smile lit Lidia's face. "He's excited. We've never been able to have children together, and we've talked about adoption a few times." She turned to Dahlia, who was walking a Bratz figure alongside Madison's doll as if the two of them were out for a stroll in the park. "Sometimes wonderful things can happen in the midst of tragedy."

I agreed with her. If Dahlia started receiving the kind of love and support rumor had it she didn't get from her mother, it would have some silver linings for the little girl. And for Lidia and her husband.

Chance ran over with a blue three-ring binder and shoved it at me. "Hey, you want to see what I did for my project?"

"Sure." I took the book from the eager boy and paged through it. Each plastic sleeve held pictures. The middle picture on each page was one of his parents or sibling. The other photos were of relatives with information about the trait the main person had inherited from them. These included talents and physical characteristics, so it was clear his mother had lent a hand. I wondered when she'd had time to help him with everything else going on.

After his family, there were pictures of me with my parents and grandparents and the qualities I'd gotten from them. Following my page was one with photos of Dahlia with shots of Lidia and Valerie on the sides. The picture of Dahlia was of her in Tad's arms as they laughed together—probably one of the few taken of Dahlia the night of the murder. The comments on the page were strictly about the characteristics she'd gotten from her mother and aunt. I found my eyes drawn back to the picture in the middle, studying both faces. Valerie wasn't the only person Dahlia resembled. My mind started to race.

I needed to think this over before sharing it with anyone, so I flipped the page again and finding nothing else, handed it back to Chance. "That's awesome. You did a great job. I bet your teacher loves it."

He beamed at me and rattled on about the science fair and how excited he was. While I tried to focus on him, I kept finding myself looking back to Dahlia. Could it be a coincidence? Something told me it wasn't, and I needed to make another trip to Prescott to chat with Tad.

When Honey redirected Chance to the table to finish his homework, I caught Lidia's eye. She seemed to be watching me, but I pushed back my suspicions and changed the subject. After a few more minutes I looked at my watch. "I need to head home. I'm supposed to meet Shawn to go to the Silver Spur tonight. I have less than an hour until he comes to get me." And a ton of stuff to unload from my vehicle.

"Have fun." Honey winked. "I expect a full report."

"I'll call you in the morning," I promised and said goodbye to Lidia and the kids.

Chapter 27

On the way home, I thought about the dynamics of the situation. The bank account was getting low, so Valerie would have been looking for another cash infusion. I could imagine Analesa's feelings if she found out on her wedding day that Dahlia was Tad's child. I wasn't sure what she would do—try to convince Tad not to take responsibility? Or would she decide it was okay to take her in if Dahlia was her step-daughter? It was a moot point, since I didn't think Analesa knew the truth. And now Lidia seemed so excited about taking her niece home—would there be a big court battle? Wouldn't father's rights trump the aunt's in court?

A few minutes after I returned home, I answered my ringing doorbell to find Detective Tingey on my stairs. He was the last person I wanted to see right then. "Hello, can I help you?" I asked. The way things were going, I'd be lucky if he didn't arrest me.

"I wanted you to know that we have Millie in custody for Valerie's murder, so you'll be safe from here on out."

"She really did it? I thought for sure she had just taken advantage of the situation." Once again, I was having a problem reading people lately. I thought I was a better judge of character than that.

"Oh, that's the story she's telling right now." Detective Tingey shook his head. "Sometimes criminals amaze me with their stupid excuses."

I thought he was being a bit naïve, considering he was a

police detective—no doubt there were worse excuses. But he'd said Silver Springs didn't see many murders. "Thanks for letting me know. I appreciate it." Strangely, I didn't feel all that reassured about my safety.

"No problem, ma'am. I'll let you know when we hear more about the problems you've been having."

That reminded me. "Right. I meant to call you, but today has been rather overfilled with events. I found out who spray painted my window and I've taken care of it, so you can close the case."

His eyes narrowed and grew wary. "You've taken care of it? Miss Crawford, you *taking care* of things is why your window was vandalized in the first place."

As he wasn't entirely wrong on that point—no matter how much I wished to deny it—I decided he deserved an explanation. "It was my ex-finance, Bronson. Marge's gift shop across the street caught him on a surveillance camera. I gave him the option of cleaning it up and going home, or me pressing charges. He chose the former—which was my preference, as it got rid of him. Anyway, it's over."

"Good." He lifted a hand in farewell. "You have a nice day, and I look forward to your store opening."

"Thanks." I felt confused when I shut the door behind him. He could be right. Maybe Millie had enough of the high and mighty routine Valerie had been pulling. Maybe she and Valerie got into a fight—but it didn't feel right to me. I couldn't decide what to think, so I turned my thoughts back to my date.

I really liked Shawn. He had integrity, he was fun and intelligent, willing to help out and man, was he a good kisser! But I wasn't ready to become serious in another relationship right now. It wasn't a problem, I reminded myself. We were having fun, and that was it.

I hurried to get ready, even pulling out an old pair of red

boots I'd carried around with me for years—the same pair I'd purchased when I was sixteen. They had been worn many times over the years, though mostly when I came to visit my grandma. I wondered why I hadn't worn them before now.

As I slid them on, touching the red leather, dusting the contours with my index finger, I remembered the way I'd felt when I bought them. Grandma had taken me to the store for a pair of *real boots*, she said. I was going to do some horseback riding with a guy I had a major crush on, and she said if I was going to spend much time around horses, I'd need the right footwear.

Though I'd balked at first—they didn't fit into my idea of fashion—I found them super comfortable. They were so, so much better than the tight and uncomfortable high heels I now wore at every opportunity—though not nearly as cute. Eventually the boots were my favorite footwear, so much that I'd nearly taken them back to New York with me, but I could still hear the taunts I'd imagined from my friends. Being labeled a hick was not on my to-do list at the time, so I'd set them side-by-side on the closet floor and mourned them from New York. It wasn't until after my apprenticeship in France that I'd finally taken them with me.

Amazingly, after all these years, they still fit well and I slid the legs of my jeans down over them. Good thing we'd popped into a store to pick up some boot-cut jeans, as I'd forgotten to bring my only pair with me when I left Chicago. These were not designer, but I liked the way they fit over my rear end and the slimming look they gave my legs. I wasn't the skinniest person on the planet, but they made me look good.

I topped the outfit with a soft red shirt that buttoned up the front and a beaded necklace with a big silver amulet at the bottom. It was heavy, so it wouldn't fly around too much when I danced.

I heard the clomp of boots on the stairs just before the knock on the door. Shawn stood on the other side, a single tulip, no doubt filched from someone's yard, twisting in his fingers.

He was such a strange mixture of contrasts. His eyes slid down me appreciatively, stopped on the boots and his brow furrowed before he lifted his gaze to my face again. "Those boots are scuffed."

"Very observant of you. That's what happens when you wear them," I answered as I accepted the flower.

"Who did you borrow them from? Honey?"

I turned my back on him and moved to the kitchen for a vase, smiling at his surprise. At the last minute, I detoured to the cupboard and pulled out an old pint jam jar. Somehow it seemed more fitting than my slim crystal bud vase. "Nope, I didn't borrow them. I've owned them for years. I just haven't had a reason to put them on since I got back."

Shawn came up behind me, took the jar from my hand and set it on the counter. He turned me to face him. "You're so different than I expected." His hand lifted to my face, and his thumb ran along my bottom lip. "You intrigue me."

My heart rate picked up, despite everything I'd told myself about the non-future of our relationship. I allowed my mouth to slide into a teasing smile. "Good. I wouldn't want to become predictable."

His mouth covered mine in a sweet, lingering kiss. I felt goose bumps rise across my arms and a yearning for something more enter my chest. Shawn made me feel good about myself and I loved being with him, wanted more of it. He moved back and took my hand, pulling me toward the door. "Do you need a purse or anything?"

"Nope, I've got what I need in my pocket." My emergency

stash included lipstick, cell phone, a twenty dollar bill, my ID and the key to the apartment.

"I thought it was against a woman's genetic makeup to go around without a purse."

I followed him down the last of the outside stairs before responding. "If we were going dancing somewhere that required a slinky dress, I'd have a purse. Thankfully, these jeans have pockets."

He scanned me again as we approached his car. "Though I like the way you look right now, I admit that the thought of you in a slinky dress interests me."

"Too bad Nogales calls, isn't it? I have several dresses that would qualify." Okay, so they were all in my closet in Chicago, but they'd be in Silver Springs soon.

Shawn opened the car door and watched me sit, letting his eyes linger for a long moment. "It sure is a shame." He shut the door and rounded the front of the car to the driver's side.

I loved the way he made me feel special and beautiful.

When he'd pulled the car onto the road, he slid me a sidelong glance. "I admit, I think of you as more of a symphony and Broadway musical type of gal than as a cowboy bar woman."

"No reason I can't be both," I pointed out. "Diversity is the joy of life."

"True." He squeezed my fingers. "Any info about your vandal? I've been poking around, but haven't turned up anything useful."

We pulled up to the bar a while later. I'd spent the drive telling him what I'd learned about Bronson and what I did about it.

He parked the truck, then came around to my side to let me out. "I think you might scare me a little," Shawn said as he took my hand to help me out of the vehicle. Yes, he actually gave me his hand and helped me up—not that I needed assistance, but it was a sweet gesture.

"You don't act scared."

"I have a really good brave face. It comes in handy with my job." He shut the door, locking it with his keychain fob. We headed for the bar, and he didn't release my hand.

"I see. I'll remember that I can be scary, and hold that in reserve for when someone earns my wrath." Of course, Bronson had more than deserved what little I had dished out to him that morning, so I didn't feel guilty about it.

Shawn led me inside, we ordered food and he pulled me toward the dance floor as a fast song started. "Do you know how to swing dance?" he asked as he led me away from the group line dancing on one side of the floor.

I grinned. "It's been a while, but if you can be a little patient, I'll pick it up again."

The dancing was fun, the chicken strips and fries I ordered were delicious and Shawn kept me dancing until midnight with water breaks in between to stay hydrated. Not only was he a fantastic swing dancer, but he showed off smooth moves on the slow dances as well.

"Not much of a beer drinker, are you?" he asked as we pulled out of the parking lot at the end of the evening.

"You're one to talk. You didn't have one either."

"I was driving tonight, and I don't drink much anyway. Do you avoid alcohol on principle, or was this an exception?" His question was light, curious.

"It dulls the senses, and I was having too much fun for that. Besides, I think I need to keep my wits about me where you're concerned." It wasn't that I didn't trust Shawn, because I had no reason to think he'd take advantage, but keeping a clear head had definite benefits. Since I'd recently learned I wasn't nearly as good a judge of character as I'd thought, a clear head was a good thing. I had long-ago vowed to stay away from the stuff—my family history of alcoholism went back many generations.

"You may be right there." His fingers tapped on the

steering wheel, his face a study in thought. "The thing is, I like you, and I enjoy spending time with you. Nogales isn't exactly next door."

"I know. And I'm going to be honest—while I've had a great time with you, I've only been unengaged for two weeks and I'm not ready for a new relationship." I studied his profile for a moment. He was so gorgeous. And strong. And sweet. "If I were looking for a rebound relationship, though, you'd be my first choice."

His smile broadened. "What, no declaring your undying devotion? I'm only good enough for a rebound guy? I'm hurt."

"No, you're not." And though I would miss him, I found I wasn't upset that he wouldn't be nearby, that it could be months before I saw him again. There would be lingering pain over Bronson's betrayals, but I thought I could live with them, too. "And I'll admit, flirting with you has made this whole thing with Bronson easier, so thanks."

Shawn parked the car behind my building. "He didn't deserve you."

"I'm starting to think you're right." And eventually I'd be able to say that without a little ache in my chest. I decided that was more than enough seriousness. "Do you make it back here often?"

"Not as often as I'd like. But if you agree to see me again some time, I think I might find a way to work it into my schedule." His eyes lingered on mine, making me warm inside.

"In that case, I'll expect to see you knocking on my door, or better yet, coming in for a cupcake or something, before the summer's over." I'd miss him, and definitely looked forward to seeing him again down the road—when my brain had calmed and the business was established.

He came around to open the door for me, offering me his assistance to stand. "How soon do you think you'll be able to open?"

"Before Easter, with any luck. I've got equipment and supplies coming in from all over, and I have another wedding cake scheduled." The thought filled me with glee, even if it would be simple by my usual standards. There was nothing wrong with simple, and the most minimal cakes had their own built-in trials.

"Already? I have the feeling you'll hit it big here."

We reached the top of the stairs and I unlocked the door, but didn't open it, then turned to face him. "Travel safe." I couldn't help lifting my hand to run my fingertips over his cheek. His face was still smooth from his evening shave.

He caught my hand and held it there. "I will. You take care of yourself. It's become a dangerous world since you stepped into Silver Springs." He tipped his head to brush his lips against my palm, though he didn't take his eyes off mine.

I felt that little shiver of anticipation that usually precedes a first kiss. Strange, considering he'd already kissed me several times. "It seems like that, doesn't it? And I always thought of Silver Springs as such a safe haven."

Shawn stopped my words by pressing his lips to mine. There was no bitter sweetness, no promises of see you later, but it wasn't exactly goodbye, either. When he lifted his mouth, I knew I would see him again, and I looked forward to it.

I reached for the door handle behind me, twisted it and stepped back into my apartment. "See you."

His eyes were still on mine. "See you."

I turned to face my apartment and sucked in a breath of surprise. "Holy crap." Chaos. Pictures were off the walls, the knickknacks off the tables and shelves, several were broken and my grandma's CD collection was scattered across the floor.

Shawn only took one retreating step before he paused. "What?" He saw the mess in the apartment, swore and pushed past me.

I didn't know what to say, but though I may still have been in shock, Shawn didn't seem hampered by the same problem. He whipped out his cell phone and called the police. For the third time that week, they responded to my house.

"This is getting to be a habit," Detective Tingey said when he arrived at my front door.

"It's not *my* habit," I assured him. "It's something about this town."

"You say that, but you're the only one having continuous problems." He wrote in his notebook, then looked back at me, his expression apologetic. "I thought this would stop when we arrested Millie."

"Me too. Kinda makes me wonder if maybe she's only guilty of stealing the necklace," I said. He had to be thinking it too.

He nodded, though he didn't appear to like what I'd said. "Yes. Other than the window, these incidents and the murder all appear to be connected."

"Yes, they do." At least, I hoped they were connected. The thought of two more people out to get me was too much to deal with at the moment. Of course, we'd thought the window vandalism was connected too, at first.

"And do I take it from the fact that your apartment is trashed that you haven't backed down?" His expression was bland and it was clear he already knew the answer, but waited to hear it from me.

I fought not to squirm. "I suppose you can."

"Have you learned anything *else* I should know?" Detective Tingey tapped his pen on the top of the notebook.

I considered telling him about Dahlia's true paternity, but it was still speculation, though it would explain a lot. I decided it wasn't relevant, and shook my head. When I had real answers for him, I'd tell him.

His brows lifted in doubt. "I don't know that I believe you." He sighed. "Tell me what happened here."

I told him, Shawn told him, they took pictures and I sorted through things. As far as I could tell, nothing had been stolen, but Detective Tingey said to make a list of the damaged or missing items.

Shawn stayed to help me put things mostly to rights in the living room and kitchen—I didn't let him into my bedroom. "You gonna be okay here?" he asked when he stood at the door to leave again. "I could bunk on the couch, if you're worried."

The couch would be insanely uncomfortable for someone his size, so the image made me smile despite the situation. "I'll be fine. Thanks for sticking around."

"No problem. Take care of yourself, and *use* your deadbolt, will you?"

"Yes," I promised, feeling my face heat with embarrassment and consternation.

He bent his head and brushed his lips over mine in farewell, then left with a wave.

Chapter 28

When I had double-checked the locks, I picked up my cell phone and dialed a Chicago number. Despite the ridiculously late hour there, I knew Lenny was a night owl, so he should be up. "Hey, Lenny, it's Tess. I have a favor to ask," I greeted him after he answered his phone. I pulled the tiny note from my pocket. "I have a cell phone number and need you to see if you can find out the calls from last Friday." When he said he was ready, I rattled it off.

"Twice in one week. What's this all about? You're not trying to get me in trouble, are you?" he asked.

"No way. I just need your mad computer skills. This is for the murder again. I wondered who she talked to last." I dug into my cupboard, way too upset to go to bed after the break-in. Maybe a soothing cup of chamomile tea? The bags were left over from my grandmother, but I decided not to worry about how old they were—I needed something, and it was far too late for a cup of coffee if I was going to sleep before three.

"What's it to you? She a friend of yours?" His thick Bronx accent made me feel like I was home.

"No, it's complicated." After I filled the teapot and put it on to heat, I lined flour, eggs, sugar and butter on the counter, then double-checked to make sure I still had whipping cream and cream cheese in the fridge. I was set.

"Maybe it's better if I don't know," he said. "I'll check into this after I catch a few Zs. I'll call you tomorrow with results, if that's okay?"

"Perfect. You're the best." I put the butter and water in a saucepan to heat.

"Yeah, yeah. You say that, but it's DeMille's ring you accepted. I see how it works." He was such a shameless flirt.

I tried to keep my voice light as I measured out my flour and set it aside. "There's no risk that I'll be wearing it ever again." Not after everything the creep pulled.

The sound of the elevated train clattered in the background. "I thought he was romancing you this week to bring you back here."

I started cracking eggs into a bowl. "He tried. I can't do it, though. It was time I realized what a jerk he is." I whipped the eggs with fury. Some piece of my subconscious must have known all along—he'd been cajoling me into the engagement for months before I accepted.

"Way past time. Your business out there is gonna do awesome. Everyone will love your desserts. Oh, Kat's calling through. I'll get back to you tomorrow with that info."

I thought of the tattooed, pierced and bleached-hair Lenny with sweet, mousy little Kat. They were an odd couple. "Thanks, Lenny. I owe you one."

It came in handy sometimes, having friends with certain skill sets. Whomever Valerie called, they were likely responsible for her death, or at the very least, the last person to talk to her.

I'd had enough of this game and wanted some answers. I knew there was no way Detective Tingey would share with me.

When the flour was mixed thoroughly, I added the eggs to it a little at a time, blending them in until the dough was more like a batter. Had Millie torn apart my apartment tonight, or had it been someone else? And why? Were they looking for something, or just bent on destruction? Would I survive this investigation—because slashed tires, personal attacks and break-ins aside, I was getting very tired of working to get my business up and running while trying to find a murderer.

I put a round tip in a pastry bag and filled it, then piped the éclairs onto a cookie sheet before sliding them into the oven.

I looked at the clock. It was late. I needed to talk to someone, but was it fair to wake Honey up? I considered for a moment before sending a text. **You up?**

A minute later, as I started mixing milk into my softened cream cheese, my phone rang. I snatched it up. "Hey, I hope I didn't wake you."

"No," Honey said. "Zoey's cutting teeth again. She's been fussing for the past half hour." The sounds of a crying baby came through the phone to verify Honey's story. "What's going on? How was the date with hunky Shawn?"

I grinned. "It was great. Seriously great. Well, until we got back here." I started whipping in the pudding mix.

"Did you fight?"

I filled her in on my newest excitement. "I have a couple of theories I want to pass by you."

A giant yawning sound came across the phone line, and I realized Zoey had stopped crying. Honey spoke again. "She's finally asleep. Give me a minute while I put her down. I'll call back."

I agreed and set aside the filling. It was perfect. I scrubbed the original pan—I really needed to bring my nice set from Chicago—and tossed in chopped chocolate, water, heavy cream and a little vanilla.

The phone rang and I picked it up. "I'm back," Honey said when I answered. "So are you cleaning your place tonight or taking it easy?"

"Neither. I needed some éclairs. You care to come over in the morning and join me for a treat?"

"For your éclairs, I'd get dressed and come over now," she said through her yawn.

"Yeah, because you're not tired at all, are you? How about if

202

you pop over when you get the kids running for the day and we can finish this chat. You need your beauty sleep." I'd been making too many demands on her time this week—something I seriously needed to consider in the future.

"Thanks. I love it when you imply I look like the walking dead."

"No problem. Any time. Rest so you'll look like that fresh-faced teen so many people mistake you for."

She laughed and said goodnight.

I continued stirring the chocolate sauce until it came to a boil, then turned off the heat and checked on the éclairs. I knew precisely how long it took to bake the shells to perfection at work and at my condo in Chicago. Since I was still learning the quirks of Grandma's oven, I pulled one of the browning pastries from the baking sheet and thumped the bottom. Not quite ready. I put it back and set a timer to remind me again in a couple of minutes.

I looked over the living room, and the items the intruder had pulled from my kitchen cupboards. Cans and boxes were jumbled on the table where I'd stashed them while I cooked. The whole apartment would need a thorough cleaning in the morning, but since the kitchen mess drove me the most nuts, I started on it while the éclairs finished baking and cooled for filling.

Éclair recipe

Pastry
1 cup butter
2 cups water
2 cup all-purpose flour
1/2 teaspoon salt
8 eggs

This makes a big batch of éclairs. Preheat oven to 450 degrees F. Grease two cookie sheets.

In a medium saucepan, combine 1/2 cup butter and 1 cup water. Bring to a boil, stirring until butter melts completely. Reduce heat to low, and add flour and salt. Stir vigorously until mixture leaves the sides of the pan and begins to form a stiff ball. Remove from heat. Add eggs, one at a time, beating well to incorporate completely after each addition. With a spoon or a pastry bag fitted with a No. 10, or larger, tip, spoon or pipe dough onto cookie sheets in 1 1/2 x 4 inch strips.

Bake 15 minutes in the preheated oven, then reduce heat to 325 degrees F and bake 20 minutes more, until hollow sounding when lightly tapped on the bottom. Cool completely on a wire rack.

Filling
1 (5 ounce) package instant vanilla pudding mix
2 1/2 cups cold milk
1 cup heavy cream
1/4 cup confectioners' sugar
1 teaspoon vanilla extract
1/4 cup cocoa powder

For the filling, combine pudding mix and milk in medium bowl according to package directions. In a separate bowl, beat the cream with an electric mixer until soft peaks form. Beat in 1/4 cup confectioners' sugar and 1 teaspoon vanilla. Fold whipped cream into pudding. Cut tops off of cooled pastry shells with a sharp knife. Fill shells with pudding mixture and replace tops.

Icing
4 tablespoons butter
1 1/4 cup confectioners' sugar
1 teaspoon vanilla extract
3 tablespoons hot water

For the icing, melt the butter in a medium saucepan over low heat. Stir in 1 1/4 cup confectioners' sugar, 1/4 cup cocoa powder and 1 teaspoon vanilla. Stir in hot water, one tablespoon at a time, until icing is smooth and has reached desired consistency. Remove from heat, cool slightly, and drizzle over filled éclairs. Refrigerate until serving.

Chapter 29

"So you think they have enough real evidence that Millie killed Analesa, or is she going down just because she stole the necklace?" Honey asked me when we were seated at my kitchen table eating the éclairs with gusto. "Okay, seriously, these things are amazing! Hands down winner over the ones I brought you."

I felt more than a little smug about her compliment, but didn't allow it to derail me from the main topic. "I don't know. It seems a little too convenient to me—and the destruction of my home only reinforces that. I mean, Tingey nearly arrested me because of my fingerprints on the murder weapon—never mind how they got there or that I was nowhere near the hotel that night."

"That is pretty damning evidence," Honey said. "Especially since they didn't find a second set of prints. You're lucky Jeff agreed with your story. If he hadn't, it might be *you* in that jail cell right now."

"Yeah, and I'm not saying that lying about the theft wasn't dead stupid, because it was, but that doesn't make her a murderer." I took another bite of éclair, trying not to get it all over myself.

Honey used her finger to swipe some chocolate icing from her plate and licked it off. "You still have to talk to Tad this morning, though. Maybe he knows something more."

"Maybe. But I don't like him for the murderer and I don't know what I'm missing, though blackmail is always a powerful motivator."

"I guess we'll have to see what we can see, won't we?"

We finished eating and cleared everything out of the way before my appointment with Tad.

The drive to Tad's apartment in Prescott didn't take very long, and when I pulled up to the condo where he and Analesa lived, I wasn't sure if I was grateful for the ringing of my cell phone or not. That was, until I saw who was on the other end. "Hey, Lenny, tell me you found what I needed."

His gravely smoker's voice ground across the line. "I tracked the last call made from that number—it was about midnight your time. Then I followed the number back to a Theodore Richardson. Mean anything to you?"

Tad. So I wasn't wrong. "Oh, yeah. It's exactly what I needed to hear. Thanks. I owe you."

"You can owe me one of your chocolate cheesecakes when you get back to town. You never shared the recipe with me— what's up with that? You really didn't trust me?" The question must have been rhetorical because he continued without giving me a chance to answer. "You really staying in that hole in the ground forever?"

"That's the plan." I felt defensive, but tried to keep it out of my voice. What was everyone's problem with Arizona, anyway? And did they think I was such a city girl that I'd wither up and die if I had to drive more than an hour to a mall once in a while? "You'd be surprised at how great it is to live here. I bet you could be converted into a country boy in no time." That would be as likely as Gandhi starting a jihad, but it was fun poking at him.

"So not happening, babe. I might be serious about that job, though, if you need help in a while. Working here with Karen is enough to drive anyone batty."

"If you decide to put in applications around town, feel free to use me as a referral. You do good work, considering you went to community college." I was pushing his buttons now, but it was an old joke between us. He'd learned great things in his local classes and through his own hard work and determination—he was better than some of my former assistants who'd attended prestigious programs. I admired the way he'd managed to turn his life around, and he knew it.

"You're such a snob, but I'll take you up on the referral." A door opened and closed and I could hear footsteps on the stairs, indicating he was on his way to the diner next door for breakfast. The man was a creature of habit. "When's the boss man coming back, d'you know?"

"He'd better be at the airport headed home now. Did you get the plans for this week's cakes? Any problems?"

"Nah. It went great. Who needs your brilliance, anyway?" A door slammed and the sounds of the street rushed through the background. "Hope you figure stuff out. Don't get in too much trouble."

"Yeah, yeah. I'll stop by when I reach town, bring you that cheesecake. And Lenny, you're the best."

"I know." He hung up and I sat in the car for a long moment while I dealt with the answer I'd just gotten. Knowing it had been Tad Valerie had spoken to last didn't make me feel better. Instead, it made me wonder what I was doing at his apartment. Surely the detective had already chased this lead, but I was here now.

I saw the door to Tad's condo open and watched him step out, look straight at me and walk my direction.

Chapter 30

I'd thought I was coming to Tad's to satisfy my own curiosity, but now I wondered if it had been a mistake. Why was I so inquisitive?

I put the key back into the ignition, thinking I'd tell everything to Detective Tingey. Then Caroline pulled up behind me, blocking me in. Perfect. I did not want to have this conversation in front of Tad's mother. Did she even know about Dahlia?

On the other hand, maybe it was better this way. Not being alone with Tad when I confront him might be safer. That made me pause—did I really think he could be the murderer? My gut said no, but my gut also said Millie wasn't the murderer, so it wasn't exactly reliable.

I opened my door and slid out, then locked up behind me, greeting mother and son. "Hello, how are you both doing?" I turned my gaze on the mother. "Caroline, I didn't expect to see you here this morning."

"It seems Tad isn't surprised to see you, however. What's going on?" She was put together as flawlessly as usual with her starched peach blouse over a matching skirt that reached just above the knees. She topped it off with a pair of no-nonsense dress shoes, two inches tall with a solid heel. She was perfect from her white pearls to the matching clutch purse in her hands. The woman never missed a detail. The frost in her look could have frozen the entire metropolitan area of Phoenix in August.

"I had a picture and a question for him. Maybe this is a bad time, though?" Did I want to let the cat out of the bag if Caroline didn't know? Would he have told her?

"No, I imagine this is best." She folded her hands over her purse in front of her. "When I called earlier, he mentioned you were stopping by, but I thought you'd be done by now. I must have miscalculated."

I didn't buy her innocent act. She knew I had just arrived, that the appointment was for now. "It happens to all of us at one time or the next."

"So what was it you wanted to talk about?" Tad asked.

I was glad to see that my hands stayed steady as I reached into my purse and slid out the photograph of Tad and Dahlia at the wedding rehearsal. "I thought you might like this, since Lidia is going to be taking Dahlia back to California with her next week. I noticed how attached the two of you are."

He paused for a moment when he saw it, love and longing in his eyes, then he smiled and slid the picture into his breast pocket, all casual grace. "Sure, she's cute, isn't she? Such a sweet kid." He watched me for a moment. "But that's not what brought you into town. You wouldn't have made an appointment to drop off a picture."

I looked at his mother again and back to him. "Could I talk to you privately?"

"Anything you can say to Tad, you can say in front of me," Caroline insisted.

I glanced at her and eyed the pocket where he'd stuck the picture before lifting my gaze back to his face. I willed him to understand what this was about.

A couple of seconds passed before he nodded. "It's okay. What's going on?"

If that was how he wanted it. "I couldn't help noticing that Dahlia looks a lot like you. And the way you treat her made me wonder if she isn't more than just the daughter of your wife's best friend."

I saw the shock zip across his face, quickly replaced with an expression of amusement. He flicked a glance at his mother that said I was clueless, though she didn't seem as entertained by my suggestion. "That's quite a leap, don't you think? She's a cute little girl who happens to have blond hair and green eyes. There are thousands of others out there like her."

I decided I'd do better if I laid it out for him. He still might choose not to give it to me straight, but I knew I was right. "You had a relationship—it was before Analesa came around, so you were single and available. You hadn't planned on it, but she got pregnant. Valerie chose to keep the baby. For whatever reason, you decided to pretend the baby wasn't yours, but since Dahlia's birth, Valerie's been blackmailing you to keep quiet. From what I could see, she soaked you for twenty grand about every three months."

When he tried to speak, I held up a finger, wanting to get this all out. "Then Friday night she called you and asked you to meet her downstairs, where she probably asked you for more money. Her bank account was getting low." I flipped my hand over as if this was practically a matter of course and only to be expected.

When I stopped, he scratched his cheek and blew out a huff of breath. Again, he looked to his mom as if worried about admitting the truth, but pushed ahead anyway. "You have a lot of it right, but I've only been paying a couple times a year. I didn't like the terms or the amount, but it wasn't as though Val wasn't entitled to child support, as there was no adoption paperwork."

Caroline sucked in a breath and set a hand on her chest. The thought of her son having an illegitimate child must have given her heart palpitations. "Tad, I can't believe you didn't say anything—or that Ana would have Valerie as her maid of honor if she'd known."

"She doesn't know anything about my relationship to Dahlia, and I couldn't say anything. There was too much at stake. I'm sorry, Mother."

I ignored Caroline's comments, as they didn't get me the answers I craved. "Then who do you think's been paying on alternating quarters?" Maybe that's who I really needed to track down.

He leaned back against my car. "I didn't know someone else was paying her. It could be anyone, but my guess is Lidia."

It was my turn to be surprised. I tried to decide if I'd heard that right. "Lidia? What did Valerie have on her?" Lidia had been helping me with the investigation—why would she do that if she were paying her sister hush money?

His brows lifted. "Wait, how did you find out about Dahlia?"

"Honey's son is studying family trees. He talked about how much people look like their parents and there was a picture of you holding Dahlia—the picture I gave you. I looked at it and saw what I'd never noticed before." I gestured to his pocket. "The project wasn't supposed to be about you—just her, Lidia and Valerie."

Tad pursed his lips and rocked back on his heels. "So Lidia didn't tell you Dahlia is *her* daughter and not Valerie's?"

"Theodore Geoffrey Richardson!" His mother's exclamation showed that this shock was even worse than the first. "She's a married woman."

My jaw dropped. "What? What do you mean? I thought you and Valerie—"

He snorted. "There's never been a 'me and Valerie.' She hinted that she was interested a few times, but I wasn't. Lidia, on the other hand, is so different from her sister—at least on the surface. That's why I couldn't let anyone know I was Dahlia's father, because Lidia was already married." He shot Caroline a look of guilt and apology all rolled into one. "I wasn't in a hurry to admit that I'd had a child outside of marriage, either, no matter how common it is. Can you imagine what it would do to my future political career if word got out?"

Disappointment flooded me. This was about politics, not about what was good for his child, and though I had been ready to vilify Valerie for blackmailing him when he did owe her some child support, now it turns out she had been raising a child that wasn't even hers. If it weren't for the blackmail, I'd have to reconsider my bad opinion of her. "So how did she end up with Dahlia? Did Lidia's husband not want to raise some other man's child? She said they wanted kids, but apparently hadn't had luck together."

Tad grimaced. "Do you know what he does for a living?"

I tried to remember what Lidia had told me. "Something about military contracts, software, lots of travel. She was vague."

"Yes. And he'd been out of town for a few months when Lidia decided to visit Valerie. That was before Analesa and I started dating, but we were friends and hung out with the same people. I knew Lidia was married, and though I'm not proud of it, after a while, it didn't seem to matter all that much. He was never around, she was lonely and we became friends." Tad crossed his arms over his chest, looked away from me to his mom, explaining to her. "It started innocently enough, but we had dinner together one night, too much wine and things . . . happened."

He jammed his hands into his pockets. "In the morning, I knew I'd screw up. I refused to be alone with her again after that, but it was too late. Her husband was waylaid with some problem with a contract and didn't make it home for almost a month. I didn't think about it again. Then she came to Prescott to see Valerie."

He rolled his shoulders and looked at his mother, then at me. "Lidia came to me and admitted that she was pregnant. She was worried her husband would divorce her if he realized the child wasn't his, and not being an idiot, he would've known. She didn't want a divorce and we didn't want to get married anyway—we'd had a nice time together when we'd gone out, but the chemistry wasn't strong enough."

I wanted to make a comment about the fact that the chemistry had been plenty strong that one night, but held myself back. Sometimes my self-control even impresses me. "So whose idea was it to pass the baby off as Valerie's?"

Tad leaned back against my car, his hands stuffed into the pocket of his Dockers. "Valerie's, of course. She's so *helpful* and *good-hearted*." He grimaced. "At the time I thought I must have misjudged her, that there must be 'much more to her than I thought. Lidia stayed around for a while, then moved to Mesa for the end of her pregnancy since her husband was out of the country yet again. Valerie started talking about her new addition and how excited she was. I guess she bought or rented a couple of prosthetic wombs or whatever—you know what I'm talking about, the ones that go under your clothes and make it look like you're pregnant."

I nodded, though I'd never heard of such a thing. People actually made stuff like that? Where would you rent a fake womb? A theater costume shop? Did they really do long-term rentals?

"Anyway, when the baby got close to delivery, Valerie drove to Mesa to be with her sister. Dahlia was born and Valerie showed up the next week with Dahlia in her arms." His voice softened, his eyes took on a faraway look and his face grew wistful.

"Was that hard for you?"

"It was agony. As soon as I saw Dahlia, held her, I wanted to raise her myself, but it was impossible. I was still in school, didn't have a lot of extra money and no time." He looked at his mom, his expression pleading. "I know you and Dad would've helped out, but it would mean the end of my plans for a career in politics, and Valerie seemed to love my daughter. This way I got to see Dahlia often. Valerie let me take her for visits whenever I wanted."

The longing in his voice made my heart ache. He slid the photo from his pocket, outlined the image with his index finger. "I didn't realize then that Valerie was leaving almost all of Dahlia's care to a succession of nannies who rarely stayed around for more than a few months. Since Dahlia turned three, she's been in daycare, probably sixty or seventy hours a week." His voice cracked. "It's not right."

He looked at me now, the picture still tight in his fingers. "When she asked me for more money Friday night, I told her I'd need a few weeks to get it. I needed to help pay for Dahlia's expenses. I knew Valerie spent a good chunk of the money on herself, but I figured that's the way things were. No harm, no foul, right? She didn't want to wait, though. She wanted the money before the end of the week. I told her I couldn't get it that fast—my pocketbook isn't bottomless, and I'd had wedding expenses."

Again he looked at his mom, whose expression had softened, and tears glistened in her eyes—though I imagine she was far too dainty to shed them. Perhaps she would cry gentle, lady-like tears one could sop up with the edge of a handkerchief without marring one's makeup.

Tad continued, "She knew I'd gotten money from my parents when I'd been tapped out before, so she pressed me.

After we argued for a few minutes, I said I'd see what I could do and left." His gaze swung back to me. "I swear, she was fine when I went back upstairs. I returned to my room and didn't leave it again."

Though I knew he couldn't prove it, I believed him. "And that's why you and Lidia have been in a tug-of-war over who gets to raise Dahlia."

"Yes. Since she can still claim Dahlia as her niece, her husband wouldn't know anything unless we told the truth. I know she'd be a good mother and Don would be good to Dahlia, but I don't want them to take my daughter away. I'm used to seeing her and taking her out for ice cream or to the park at least twice a week. I don't want to lose her." His eyes pleaded with me to believe him. "The thought of her moving to Long Beach and me possibly not seeing her again for years was too much. I don't want that to happen."

"So the only way to get normal-ish visitation is to admit that Dahlia's your daughter," I said. "Which won't make things easy." Not least among the complications being the possible destruction of Lidia's marriage and maybe of Tad's future career.

"And Analesa would have a fit," Caroline said. "You should have told her about all of this before now. She's confused and deserves to know." Despite the harshness of her words, Caroline touched her son's arm, giving it a loving squeeze.

I decided to put in another plug for Bridezilla, as I could guess how I'd feel in her place. "She should know why you want Dahlia living with you, even if it is hard for her to deal with it."

He ran his fingers through his hair. "Yeah. I don't know what to do. I'm about ready to make an announcement and let the chips fall."

I let his comment go for a few seconds before shifting the conversation. "So who do you think killed Valerie, if she was

216

alive when you left? Did she say anything about seeing someone else that night?"

He shrugged. "I don't know. Valerie made her share of enemies, not the least of which was her sister."

"Valerie and Lidia were fighting?" I suppose it shouldn't be a surprise. After all, Valerie offended almost everyone on the planet. Why not her sister? And he had hypothesized that Lidia was being blackmailed for the other half of Valerie's 'child support'.

"Lidia wanted custody and Valerie wasn't having it, which meant Lidia couldn't push the point. It would make too many waves and her husband would definitely have found out—Valerie would have ensured that he did." A touch of bitterness crept into his voice.

"Unless Valerie was dead and out of the way," I suggested. "And Lidia would be free to take custody of her daughter without anyone knowing the truth." Assuming he didn't fight her in court to keep their daughter or get visitation. It was a reasonable supposition, and made as much or more sense than the other reasons people wanted Valerie dead.

"Yeah, but Lidia was in California Friday night. It wasn't until Saturday evening that she arrived here in town. I spoke to her on the house phone myself," Tad said.

That stumped me. I was running out of suspects—or were they multiplying and I was crossing them off the list too soon? I straightened and smiled at him. "Thanks for answering my questions, and I promise, I won't spread gossip about it."

"I appreciate it." He glanced at his mom.

I couldn't help giving one more piece of unsolicited advice. "And Tad, you ought to tell Analesa about everything as soon as possible. This could all come out with the murder investigation, and she'd take the news much better from you." Hey, I didn't have to like the woman to feel bad for her. Secrets, especially ones this big, could hurt.

"Thanks." He straightened and moved away from the car as I reached for the handle. "I plan to fight for custody, if Ana will support me, so I'll tell her today."

"That's a good idea, and good luck."

Caroline came around behind me, wrapping her son in a hug. It was sweet, and made me ache with missing my own mother. I opened the door and climbed in, and Caroline moved her car so I could leave. Before I pulled onto the road, I glanced back and saw Tad and Caroline heading to his condo, arm in arm.

Chapter 31

As I drove along, I replayed Tad's words in my head. I thought they were true, but were they? And could Lidia have come into town a day earlier than we thought and killed her sister? He'd called her at home, though, so she must have been there. My cell phone rang and I picked up.

The voice on the other line wasn't familiar. "Hi, Tess, This is Lois Hardcastle. I heard you were opening a bakery and I wondered if I could book a cake for my parents' anniversary party next month."

I felt my heart leap with excitement. I wasn't even officially open for business and this would make two major events—assuming she came up with the deposit. "Sure, what's the date?" I asked and pulled over to the side of the road to check my planner. The date would work well, as it was the week after Easter and I should have everything ready to go in time. "How about if you stop by in the next couple of days and we'll talk about budgets and the number of people you're feeding and what kind of design you want."

"I'll swing by this evening, if it's okay by you."

"Great." I penciled in a note on the date she wanted, already excited.

"Is this the best number to reach you? Are you going to add another line for the business once you open?" Lois asked.

It occurred to me that I didn't know how she'd been able to reach me. "How did you find this number?"

"You've never taken the line out of your grandma's name. It's in the phone book. That's okay, isn't it?"

I'd forgotten that I'd forwarded the house line to my cell. "That's fine. I appreciate you thinking of me for this special occasion. This will be a cake to remember, I promise." I jotted her name and number, and made a mental note to call her back the next day if she didn't pop by that night.

When I hung up, I realized the only way we knew Lidia had been in California the previous weekend was because Tad said he'd called her at home. But if she'd forwarded her home calls to her cell as I did . . . I pulled back onto the road. I had no idea how I was going to discover if Lidia was in Silver Springs on Friday night, but I'd figure it out.

Of course I found Honey at home, pounding away on someone's website while the kids ran amok around her.

"How do you get anything done?" I asked as I lifted my arms to prevent them from being taken off by Chance and one of his friends as they zipped around me in a game of tag.

"I mostly do this at night, but I have a deadline. George is supposed to be here to corral them, but he got called down to the store on a bottled water emergency." She rolled her eyes, giving the impression that he responded to a lot of emergency calls from work. The joys of running a business.

"There are emergencies about bottled water?" I was amused, despite my brimming excitement.

"Apparently." She hit a couple more buttons, then slid away from the computer desk and looked up at me. "So what did Tad say?"

I pulled over the soft, cushy ottoman that matched the sofa and sat on it. When Zoey toddled over, I scooped her up, covered her face in kisses, then released her to run off again. During this, I filled Honey in on all the details.

"So you think Lidia came up Friday and killed her sister that night, then holed up somewhere and waited to be notified of her sister's death?" Honey scribbled notes on a piece of paper—she'd always done that, claiming it helped her process information.

"That's what I think. She probably headed for either Prescott or Phoenix, though the second choice would be smarter, since she'd have less chance of running into someone she knew. The problem is proving she wasn't in California when they called her." What did I know? Maybe I was headed in the wrong direction. Millie had the jewelry—maybe she did kill Valerie. Would Lidia really kill her own sister?

"You should tell Detective Tingey. He can subpoena cell phone records and stuff."

"True." I sighed. The detective would have a fit when I told him I was still digging. At least I'd be able to diffuse things somewhat, telling him that I was voluntarily turning over what I knew. I pulled out my cell phone and asked him to meet me back at my apartment, and said goodnight to Honey.

It wasn't long before the detective showed up, though he wore blue jeans and a T-shirt with the Phoenix Suns logo on it instead of his usual dark suit. "What can I do for you, Miss Crawford? You do realize we've caught the murderer, so you don't have to keep calling me anymore."

In that case, I was surprised he'd bothered to see me instead of taking the information over the phone. I let him into my apartment and we took seats, then I threaded my fingers together on my lap. "I wasn't sure if you knew and decided I needed to tell you, just in case. Lidia is actually Dahlia's mother."

His brows lifted. "That's an interesting tidbit. How do you know that?"

221

"I'll tell you, but you have to promise you'll keep Dahlia's parentage secret unless it's important to your case."

He gave me a look that asked if I was for real, and who did I think I was fooling, anyway? He was a detective, I was a peon. A peon who had information he hadn't gathered himself. "Demanding an awful lot, aren't you?" he asked. "Do you know the consequences for impeding a murder investigation?"

"I'm not trying to get in your way." I paused to scowl at him when he snorted in response. "Look, Valerie, Lidia and the father went to a lot of trouble to keep this a secret. If it's important to the case, that's fine, but if it's irrelevant, I don't want to mess up all their lives. It may come out anyway, but that should be their choice."

He nodded. "I understand, and I promise to be discreet." His notebook appeared almost out of thin air and he poised a pen on a page, looking at me for the news.

I nodded and filled him in on what I'd learned in my conversation with Tad, and on my conjectures about Lidia.

"That's a nice thought, and it would tie it all up in a nice bow. She's sick of paying child support—and I use that term loosely since it's more like extortion—and wants to raise her own kid, so she offs the sister, who's in the way. No one's looking at her because she's in another state, and she ends up with custody, clearing the way for her to introduce her husband to Dahlia." He tucked the notebook back in his pocket without writing anything on it. "There's just one problem."

"What's that?"

"We didn't call Lidia to tell her about Valerie. We sent a couple of uniforms to her house to tell her instead. She was in Long Beach."

My heart sank. "What time was that?"

"You didn't even find the body until after ten, and it was a good hour or more after that before we sent someone to tell Lidia. So eleven o'clock our time."

222

I tried to figure out how she could have done it, my mind racing through the options. "That's ten hours after Valerie died, plenty of time for Lidia to hurry back to her home in Long Beach before the police arrived."

He gave me a disbelieving look. "I think you're stretching, but I'll look into it." He stood. "Now, if you don't have anything else to tell me, I have to get back to my family."

He didn't believe me. He thought I was 'stretching.' Apparently nothing I'd told him so far had been worth consideration—well, except for Millie having the jewelry, which was purely circumstantial. "No, that was it."

"Fine. Try to stay out of trouble, will you? You've had enough problems the past week without digging even deeper into this." He crossed the room to my door.

"Yeah. Okay," I lied. There was no way I'd leave it to him, not when he didn't believe me.

The bland expression on his face said he saw the lie. "Sure, you'll totally stay out of things. Because you're smart like that." He walked out, pulling the door shut behind him.

I retrieved my cell phone and called Honey to fill her in while I double-checked the doors and windows. The chances of being bothered again tonight were slim, but I wasn't going to take a chance.

"Do you know how far it is to Long Beach from here?" she asked when I told her everything.

"No. I guess I could check."

"Give me a minute." There was silence on the line for a long moment, and Honey came back. "The online mapping program says six and a half hours."

"So she could easily have gotten back home again." This was my strongest lead so far.

"Yes, but can you believe she'd do this? She seems so nice."

I had to agree that it was hard to believe, "But, the jails are

223

full of people who seemed way too nice to be pedophiles and serial killers."

"I know." Honey sighed. "I hate that we've been suspecting everyone we know of being murderers."

"Not everyone we know," I suggested. "I don't think George had anything to do with it."

"Give me a break."

"Sorry. Hopefully it won't be a problem much longer." I grabbed some crackers from the cupboard to soothe my hungry stomach, then paused with one halfway to my mouth. I had an image of the oil change sticker in Lidia's windshield. What had it said? "I have an idea. I need to go check something on Lidia's car. I may have proof that she's made the trip twice."

"Do you think that's a good idea?" Honey asked.

"Doubtful. I'll call when I get back." I grabbed a Dr. Pepper from the fridge and headed out the door with my snack.

Chapter 32

When I reached Prescott, I went straight to Valerie's building. I found Lidia's car in the parking lot and immediately located the window cling I'd remembered from my ride with her. My eyes practically crossed as I stared at the backwards numbers written on the oil change reminder. Didn't they date those three months out? I smiled as I realized my memory was correct and her oil had been changed on Thursday—the day before the wedding rehearsal. Unfortunately, the car had a digital odometer so I couldn't see how many miles she'd driven, but maybe with the information I had, Detective Tingey could check on it. I reached for my cell phone.

I heard a voice call my name and looked over, finding Lidia sitting on her doorstep in the dusk. I couldn't walk away now. I waved and approached, trying to pretend nothing was wrong.

Lidia was drinking a glass of soda with ice while Dahlia snuggled a doll beside her on the sidewalk, talking to it. Dahlia looked up and grinned at me. "Hi, Miss Tess. How are you?"

"I'm fine, kiddo. What's your baby's name?" I did my best to be nonchalant.

"Her name's Vanessa," Dahlia answered. "It starts with a V, like my mommy's name."

I glanced at Lidia out of the corner of my eye and saw her knuckles go white on the glass. I wondered how it must have felt for her, having her daughter refer to someone else as her mommy. The fact that she wanted children and hadn't been able to conceive with her husband must have been painful. "Yes, that's a pretty name. How long have you had Vanessa?"

"Two days. Auntie Lidia said she is going to be my new mommy and we're moving to the ocean. She said I can call her Mommy if I want."

"That sounds like fun. I love the ocean."

"What brings you here tonight?" Lidia asked. "I heard they arrested Millie."

"Yeah, who knew she had such a vicious streak? It's crazy." I had to stop my hands from fluttering at my side. "I was feeling restless, I guess. Went for a ride and realized how close I was to you, so I popped by. How is the packing going?"

"It's coming along. I hope to have everything worth keeping either in storage or shipped by Wednesday so we can go home to Long Beach."

I would take whatever opening I could get, so I could read her response. "I hear you've made that trip a few times. You must be getting used to it."

Her eyes grew sharp, assessing. "Why do you say that?"

I leaned back against the porch railing. "No reason—Tad just mentioned you'd been here to visit your sister. That's quite a drive, but the way should be familiar by now."

Her wary gaze softened, as if trying to dispel any idea I might have that her question had meant anything. "Of course. You've been talking to Tad?"

"Yes. He said you've been friends for years. Six or more. I had no idea you'd known each other before last weekend."

"Sounds like he's been very forthcoming." Her voice was even, but her eyes grew sharp.

I shrugged. "Yes and no. Unfortunately, he still has no idea who might have—" My eyes cut to Dahlia, then back, "—visited your sister that night. It doesn't seem like Millie's nature to do something like that for a few baubles, but I don't really know her—and she does have the necklace."

"That's true, but if it's not her, my bet's on Tad. Who else had the opportunity?"

Strange how I hadn't mentioned before that Tad had seen Valerie that night, and yet, Lidia took it as if she'd already known. I remembered that all the entrances to the hotel had cameras on them, unless there was a secret entrance through the kitchens that they didn't bother to film. And if Lidia had thought to use that way . . . Now that Deputy Tingey knew who to look for, maybe he'd be able to prove Lidia had been in the hotel after all. That, coupled with the odometer readings, might be enough to get Millie free and Lidia where she belonged.

My head was still reeling, thinking about this woman possibly being a murderer.

"Did Tad have anything interesting to say?" Lidia took another sip of her drink. She seemed so calm until you noticed her hand shaking the glass, pale face and determined eyes.

"Just old news. From when you first met. Nothing important." I pulled away from the railing, hoping to head back to my car. I yawned to give myself an excuse to leave.

She stood and stretched, smiling at her daughter as spoke to her. "Hey there, baby. It's getting late. How about if you go change into your jammies for me?" she asked Dahlia.

"Not yet!" Dahlia wailed. "And you promised I could sleep over at Jenny's tonight."

She brushed a hand down Dahlia's hair and a sweet smile popped onto her face as she looked at her daughter, her eyes glowing with love. "So I did, and if you change into your jammies, you can go over. Do you want me to time you to see how fast you can do it?"

"Yeah!" Dahlia jumped up and ran into the apartment, her doll tucked under her arm.

Lidia watched her until she was out of sight, then stepped

closer to me, her voice lowering. "If you think you can threaten me like this, you'll soon find out how wrong you are."

"You and Tad made a one-night mistake. It's really none of my business, and what matters now is Dahlia's happiness."

A long moment of silence ensued as Lidia studied me, then she nodded. "You have it exactly. I want to take my daughter home with me, like I should've done in the first place. I made a mistake and I've lost out on years of time with her." Her eyes were hard and dark.

I hadn't felt menaced by her before. In fact, I hadn't felt like she could be the least intimidating or dangerous, but now I wondered. This was a woman who would do anything to get her child back. Even murder her own sister. I inched farther away.

Dahlia ran back out, breathing heavy with her pajama top on backward and her feet bare. "I'm ready. Was I fast?"

"Oh my goodness, I think you were faster than lightning," Lidia said as she scooped up her daughter and pressed a kiss to her cheek.

"Now can I go to Jenny's?" Dahlia asked, giggling, but pushing away from Lidia.

"Yes, you can." Though Lidia smiled, she looked a little disappointed as she set down Dahlia. "Run along." She watched as Dahlia scampered to the apartment four doors away and rang the bell.

I continued to inch away. But didn't want to turn and flat out run.

When the door opened, Dahlia said something fast and excited and went inside. A dark-haired woman stepped out and waved to us. "Thanks. I'll call you if she gets scared, but they'll have a great time."

"I know they will," Lidia said with an answering wave. As the door shut, she stepped closer to me.

I moved into the parking lot. "I guess that's my cue to leave."

"Yes, but not like you think." She reached into a concealed holster behind her and pulled out a tiny black derringer. "I hoped to distract you, send you off in the wrong direction, but you wouldn't stop or go away. I tried to scare you off the search, but that didn't happen, even when your fiancé left that love note on your window."

"My *ex*-fiancé," I corrected for what seemed the thousandth time since his arrival in town. She ignored it and gestured for me to head toward her car. I don't like guns, never did, and having one pointed at me freaked me out. I had to talk my way out of this somehow. "Look, right now all I know is that you're happy you get to take your baby home."

"If Tad doesn't put up a fuss, and I just bet he will. But either way, I can't have you running around looking for answers. You're far too nosey for your own good."

I took a couple of hesitant steps, keeping my eyes on the gun, which she had tucked up close to her body so no one would notice it. "I don't think you want to do this."

"I didn't want to kill Valerie, either, but she didn't leave me much choice." Lidia opened the car door with a beep of her keychain and gestured for me to climb in. I did so against my better judgment and planned to jump out again before we left the parking lot.

She seemed to guess my plan, because when she got in beside me, she reached over and squeezed a spot on my shoulder. Her training as a masseuse must have paid off because the last thing I remember was her saying that I should have a nice catnap.

Chapter 33

When I woke again, we were parked behind my building and it was dark outside. My hands, feet and mouth were bound with silver duct tape, making escape nearly impossible.

"Awake again finally? You must have been more tired than I thought. You need to do something about your schedule." Lidia tsked.

She got out of the car and I tried to open the door, but she'd locked it remotely before she got out, and in the dark I couldn't find and push the button to unlock it before she stood on the other side. "You're going to worry yourself to *death* if you aren't careful." She tsked again.

"Come on." She pulled out a knife I hadn't seen before and sliced the tape on my ankles, then pulled it off before grabbing me under the armpit and heaving me to my feet. The woman was stronger than she looked.

"I know if I let you talk you'd probably say you wouldn't tell the police it was me, that you want Dahlia to have a secure future, but you'd be lying. It's funny how police find pesky details like forensic evidence once they know what they're looking for. So before you can speak to anyone else, let's take care of this." She reached into my pocket and pulled out my keys, then stood me against the wall of the courtyard at the back door to the shop, her gun trained on me as she flipped through for the right key.

I kept my eyes moving, looking at her, around the area,

back at her, then around again, desperately hoping for a weapon I could snatch up—even while my hands were taped together. What was I thinking when I went to her apartment? Did I think the police couldn't catch her without my help? Stupid.

After a couple of tries, she found the key and got the door open. She pushed me into the building. We crossed to the front and she pulled down the sunshades before flipping on the light in the kitchen area.

She pushed me into the chair and began to talk while she moved around, opening drawers and cupboards. "You never had to make a decision about keeping or giving away a child, did you? Even if I had no better choice, you blame me for cheating on my husband, for giving up my child, then for killing Valerie when she refused to be reasonable. She wanted everything I had and was sucking the life out of me. It was only a matter of time before my husband noticed the money disappearing from our account. It couldn't go on this way."

I looked behind me and saw her kneeling at the wall where the oven would go, messing with something. I had a very bad feeling when I thought of that exposed natural gas line.

She stood. "So I'm solving my problem, and I'm taking Dahlia home where she belongs. I'm sorry you're not going to be here to run this business—I think you could have made a go of it." She looked around. "I love what you've done with the paint."

I growled low in my throat.

She looked at the tape over my mouth and smirked. "Sorry, I can't risk removing that. The fire should burn it off though, and the explosion will destroy any evidence." She pursed her lips and frowned. "Too bad about the fabric store next door, but sacrifices must be made." She touched her fingertip to her chin. "I hope they have good insurance."

She sniffed. "Do you smell that? That's natural gas, from

the line hanging out of the wall. I noticed it when I was in here before. Don't worry—it might kill you before the fire hits, but if not, the explosion will be instantaneous. You won't feel a thing." She ran her fingers over the edge of my counter.

I wished I believed her, but it was hard to accept her words when I could already imagine the flash of heat as it scorched, the pounding of equipment as it hit me, as I hit the wall. Terror rose inside me like nothing I'd ever felt before.

She pulled out a lighter, selected one of the emergency candles that were still stacked on the counter, and lit the wick. She set it on a shelf near the window, as far from the natural gas as possible, and higher than my head. I might really die from the gas before the world went white after all. I wasn't sure if that was a good thing or not.

I watched her every move, desperate, knowing I couldn't allow this to happen and that I needed to take a chance. I looked everywhere for anything that would help me pull off the tape, and my eyes caught on the razor blade still sticking out of the cabinet. I'd completely forgotten about it in the stress caused by Detective Tingey's request for fingerprints. I glanced at Lidia again, saw her back was turned and rubbed the tape along the blade, wincing as it cut my skin as well.

"I really did love that cake. It was fabulous. I wish I could get the recipe, but I suppose it's a secret, written down only in this building, where it'll be destroyed. Pity."

I felt the tape rip and rejoiced inside while I watched her. I carefully separated my wrists, waiting for a moment to take her down. A glance said the cut wasn't bad, thank goodness, and though it was bleeding, it wasn't much.

The smell of gas grew stronger and my stomach turned. I felt the sweat begin to trickle down my temple. Stress always makes me sweat. It was so irritating.

Lidia looked around with satisfaction, her hands on her

hips, her dark hair flowing down her back in a long, shiny braid. "I guess I ought to go before it gets any later. I want to be long gone before the fire trucks arrive, alas, too late to save you. It wouldn't be right for my car to be seen anywhere around here." She twirled my keys on her finger. "Don't worry, I'll make sure your car ends up in your parking lot. I need to get my beauty sleep—I have a funeral tomorrow."

I saw a shadow against the window, and then there was a knock on the glass of the front door. She whirled toward it. I took the opportunity of distraction to knock her down. The gun went off as our bodies collided with the ground and I felt a tearing sensation in my shoulder.

I sucked in air through my nose and tried to focus through the pain. I had to get out of here alive.

"Get off me," Lidia screamed as she twisted and tried to flip us over so I'd be on bottom.

I saw her hand coming down toward my good shoulder, aiming for the pressure point again, but I wasn't going to let her do it. Before she could get a grip, I grabbed her wrist and dug my fingers into the pressure points on her hand that I'd learned in my self-defense classes. Her fingers opened reflexively and I had to turn my head as her other wrist broke from my grasp and she aimed at my temples. I caught the blow behind my ear instead and winced. Words I didn't normally utter ran through my mind and would have poured out of my mouth, if I didn't still have duct tape on it.

I saw her gun a couple feet out of reach, and not sure if it held more shots or not, I rolled us away so she couldn't grab it— which put her on top, but gave me better leverage. I thrust a knee in her groin—not as effective as it would be on a guy, but women aren't exactly immune to pain in that region, either.

She groaned and weakened for a moment, and I took advantage of the break. The pain in my shoulder screamed, but I did my best to ignore it. The natural gas smell grew stronger in the air around us and I longed for fresh air as I struggled to breathe enough through my nose. Lying on the floor right now was not the best choice, all things considered. I twisted toward the cupboard, knocking Lidia's head against the side. She grunted and came back swearing.

I saw her glance toward the gun and lunge that direction. I followed with a punch to the side of her head that had me wondering if I had broken my hand—hadn't I learned anything from hitting Bronson? Still, she screamed and began yelling more invectives at me.

It occurred to me to wonder who had knocked at the door and where they had gone, but the thought was fleeting as I threw myself on top of Lidia again, grabbing her arm, trying to keep her away from the gun.

"Police, open up!" a voice called from the other side of the glass.

I yanked off the tape from my mouth and wanted to cry as it ripped all of the hair off of my face. I ached all over, and this didn't help. "Help! She's got a gun! Come around back!" I yelled before Lidia started to rise onto her knees. I guess letting her get on her stomach was a bad move on my part.

"Shut up!" she yelled and grabbed my hair.

Blood dripped from my wound onto her shoulder, and between the smell of that and the gas filling the room, my stomach roiled. I was starting to feel light-headed and was afraid I might hurl, but the hair pulling helped focus my attention again. I rose up enough to bring my elbow down on the back of her skull as hard as I could, which forced her forehead to hit the ceramic tile floor. Pain radiated up my arm, followed by the tingling that meant I'd hit my funny bone nerve. It made the gunshot wound on my shoulder burn even worse, but she collapsed beneath me.

The police burst through the back door into the kitchen, guns outstretched. "Hands in the air!"

I rolled off Lidia and pushed myself up so I leaned against the cupboard. I lifted a throbbing arm and pointed to the natural gas valve. "Could someone turn that off before we blow everything sky-high?"

The first officer was already taking care of Lidia, who groaned and started moving around again. He pulled out handcuffs and slapped them on her.

A second officer flipped the valve and came over to me. "You're bleeding all over." He grabbed a nearby rag and pressed it to my shoulder. "Is your back or neck hurt?" When I shook my head, he helped me stand. "Let's go outside where we can breathe and you can tell me what happened."

As I looked up and met his gaze, I recognized the man who had responded when my tires were slashed, Officer Lambert. "She killed Valerie. She's behind everything."

"Okay, Come on, let's go out." He wrapped my good arm around his shoulder and helped me through the door.

Detective Tingey was getting out of his squad car when we exited the building. "Can't stay out of trouble, can you?" he asked.

"Apparently not." I was grateful when the officer sat me in the chair on the back patio. The other officer took Lidia straight to a squad car and put her in the back seat, then climbed in the front and pulled out his notebook.

Detective Tingey turned my attention back toward him. "Anyone else in there?"

"No, it was just her and me, duking it out." I ached all over and desperately wanted something for the pain in my bleeding shoulder. "There's a candle burning inside."

The detective turned to the road officer. "Tell the paramedics they can come over." He turned back to me. "What about a candle?"

"There's a candle burning inside a room filled with natural gas. Someone needs to blow it out." I winced when gesturing with my hand caused pain to shoot through my elbow. And my shoulder throbbed.

He turned and asked someone to take care of it, then looked at me more closely. "Looks like you got in the way of her gun."

"I'm fine," I said, but even I didn't believe it, and the detective's snort was more than enough proof that he didn't either. Still, I tried to make light of the pain. "It grazed me. I'll live."

He looked at it again and gave me a withering look. "It didn't graze you—it went all the way through. You're lucky it didn't hit a major vein or something. You're bleeding everywhere."

Surprised, and more than a little dazed, I looked at it more closely and realized he was right. From the amount of blood I was losing, I thought maybe it *had* hit a vein. I hadn't realized the back of my shirt was shiny red.

The ambulance pulled up and Jack and his partner popped out. Again? Really? Did the man never take a night off? Jack came to me while his partner went to check on Lidia.

"It's a flesh wound," I said with a half-smile. "Just going into shock. Nothing serious."

"Right," he said in a smooth voice. "Because shock's not serious at all."

People were shocked on a regular basis, weren't they? I wasn't sure how he managed to sound sarcastic and soothing at the same time. Perhaps I was going light-headed, and seeing his face calmed me.

He turned to one of the other officers and asked him to get an oxygen tank from the rig and to grab a handful of four-by-fours—that had me wondering how he intended to use blocks of wood to help me. Or did he mean a truck with four-wheel drive? My head swam. He started asking me where I hurt.

236

Someone came back with some packages of gauze. I glanced at one as Jack ripped several open and noticed it said "4x4" on it. Oh, okay. His partner put on the blood pressure cuff and started pumping it up. Officer Lambert brought over the gurney.

"I don't need an ambulance," I said. I knew if they got me in there, he was going to try to stick a needle in me. I hate needles.

Jack scowled at me. "You are so stubborn. You're going to pass out from blood loss if we don't get you to the hospital soon."

"I can drive myself." Except my Outlander was still in Valerie's apartment parking lot.

"Forget it." He put a hand under my good shoulder and helped me stand, then turned me to sit on the gurney. I shot him a dirty look, but was too tired and achy to argue. Dang it, he was right.

"Hold this," he said as he put the gauze on the front of my bleeding shoulder and set my hand on it. "Apply plenty of pressure if you can."

I felt light-headed and trembly, but did the best I could.

He opened some more packages and threw them on the exit wound in back. "You're lucky it's not worse." Someone kept a hand under my shoulder, holding pressure on that wound while we moved to the ambulance. Once inside, a couple of other EMTs I'd never seen before hopped in with him, and one held pressure on my wounds, while another cut my shirt from the sleeve to the neck, then wrapped a roll of gauze around my shoulder, under the arm pit, to hold everything in place.

The one holding pressure started asking me all the same questions Jack had asked me on the day I was attacked.

After answering a few I turned to Jack. "Do you ever go home?" I watched him opening packages of tubing. The man had been everywhere this week. I thought he could use a cheesecake.

He smiled. "Not nearly enough. I've been pulling extra shifts because someone's out sick."

Oh, that explained it.

"What happened?" he asked.

"She was trying to kill me. She shot me; I managed to get away." I squeezed my eyes against the white-hot agony in my shoulder. "Can you give me something to numb the pain?"

"Sure. Just a minute." I looked up when I heard a tearing sound and saw him adding the tubing onto a bag of the clear liquid they hook to IVs.

"Oh, no. No needles." The ambulance careened around a corner and bumped through a pothole or something. I groaned as the pain spiked.

"If you want pain meds to get to you fast, this is the best way," he said as he wrapped a rubber strip around my upper arm. "Besides, you need more fluid. You've bled quite a bit and your blood pressure has looked better." He tore open a small package and pulled out a red-brown square.

I looked away, even more sure I was going to puke. "I might need something to vomit in," I warned them. One of the other EMTs handed me a barf bag faster than you could say "ralph." "I hate needles. I don't want an IV." The words came out more as a whine than a refusal.

"Fine I'll wait until you pass out and do it anyway. It should take all of two minutes."

I scowled.

As the IV needle went into my skin a minute later despite my half-hearted arguments, I decided Jack didn't deserve the cheesecake after all.

Chapter 34

It seemed to take forever for the doctors to sew up my bullet wounds and check for anything else that might be wrong. By the time they left me in peace to answer all the police officers' questions, I had been given almost a pint of blood and a full bag of the clear stuff. At least they gave me some good pain medication, I thought as I looked into Detective Tingey's grim face.

The detective asked, "Feeling better?"

"I'm pretty sure I'm not going to pass out or puke on you," I answered. I thought those were relevant issues.

He seemed to agree as he took the rolling chair next to me. "What happened?"

I gave him a brief summary from the time I'd spoken to him earlier that afternoon. "There are videos. My surveillance system's on. She tried to kill me, to make it look like an accident. To shut me up."

He scribbled notes. "Why would she do that?"

I gave him the short version, not sure if my words made sense.

"Where's the security system set up?" Detective Tingey asked.

I told him and he made another scribble in his notebook. "I'll have Officer Lambert retrieve the videos as evidence. Someone phoned Honey and she said she'd lock up for you. I'm sure she'll be here soon."

"Good. Are you going to let Millie go now?"

"Yes, as soon as I talk to the judge. She may be out of jail tonight. Of course, there will still be charges for theft, but they'll be minor in comparison."

I decided now was a good time to ask the question that had been nagging me for the past half hour. "How did you know I needed help? Why did the police show up?"

"A woman stopped by to talk cakes with you—said you were expecting her. She heard the gunshot, so she called for help." He gave me a hard look. "Apparently she's smarter than *some* people I could mention."

I felt my face heat with a blush, but didn't respond.

He studied me for a long moment. "Looks like it's a good thing you still have insurance with your old job," he said.

"Two trips to the ER and an ambulance ride in less than a week. It makes me think this small town might be more exciting than I remembered." And I'd thought things were supposed to be slow-paced in Silver Springs.

He shook his head like he couldn't believe my comments. "It's only exciting when you're around. Do I take it you're going to stay?"

I smiled weakly and nodded. "Yeah. Looks like it. I have to head back to the city to settle things there, but I'll be open for business by Easter."

"I'll stock up on Tums."

I laughed at that, which meant the drugs were probably doing a great job.

He handed me a couple of papers. "Now, I know you told me what happened, but can you write me a full report from the moment you pulled up at Lidia's? Do you feel up to it?"

"I'm a little fuzzy right now. Do you mind if I take care of it later?"

"That's fine. I'll come by for it tomorrow. I may have some more questions for you by then." He stood and took one more look at me. "Try to stay out of trouble, will you?"

I grinned. "I'll do my best."

He disappeared through the curtain.

Honey arrived a few minutes later and fussed over me. "I can't believe you went out there alone," she said. "I should've gone with you."

"And she would have tried to kill us both." I wasn't about to put her life in danger. She had a husband and children. Besides, it was only supposed to be reconnaissance, not a confrontation. Apparently I needed to work on my sneakiness in the future.

"No way—she would have been stealthier and tried to take us out individually," Honey protested. "You wouldn't be here at all if we'd used the buddy system."

"She's probably right," Jack said as he entered the screened room where I lay. His eyes studied mine. "You look better. More color. Has the doctor said you'll live?"

"Yeah. I'm harder to kill than Lidia thought. How is she?"

"She'll survive to face the courts, despite her concussion. Remind me never to get in a fight with you." His mouth quirked up on the right. "You know, when I first met you, I thought you were one of those city women who were focused on their careers to the exclusion of everything else. You proved differently. I'm sorry if I was a little cold."

His words somehow made the pain a little less acute. "Thanks. I appreciate it."

He stepped back, as if needing to put space between us. "So when are you going to open your shop?"

"Before Easter." I plucked at the blanket covering my legs. I wondered if I could really get everything together that fast, then made up my mind to be sure I did.

"Good. Count on me to stop by for some treats."

"See you then."

With a wave, he disappeared down the hall.

Maybe he wasn't as bad as I'd originally thought. Perhaps, if I could go more than two days without him coming to check my wounds and poke holes in my veins, we could even become friends.

Nah.

Honey turned a wide grin on me. "*Now* what do you think of him?" She wriggled her eyebrows.

"You can't be serious." I gave her my best scowl. "He stuck me with a needle. No way am I going to go out with a guy who stuck me with a needle."

"Lamest excuse of the century." She straightened the blanket on my legs. "What? Is he not good enough for you?"

I shook my head. "He seems nice, but guys are totally off the menu for me right now." I looked at the IV bag and noticed it was almost empty. "Can you go find someone to disconnect this thing?"

"I'll let you change the subject—this time." She disappeared out the door and left me smiling.

Now if I could get through a week without a major catastrophe, life would be good.

Epilogue

A week later I was amazed how much I could accomplish toward getting the business set up when I wasn't running around interviewing murder suspects. As I waited for Honey to pick me up for the drive to the airport, I took stock of the restaurant-turned-bakery. My sign was in the window, the paint and trim finished. All the supplies and equipment that had come in were put away, my oven was installed and I'd placed an order for baking supplies, the delivery for which Honey would come accept on my behalf while I was gone.

I'd even had a display case delivered the previous afternoon to show off my cupcakes and cookies and any other fun desserts. I was proud of what I was doing, and couldn't wait to hear the bell ringing as customers came in to buy something to please their sweet tooth.

I heard the kitchen door open and crossed back there to see Honey standing in the doorway. "About time you made it," I teased, though she was less than two minutes late. "I have a plane to catch, you know."

"Yeah, yeah, tell it to someone else. You ready to go?"

"Definitely." We went out and she loaded the bags I'd left by the back door into her trunk—I claimed that lifting hurt my wound, which was true. I locked the door and turned to hand the keys to Honey. "You'll remember to let the delivery guy in on Wednesday?"

"Yes. Don't worry about it. I have everything under control."

Of course she did. She was superwoman. I slid into the

passenger seat and buckled up. "I heard Dahlia is staying at Tad and Analesa's," I said when she had started the car.

She sent me a sideways glance. "Been talking to Shawn again?"

I allowed a smile to curve my mouth. "I might have. He said Analesa got over her anger pretty fast when she got all the facts. It could hurt Tad's chances at a senatorial seat someday, but they've decided not to worry about that now. I guess her parents and Tad's are over the moon about having a granddaughter."

"Yeah, but rough on Dahlia, don't you think? Can you imagine being in her place?"

That was one issue I hadn't been able to resolve. The poor baby. I still woke at night with visions of her running into that room, crying for her mom. "No. She's the biggest victim in all of this. How confusing for her."

"But back to Shawn—so, you know. What's up?" She maneuvered the car onto the freeway and we headed south for Phoenix as I laughed.

"I guess the only thing that will answer that question is time." And as I looked ahead, I knew there would be time to figure out answers to all my questions.

Pistols & Pies

Sweet Bites Book 2

Tess thought her sleuthing days were behind her after she nearly died solving her first murder, but when a city councilman is killed at the opening of the new fitness center, and his step son is the detective's favorite suspect, she gets roped into proving the teenager is innocent. When the killer ups the stakes, Tess is forced to put herself in danger or risk the life of someone she cares about.

Acknowledgements

Many thanks to my terrific critique partners Mary Greathouse, Kathleen Brebes, Rebecca Blevins and Nichole Giles, for their help and feedback on this story. I couldn't publish a book without the help of others whose notes and thoughts make my stories so much better. And special thanks to Tristi Pinkston for her time fixing all of my misplaced commas and funky sentences when I know how busy she's been.

Thanks to my test kitcheners, Lisa Swinton, Laurel Wilson, Jordan McCullom, Kristen Robison, Monique Leutkemeyer and Jenna Swinton. The alternate suggestions on the recipes and some adjustments came from them. And thanks to my parents, husband and friends who got to be guinea pigs for my many variations and tweaks when I was still in recipe-development mode.

Thanks to my sweet husband, Bill, for doing my cover, building and updating my website, and just being a constant support in everything I do. I truly would not be where I am in my career without you. I love you, honey!

About the Author

Heather Justesen remembers making her first scratch cake when she was about thirteen. Thankfully, her baking skills have improved dramatically from the lopsided, but tasty mess she made that day. When she's not writing or developing recipes, she runs with the local volunteer ambulance, enjoys gardening, playing with her chickens, cake decorating and working with her husband in their small business.

Learn more about her at her website at http://heatherjustesen.com/ or her blog at http://heatherjustesen.blogspot.com/ Follow her Facebook fan page http://www.facebook.com/pages/Heather-Justesen/273141090197?fref=ts or on Twitter https://twitter.com/HeatherJustesen/